HOLE PUNCHED

By Susan Renee

Cover art by Samantha Roth of Grothic Designs
Editing by Nikki Rose
Formatting by Douglas M. Huston

Other books by Susan Renee
Seven
Solving Us

Table of Contents

To Mary Lee,
who inspired me to bring the
word JIZZ to life.
I adore you!

CHAPTER 1
Wiffy Sticks
Jenna

"Excuse me ma'am, but do you guys carry those umm…one of those wiffy sticks?" a lady asks me as she approaches the counter. I look up with a cocked eyebrow surveying the customer standing in front of me. She's a stout older lady with her hair still in the curlers she must've put in last night, or maybe a week ago for all I know. She's missing a couple of front teeth and seems to be a few fries short of a happy meal. I blink my eyes and force a smile, reminding myself that a good retail manager doesn't judge. I'm here to serve. Except, in order to serve this lady correctly, I have to know what the hell a wiffy stick is.

"I'm sorry ma'am," I say to her. "What was it you were looking for? I'm not sure I heard you correctly."

"A wiffy stick."

Yeah…I heard her correctly.

"A…wiffy…stick." I repeat slowly, closing my eyes and trying my damnedest to figure out what the hell a wiffy stick is.

"You know, one of those sticks I need to use the interweb system," the lady explains to me. When my eyes meet hers again, her eyebrows are raised in anticipation of my understanding. With her explanation, I think I may actually know what she's talking about, but before I get the chance to answer her, I catch the eye of the man in line behind my confused customer. It's not the first time I've seen him in the store. He's sort of a regular by our standards, or at least by mine. He comes in at least once if not a couple of times a week, always for the same items. His body is trembling slightly in quiet laughter, and when my eyes meet his for a fleeting moment, I can tell he's trying to hide a shit eating smirk. He's attractive yet has a bit of a rough-around-the-edges look to him. Though he's a regular, I've never really taken the time to make anything more than small talk with him. Being a retail manager at The Hole Punch is draining enough with customers like this lady in front of me. I don't care to spend much more time getting to know customers that I may only see once in my lifetime if I'm lucky. Anyway, he's scrolling through his phone now as he chuckles, so I can only assume he got some sort of funny text.

"Ma'am, do you mean a Wi-Fi adapter? A Wi-Fi adapter is for a machine that doesn't already have a Wi-Fi card in them, like an older computer, so that you can use the internet."

"YES!" The lady exclaims. "That's the one! I'll take one o'them if you please."

I smile at her, biting my tongue so that I don't laugh my ass off at the absurdity of hearing them called 'wiffy sticks'.

Seriously, what the hell will people come up with next?

"Ok Ma'am, our Wi-Fi adapters are in our tech department. If you'll wait here one moment, I'll get Adam up here to help you out." I reach up and push the button on the microphone cord hanging in front of me, the other end attached to my ear piece. "Adam, I have a customer here who needs a Wi-Fi adapter. Can you please help her find what she needs?"

Immediately I hear Adam's voice reply to me, "On my way."

I nod to nobody but myself since I'm the only one who was able to hear him. "Adam is on his way ma'am. He'll take you back and help you choose which one will work best for you. Please let us know if you need anything else, ok?"

"Thank you dear. I appreciate the help," the female customer says, smiling and showing off the empty spaces in her mouth. She steps to the side and out of the way so that I can check out the customers who have lined up behind her. The attractive guy I noticed a minute ago walks up to my register and places his items on the counter in between us.

"Hello," I greet him.

"Good morning." His voice is soft, smooth, and captivating when he speaks.

I hear Linda's ornery whisper seep through my ear piece. "Hey Jizza look! It's Mr. Tall, Dark, and Handsome!"

"It's Jenna." I reply to her.

Hot Guy cocks his head, confused. "Jacoby."

"Shit," I mutter. "I mean shoot!"

Oh my God, I just said "shit" to a customer.

Tall, Dark, and Handsome laughs, his head still cocked to the side like he's trying to figure me out.

I take a deep breath at the off-kilter feeling going through my chest. "I didn't mean that for you."

He chuckles. "Oh, so you weren't introducing yourself just now?"

"No. Well - I mean…"

"Mmm…he's good eye candy don't you think Jizz?" Linda says again through my earpiece.

I laugh out loud at my best friend's remark even though to everyone around me it looks like I'm laughing to myself. "I don't need candy." I mumble, shaking my head.

"Hello girl named Jenna who doesn't need candy." Hot Guy says, grinning. "It's a pleasure to meet you."

Dammit, I did it again!

"Sorry, I…yes, my name is Jenna."

"I gathered that since it's the name on your nametag." He smiles. "I'm Jacoby." He crosses his arms and leans on the counter where his purchases sit. "Why don't you like candy?"

"I do like candy."

"Oh. Ok." He gives me a confused smile as I swipe the printer ink cartridges he's purchasing over the scanner and place them in a plastic bag.

"No I mean…" I can feel the heat rise in my cheeks at my embarrassment. "I'm sorry. I have a colleague talking to me in my ear. She's trying to distract me from my job and right now it looks like she's winning." I shake my head, smiling as my eyes quickly glide over to the copy center where Linda holds court. She's laughing loudly enough that I can hear her from where she stands, though nobody knows she's laughing at me.

"Oh. Well I guess that explains things better than my thinking you're some sort of girl who randomly vomits weird phrases out her mouth to unsuspecting customers." When I look up at him from ringing out his purchases my eyes fall to the dimple on his left cheek. He has an attractive smile.

Laughing, I reply, "Well I'm sorry if I gave you the wrong impression. It's been a weird morning already around here. Please forgive me. Did you find everything you were looking for?"

"It's totally fine," Jacoby says. "And yes, I did - for now - thank you." When my eyes flash up I'm taken aback by the fact that he's watching me, holding my gaze. This whole day has been weird for me since I opened the store. Customers walk in here looking for the weirdest stuff. It's either old people asking for things that they can't pronounce or young assholes who walk in and ask if we in fact do carry hole punches. The answer is yes, twenty different varieties, actually.

I finish ringing up his items and quickly give him his total. "That will be sixty-nine…dollars." I blush having to say the words sixty-nine to him. Usually it wouldn't bother me except, well, he's attractive and it's sixty-nine. That's why.

"Hell yeah he'll give you sixty-nine Jizza!" Linda says into my earpiece as she walks by, hearing my conversation with the hot guy in front of me. She's obviously trying to rile me up so I do something stupid in front of this guy. I swear this woman thinks about nothing but men all day long. No, scratch that. Men and sex and alcohol. She's like a walking Las Vegas Strip.

I gasp at her comment. "Oh my God!"

"What?" Jacoby's head snaps up from looking at his wallet. "Is everything okay?"

Shit!

"Yes! Yes, it is. I'm sorry again. This stupid thing…" I pull my earpiece from my ear and let it dangle around my neck. While Mr. Tall Dark and Handsome is inserting his credit card into the machine, I quickly flick the switch to turn off my microphone in hopes that I won't say any more embarrassing things to this good-looking man in front of me. As he enters his pin number in to the credit card machine I take a second to give him a once over for probably the third or fourth time in the last couple weeks.

His facial features are dark and striking. His hair could be described as almost surfer-like, except that it's jet black instead of the stereotypical blonde. It sweeps around his head, framing a pair of beautiful gray eyes. His stubbled beard gives him a roughed-up look that I find way more appealing than a freshly shaved baby face. He's dressed in jeans and a vintage Coke t-shirt that sits comfortably around his body, pulling ever so slightly at his chest. Peeking out of his right sleeve is the bottom of a tattoo on his nicely-sculpted bicep. I can't tell what it looks like, though part of it sticks out almost like a feather. As someone who loves art and design, I'm definitely intrigued, but not enough to ask him if I can see it. His comfortable and casual look so early on a Wednesday morning tells me that he most likely does not have some sort of corporate job. Either that or he's on vacation. I would ask him, but given that I don't even know the guy other than I've seen him in here before buying paper and ink and post-it notes and highlighters – not that I pay attention to what he buys - I would say it's none of my business why he's here.

"Thanks for the ink." He nods his head in the direction of the first customer that I helped this morning and winks. "I hope she finds her wiffy stick."

"KitKat!" I blurt out loudly.

Why the hell did I just say that?

"I'm sorry?" Jacoby tilts his head perplexed by my outburst.

"My favorite candy," I start to explain. "Umm, KitKats are my favorite candy, so see? I like candy. Anything chocolate really but there's just something about those wafer things and chocolate together, so those are my favorite."

Stop vomiting all the words Jenna!

He nods, clearly amused, or he wants to make fun of me for being a stupid word-vomiting idiot. "Good to know," he says. "Those are my favorite as well."

Not knowing what else I can or should say to this guy, I simply thank him for shopping at The Hole Punch. He steps away to leave but turns back for just a moment before staring me down. "I'm always up for the hole punch." He smirks with a wink and walks out the door. I watch as he proceeds through the parking lot, gets into his dark blue truck and pulls away.

"So, who the hell was that? Did you finally get his name and what were you two talking about for so long? Did he ask you out? Oh, my God you're so getting laid. I can feel it!" Linda whispers, tossing all her words at me at once when she comes back over to the register. I hastily finish checking out the last customer in the line and then turn back to chat with her.

"Whoa! Slow the hell down girl! First of all, I don't really know the guy other than the fact that his name is Jacoby."

Linda crinkles her nose. "Jacoby? What kind of name is that?"

Exasperated, I reply, "An easy one to remember! It's Jacob with a Y. And we were talking for so long because some bitch on the other side of the store wouldn't shut up in my ear piece, which kept causing me to spit out weird phrases as I answered her…except he was only hearing one side of the conversation!"

Linda laughs maniacally before jutting her hip out to the side, narrowing her eyes and asking, "So does that mean you're not getting laid tonight then?"

I sigh loudly even though I can't help but laugh with Linda. She's always giving me a hard time about the guys I have dated. And by dated, I mean slept with once, or maybe twice if I was feeling like a horny slut, but then refused to ever talk to again. I guess that makes me the human one-night stand, which I suppose for now, I'm okay with. I've yet to find a guy who complains when I don't badger him about calling me in a day or two, and those who have called me in a day or two I've deemed as too needy or desperate for sex and turned them down anyway. Life is way easier that way. No attachments. Just me, myself, and I…and sometimes a guy and his hole-punch to take the edge off when I'm stressed.

"You're so lucky you're my best friend or I might have had to tit-punch you for that stunt; in fact, I may decide to do it anyway!"

Linda doubles over laughing at me, like always.

"And I never said I wasn't getting laid, but it sure as hell isn't going to be Jacoby if that's what you're implying. I don't fuck every guy I meet you know. I don't need to have a different guy in my bed every night to be a happy woman, and I have a lot to do in the next few days anyway. Besides, it's only been a couple weeks. I think my lady bits will be just fine…until the next wiffy stick comes along." I smirk.

Linda laughs dramatically. "I'm sorry, what did you say? A wiffy stick? What the hell is that?" I watch as her eyes grow large as she thinks to herself. Smoothly, she bends over the counter between us and whispers, "Ooh, please, tell me it's another vibrator!" She props up her chin with her right elbow on the counter. "I'm all ears. Tell me everything. Does it swivel? Does it have those beads? Do they come in multiple colors? Short and stubby or long and bulbous?"

"Oh my God, you don't stop do you?" I ask her, shaking my head in amusement. Seriously, this girl. "You know what, you should Google it." With that I wink at her and move from the counter to head to the tech desk.

"So if you still have shit to do, does that mean no wine and girly chat tonight?"

I nod my head. "Most likely. How about a rain check for tomorrow night, okay? I have a few more pieces to finish tonight and then I'll be free to hang out tomorrow."

"Deal. I can't wait to see the finished products this time. That red and purple one is still my favorite." She winks before heading back to the copy center to fill a few more standing orders before the afternoon rush. "Hey do me a favor and remind me to buy batteries before I leave today, okay?"

"For what?" I ask.

Linda spins around walking backwards to the copy center. "Well since it's just me tonight…I may as well spend some time with B.O.B." She winks again and I roll my eyes in response. I don't know why I even asked. I knew her answer would be something sexual like spending an evening with her battery operated boyfriend. The girl has no shame and no filter, but I kind of admire her for that. Being yourself, who you want to be, and who you're meant to be, and owning it, is a lot harder than anyone thinks it is.

CHAPTER 2
Rise and Grind

Jenna

"Anybody want a coffee or something from Rise & Grind? I'm heading over to get breakfast before we open," I ask the associates – or asshats as I like to call them -working with me this morning. They each give me their order which I write down on the back of my hand like I don't work in an office supply store with notepads all over the damn place. I start to collect their money but then decide to just treat everyone from our petty cash stash. I'm tired of the usual Friday pizza lunch thing. Nobody says I can't treat the morning crew to Thursday coffee and scones.

"Be right back guys," I say before heading out the door. Rise & Grind Café is just across the parking lot from The Hole Punch, which makes break times pretty easy when you're hungry and don't have a lot of time. The crew at the café pretty much know all the associates in the store since we all frequent each other's establishments. We go there for food. They come to us for office supplies to run their business. I try to remember to give them a little discount whenever they come in and every once in a while, I get a free scone. Maybe I should consider the fact that those free scones are most likely ones that got dropped on the floor, but when they're melting in my mouth I don't give it a second thought.

I walk into the café and look at the menu like I don't already know what I want or have four orders written on the back of my hand.

"Mornin' Sunny-J!" Paul says with a smile to greet me this morning.

"Good morning Paul. How are you this morning?" I ask.

"Very well, thank you. Did you catch *Big Brother* last night?" Paul has become a great friend since I started at The Hole Punch. He's my sassy black woman in a man's body. We know enough about each other to know that we're both huge fans of the CBS reality show. We look forward to summer time like crazy just so we can talk *Big Brother* all the time.

"I sure did! Can you believe who was evicted? I was elated. That douche needed to go." I could talk about this for hours.

"Giiiirl, you know it. I couldn't agree more. I just hope Nicole stays because she's totes adorbs and Paulie is a fine piece of ass," he says in his best diva voice. "What can I get you this morning sweetheart? You buyin' for everyone?"

"Yes, sir. I am. Let me see here…" I turn my hand over so I can see everyone's orders. "Adam wants a small iced latte, Sonya needs a tall black roast, Linda wants a damn chocolate milk." I roll my eyes. "And Jason wants a tall roast, two creams, two sugars."

The bell above the door to the café rings as other patrons arrive. While I'm studying the menu for myself, Paul looks back behind me, welcoming one of his regulars. "Good morning, Mr. Malloy. I'll be just a moment."

"Coming right up, sugar," Paul says to me quietly as I watch him punch my order into the screen in front of him. "What else? You forgot yourself."

"Oh yeah. I'll have a colossal iced mocha and at least a dozen scones. Mix 'em up for me will you? Linda hates the orange ones but they're my favorite."

"Got it. Hang tight just a minute and we'll have it all packaged up for you. I'll get you your coffee to drink while you wait." Paul winks as he turns towards the coffee maker.

"Thanks, Paul."

"Need a lid?" he asks.

"Nah. I'm just walking next door." I watch him prepare my drink for me. I'm already salivating over the taste of the ice-cold brew. The weather is getting too hot these days and running around the store in a long-sleeved shirt does me no favors.

"Here ya go Sunny-J." Paul hands me my colossal drink. Good lord this cup is huge. Nobody really needs a drink this big, but something this size should last through my entire shift, God willing.

"Thanks so much Paul. Here, I'll just give you this now. Keep the change." I wink back at him, smiling as I hand him fifty dollars.

"Thanks!" He nods.

"Sure! I'll go sit and wait for the others to be ready," I tell him. I turn around to head back to the booths along the wall to wait for the rest of my order. As I skirt around a few people, I take a quick sip of my drink so that the filled cup doesn't spill. At the same time, a woman behind me on her cell phone turns to motion to her friend when she bumps into my arm.

"Shit!" I curse quietly as the shocking chill of my iced mocha cascades down my shirt, my leg and onto the floor, splashing those standing around me. I look up to see the girl grimacing at me apologetically, yet she's not ending her phone call to help me out at all.

Bitch.

"Whoa. Slippery little sucker. Let me help," a man says beside me as he bends down to grab my plastic cup. I would usually wave someone off and tell them not to worry about it but that voice, the sincerity mixed with teasing humor, flabbergasts me enough to want to look up and tell the jack-ass to fuck off. I mean what kind of asshole would laugh at a damsel in distress?

"Jacoby." I squeak. I want to roll my eyes at the obvious quandary I seem to find myself in whenever he is around. First it's Linda saying inappropriate things in my ear when he's in the store, and now it's spilling my colossal iced mocha all over myself and…him, or his shoes at least!

"Oh God! Shit! I'm so sorry," I cry in a sudden state of panic. I had no idea anything had landed on him. I had no idea he was even here. Quickly my eyes dart around for a napkin…or twenty napkins…to wipe up my mess. Out of the corner of my eye I see my savior, one of the café workers, walking towards me with a bucket and mop.

To my astonishment, Jacoby beams at me, his dimple on display for the world to see. "Good morning Jenna who likes KitKats and obviously…iced mocha?" He laughs.

I stand up straight, surveying the mess in front of me, my hands on my hips.

Panic or shake it off.

Panic or shake it off.

"Well not really." I decide to shake it off and try to find the humor in my hot mess of a morning. "Truth be told, I don't even like coffee, I just like to start my days off by getting a gigantic cup of cold liquid and throwing it - with force I might add - onto the floor and splashing whoever may be in target range." I shrug. "Guess you were too close to me. Sorry – not – sorry."

Jacoby's smile widens. "Oh really? So that's the best way to start the day huh?" I watch as he licks his bottom lip, which causes my insides to wake up and take notice.

"Yeah well, I try to beat my record at least once a week. You know, see how many customers I can destroy before the day even gets started. The good ones will know it's coming and spring out of the way. In fact, the really smart ones will just wait until after eight to even walk in here so they know I'm already gone."

"Ah. I see. I'll make sure to set my alarm tomorrow morning then so I know when it's safe to come in." He tries to hide his soft smile. "Are you okay?"

I don't even have to look down to know that my shirt is sopping wet. My nipples, now standing at attention for the world to see, are not so subtly reminding me that the liquid poured all over them was damn cold. It's not lost on me that Jacoby takes notice, but I decide not to say anything, because really…I would let him look all he wants. He's hot in that I'm-not-sure-if-he's-a-good-guy-or-bad-boy-but-either-way-is-okay kind of way.

"I'll be alright, thanks." I take the front of my shirt in my hands. "Excuse me a minute, I need to go wring out my shirt." As I walk to the door I hear Paul say "Don't worry Sunny-J, I'll have another one waiting for you!" I wave him off in appreciation and continue to the door. Stepping outside, I quickly wring out my shirt, letting the excess liquids fall onto the parking lot pavement.

Thank God the asshats can't see me from the store.

"Don't go anywhere. I have something for you." Jacoby had followed me outside. I watch him walk to his truck, a truck that looks nothing like the truck I watched him get in the other day. This one is a classic of some sort, that I know. He heads back toward me with something balled up in his hands.

"Here. Put this on." He hands me a gray t-shirt. "It beats a soaking wet shirt that will now smell like mocha all day…not that smelling like mocha is a bad thing…" He trails off for a moment and I catch him ogling my wet chest. "Come to think of it, neither is looking at a girl in a wet t-shirt, but, you know." He shrugs. "I wouldn't want all your customers staring at you all day."

I raise an eyebrow at his somewhat cocky statement. "Oh? And why not? Because my chest is for your viewing pleasure only?"

Holy balls! Did I just say that out loud?

"That's not what I meant, although if you're offering your chest up to my eyes only I would probably be a fool not to take advantage at least once," he responds.

I scoff. "Are you saying my chest isn't pretty enough to look at more than once?"

"Uh…no." Jacoby clears his throat, holding his hand in front of his mouth to hide his smile. "What I'm saying is that you're a girl standing in front of a guy and you look like you've just been crowned winner of a wet t-shirt contest. Now I don't have all the facts because I've never seen your chest, but I'm pretty damn sure if I looked at it once, I would want to look at it again." He clears his throat a second time. "And maybe even a few more times."

My breath escapes me with his stare. I didn't quite expect him to say that, though in hindsight, what guy is going to tell a girl that her rack is ugly? I imagine any heterosexual guy would take advantage of a peep show right? At least Jacoby is honest.

"I'm going to pretend for a minute that we know each other really well so that I don't have to feel weirded out that you're talking about looking at my chest," I resolve.

He shrugs, and smiling, says, "Whatever helps you sleep at night, KitKat."

"KitKat? Now you have a pet name for me?"

I watch him shake his head back and forth as he laughs. "Are you going to put that shirt on or stand there all day showing me your grand-champion status?"

Letting out an exasperated sigh, I unfold the t-shirt he handed me, looking it over to make sure I'm not about to put something on that has naked women all over it or something. "What the…?" I nearly yell before turning the shirt around to show him. My jaw almost hits the ground. "Jacked Up? You want me to wear a shirt that says 'Jacked Up'? To work?"

Jacoby chews on the side of his mouth as he thinks about my conundrum. "Well, to be clear, there's a picture of a truck on the back. It's for an auto-repair company."

"Dude." I protest, waving my hand furiously up and down like an angry showgirl on *The Price is Right*. "It says 'Jacked Up'. I can't wear a shirt that says that while I'm working! I'm a manager." I hand the shirt back to him. "Thanks, but no thanks."

"No, wait. You're right," he answers. "Here." Jacoby reaches back with his right hand and lifts the shirt he's wearing, a navy-blue V-neck shirt, over his head and hands it to me. "Wear this one. I'll wear the other one." Before I can move he snaps the Jacked Up t-shirt from my hand and replaces it with the shirt he literally took off his back to give to me. I'm probably supposed to be impressed and grateful, but this guy I barely know is standing in front of me with no shirt on because he actually took it off and handed it to me. And now my eyes are stuck in the staring position. His upper body is sexy as hell and I can't stop looking at it.

Shit.

Tattoos AND a nipple ring.

Dear sweet Jesus, Mary, and Joseph.

"Hey KitKat, my eyes are up here." He chuckles.

Fuck! Pot calling kettle! Pot calling kettle!

I shake my head, trying to escape the trance I was just experiencing. "Sorry, I'll uh…" I hitch my thumb over my shoulder. "I'll just…go…change. Yeah. Be right back." I can't turn around fast enough before retreating back into the café. Briskly I move to the back of the store where the restrooms are. I open the handicapped stall because…well, my boobs are wet, which means my underwire is going to chafe eventually and I don't have a clean dry bra, so I'm considering that a handicap. I pull off my work shirt and replace it with the one Jacoby gave me. It's slightly baggy on me which makes me feel good, and it smells like…cologne and coffee and hotness personified. I grab the front of his shirt and hold it up against my nose, committing this smell to my memory. I'm sure I'll give his shirt back at some point but I secretly hope he doesn't ever want it back.

Walking back out to the café I see Jacoby waiting for me inside with a large bag tucked under his arm and a drink carrier in each of his hands. He looks like a completely different person than he did five minutes ago. First he was the clean cut good guy in the coffee shop and now, in that t-shirt, he looks like the resident bad boy. Maybe it's because I now know what's hiding underneath the gray cloth.

"Order up Sunny-J" I hear Paul say. I turn back toward the counter to see Paul nod to Jacoby. "Mr. Jacked Up said he would help you out." He winks at me before turning around to carry a few things back to the kitchen.

"You look good in blue." Jacoby approves.

"Uh, thanks. You don't look so bad either…um, yourself. I mean, you don't look so bad yourself."

Now is not the time for word vomit, Jenna.

"Let me help you carry these. You walked from the store I assume?" he asks.

"Yeah. I did. Thanks."

"After you." He nods toward the front door. I grab the door and hold it open for him, the least I can do.

We walk slowly together across the parking lot toward The Hole Punch. There are a million thoughts going through my head as we walk in silence, but the only one I wish I knew the answer to is what Jacoby is thinking right now. I can't even think of anything cute to say. I'm afraid I'll just spill all my words out at once and scare him off.

Meh, it wouldn't be the first time.

"Hey thanks, Jacoby for the shirt. You really didn't have to but…"

"I wanted to." His voice is comforting, his demeanor now charming, a slight switch from the presumptuous personality I saw ten minutes ago.

"I'll have it washed and waiting for the next time you…"

"There's no need." He interrupts. "It's just a shirt. You can have it."

Praise Jesus! He said I can have it!

"Oh, umm, okay. Thanks. I'll just keep it in my purse then." I nod.

My response makes Jacoby stop in his tracks. "That's a pretty weird thing to just keep in your purse isn't it?" he asks.

"Well…you know, for tomorrow morning when I go to the Rise & Grind and throw another colossal iced mocha on the floor. At least this time I'll be prepared." I smirk playfully.

"Ah yes. Good point." He grins.

"Did you get a new truck?" I ask.

"Nope. What makes you ask?"

"Oh. Um. No reason, I guess. I just…thought you drove a dark blue truck." Ugh am I admitting to him that I've watched him before?

"So you're stalking me now, eh? As a matter of fact, I do drive a dark blue truck," he teases.

"I don't stalk you." I roll my eyes.

"Oh, you don't? But you've watched me enough to know what color car I drive?" His eyes are dazzling and I can tell he's enjoying this game of 'Tease-Jenna'.

"Okay, okay. I know you drive a dark blue pick-up truck because I saw you get in it and drive away the other day when you when you left the store, and that," I say, pointing to the bright blue classic truck in the parking lot that says Studebaker on the back. "...is not the same truck you had the other day."

Jacoby smiles and nods silently. "You got me. I'm a truck whore with a bad habit. I steal trucks and drive a different one each day so my would-be stalkers are thrown for a loop and can't track me." When I look over at him, laughing, he winks at me. I guess if nothing else he's easy to talk to. I don't mind playing along.

"A truck whore huh? I would've never guessed with all the highlighters and post-it notes you..."

"A-HA!!" He stops and looks at me, his eyebrows raised. "So you DO stalk me! Hmm...I'm going to have to figure out how to buy my supplies incognito from now on." He whispers to himself but loud enough that he knows I hear him. "Maybe a mask, or a wig..."

"Oh, touché." I laugh. "Okay, I promise I don't stalk you. It's my job to know what my regular or semi-regular customers buy."

"And why is that?" he asks.

"That way I always have what you need, when you need it." I answer. Jacoby's chest swells as he watches me for a minute. His eyes pierce mine with a look I can't describe. Contentment? Attraction? Pain? I have no idea.

I take a deep breath and then change the subject. "Anyway, I don't think *two* trucks makes you a truck whore, but that classic one is beautiful."

"Yeah? You like it? Maybe one day I can take you for a ride." I swallow the giggle that is aching to escape my mouth at Jacoby's innocent statement filled with sexual innuendo. I'm sure he didn't mean it like that, but it's funny nonetheless. Linda would never let him get away with a comment like that.

"Nah…I prefer tow trucks," I reply.

"Tow trucks?" He laughs. "Why tow trucks?"

"Sexual fantasy," I say proudly while sporting a straight face.

Jacoby trips over his own foot and almost drops the cup carriers he's holding. The bag of baked goods drops from under his arm, but I catch it just in time. "I…I'm sorry." He stutters. "Did you just say sexual fantasy?"

"Yeah."

"Tow trucks?" he asks, his voice growing higher in pitch. I'm pretty sure he's dumbfounded. This is hilarious! Woohoo! Point for Jenna! The tides of this game have turned.

I look at him with my head cocked innocently to the side. Inside I'm dying, but teasing him is proving to be a fun activity. "Yeah. You mean guys don't have sexual fantasies involving tow trucks? You know…" I shrug. "Hooking your tow bar up to her chassis?"

I would love to hear his response but I don't give him the opportunity. I nonchalantly open the door to the store, holding it open for Jacoby to walk through with our drinks. He steps inside and turns his head to look over his shoulder at me. All I can do is shrug innocently like the conversation we were just having was all about the weather and not sex a la tow truck. He smiles devilishly as he follows me into our breakroom and sets down the drink carriers on the table in front of us.

"Thanks so much for your help Jacoby, and for the shirt. I really do appreciate it." I try to be as sweet as punch like I wasn't just talking about tow trucks and sex.

"It was absolutely my pleasure." He hasn't stopped smiling even as he shakes his head back and forth. "There's something about you…" He lightly brushes a few stray strands of my hair away from my face and damn if his touch doesn't send sparks straight through my chassis. "I should go and get some work done though."

"Yeah." I'm mesmerized. "Okay. Me too."

"I'll see ya around, KitKat," he says quietly before turning from me and heading out the door.

"Yeah. Okay. Me too." I repeat to myself as he leaves.

I don't know what it is about that guy that makes me drop things, and spill things, and vomit words like no other, but deep down, even though I don't really want to have to admit it, because it's not what I do, I think I could like him.

CHAPTER 3

The Art of a Thorough Oil Change

Jenna

I don't see or hear from Jacoby for the rest of the day, or even the next day, for that matter. It's harder than I expected pretending not to be disappointed. I mean, what did I expect? It's not like I thought he would show up here every day to buy pens or packing tape or a filing cabinet just to see me.

Okay, maybe I thought that.

He said there was something about me. Maybe that something is that I'm a weirdo freak who word vomits way too much and says inappropriate things like how tow trucks are a sexual fantasy of mine.

"You really told him that?" Linda laughs. "Tow trucks? That's clever even for you!"

"Yeah I did. I was in the moment and he had been pretty flirtatious so I gave it right back to him. Figured he could handle it."

"Well, either he went home and handled it for sure or you scared him off with your creative imagination." She giggles. I snap my head up from my paperwork to look at her with a pained, doubting-Thomas expression.

I wonder if he thought I was serious.

I suppose if he got to know me even more, he really would think I was weird…or he would think I'm some sort of nymphomaniac based on what I do with my personal time. Yes, okay, I enjoy sex. I'm a woman in my twenties. It's my sexual prime…I think. So I take a dip in the semen pool once in a while. That doesn't make me a slut. I have mad respect for the penis.

"Don't worry." Linda pats my shoulder like I'm lost puppy. "I have a feeling he'll be back. Maybe he's just been busy."

"Yeah," I agree. "Hey, I finished the red one last night. Want to stop by this evening and take a look? Tell me what you think?"

"Hell yeah I do! You know I love your designs. I'll stop over tonight, and I'll bring wine." She winks.

"Perfect," I whisper as Linda walks out the office door.

"Hey Jizza!" Linda calls for me through my ear piece. "Crazy Larry is on the phone. It's your turn."

Sneering to nobody but myself, I hit the button on my ear piece to answer Linda. "Ugh. Okay. I'll take it." Ripping the ear piece from my ear I walk over to the phone at the Customer Service Desk and prepare to take the call from 'Crazy Larry', the guy who calls umpteen times a week to bitch about whatever is on his mind, and who also has a million conspiracy theories about how he thinks the government is constantly watching him. We've worked on his computer more than a dozen times because honestly, I'm not sure he really knows what he's doing with it. He's constantly getting viruses and odd messages that pop up. Clearly he spends all day surfing the internet and downloading God knows what. Talking to Larry is about to make a depressing, not-great day even worse.

"Hello, this is Jenna," I announce into the phone with as pleasant a voice as I can muster.

"Jenna! It's Larry Seymore and I've got to tell you that I'm pissed off today! I'm just fucking pissed!" he begins.

Well good morning to you too Larry.

"I'm sorry to hear that Mr. Seymore. What can I do to help you this afternoon?"

"My fucking computer is on the fritz again. I push all the right buttons but the fucking thing just keeps telling me to do the update so I did the update but then the fuckers said I may have a virus

MAYDAY, MAYDAY!" he shouts dramatically. I pull the receiver away from my ear because he's so damn loud.

"Okay…" I begin, but Mr. Seymore interrupts me.

"Well I'm sorry to be saying fuck so much but fuck this! It's fucking pissing me off! I'm done. I just want to kill all those government people who work on these damn computers because they keep messing with my stuff. Maybe I'll just invite Bill Gates to come over and have a good time. I'll show him all about fucking up computers. I'll just pull them into a warehouse. I know how to use chemicals. All I need is a wide-gauge syringe."

Oh good fucking grief.

I don't get paid enough for this.

"And that's another thing…" Mr. Seymore continues. "Why the fuck when someone's on death row, do they bother using alcohol wipes to clean the area for the needle? Are they worried those fuckers are going to get AIDS? Are they worried they're going to get sick and die? I mean…they didn't care about the person they're killing in the first place so why bother fucking sterilizing the area before they kill the guy?"

"Mr. Seymore?" I attempt to interject.

"That's what I would do to all them fuckers. And to the FBI, because I KNOW you're listening to this phone call, fuck you too! I know I'm on the no-fly list to anywhere because you hear all the shit I say. And I know you're on the call right now."

"Mr. Seymore?" I say a little louder, rolling my eyes at this ridiculous phone call.

"Besides, I'm not taking my shoes off for anyone. I'll drop my drawers, then they can all kiss my fucking ass. Then I'll pull my pants back up. Then we're good. FBI, Fucking Bureau of Idiots. That's what I call them."

I clear my throat. "Mr. Seymore, if you're having a problem with your computer we would be more than happy to look at it for you if you'll bring it in."

"Nope, nope, nope. I'm all done. I just needed to call over and tell you what was going on, but I'm all done now so that's it. I'll talk to you later." I don't even get the chance to finish the phone call and tell him to have a nice day before he hangs up.

"Well there's ten minutes of my life I'll never get back. Thanks a lot, Mr. Seymore," I mutter as I slam down the phone and head back to the office. I turn on the microphone to my headphones before announcing to my asshats, "If anyone needs me I'll be in the office finishing up the schedule and then in the warehouse unloading the truck when it comes." Sometimes I hate that having a retail management job means working with people. I much prefer being on my own, working on my own, and answering to nobody but me. One day…maybe one day…

By closing time, I'm more than ready to get out of the stale air that fills the store. I'm tired of dealing with cranky, disrespectful customers. I'm tired of listening to ridiculous rants by crazy people on the phone. I'm tired of watching Tonya and Vanessa fight with one another over who can do their job better. Come to think of it, I'm tired of all the drama surrounding the associates working from day to day. Although every day is different in terms of the customers I see or talk to, or the exact tasks I complete, retail life is monotonous, and uninspiring. I'm glad I have my projects to go home to at the end of the day. At least I have something to be passionate about other than selling office supplies all day long.

I mean we sell fucking pencils for Christ's sake!

Get over yourselves people!

After stripping off my gray manager shirt down to the pink tank underneath, I can finally feel the fresh air on my shoulders. I hop in my Ford Fusion, start the engine and peel out of the parking lot as quickly as I can. The faster I get home, the more time I have to spend doing what I love. Mystic, Connecticut can be a very pretty town driving near the water early in the morning or even during the mid-evening sunset, but right now, my yoga pants and flip flops are calling my name. Who cares that I'll be the only girl sitting at home alone on a Saturday night. Well, I guess that is pretty lame. I'm sure I can talk Linda into coming over for pizza, beer, and a some kind of silly chick flick.

Ten minutes down the road my thoughts are interrupted by a clicking sound in my car. I know nothing about cars except how to drive them so any odd sound they make cranks my anxiety up. I haven't even been driving for fifteen minutes when the car sputters and shakes under my feet.

"Shit!" Something is wrong and I have no idea what it is. I try not to panic as I glance in the rearview mirror to make sure all is clear behind me. I have just enough time to pull over to the side of the road before my damn car sounds like it's hacking up its lungs and then stops. Silence surrounds me. The engine won't turn over even a little bit. I throw my head back on my headrest and punch the steering wheel, which of course, causes the horn to beep loudly.

Shit!

Seriously?

This is how tonight is going to play out?

"This is all Mr. Seymore's fault," I mutter. "I should've known the moment he called that the rest of this day was going to suck ass." Grabbing my phone out of my pocket, I quickly call Linda to see if she can turn around and come get me, but she doesn't answer her phone. None of us usually have our ringers on while at work, so it doesn't surprise me that she doesn't hear me calling. I push the button to turn my hazard lights on before sending Linda a quick text. That girl always has her phone near her. She's bound to get my message.

Me: Hey. Car is dead.
I'm stuck on Holmes St. Bridge.
Come get me?

Linda: lol. Sure.
Just a few minutes. Turning around.

Me: Thx

I sit in the car for a few minutes and force myself to breathe after such a tedious day before getting out to do a quick walk around. I should probably make sure nothing looks out of place on the exterior of the car, or that I don't have some sort of car part hanging from the back of the car, not that I would know what it is if I found something. Fortunately, all looks as it's supposed to be, so hell if I know why my damn car won't start.

I'm walking back to my car door when a red truck drives by. The driver, who I can't see well in the dark, looks at me as he drives by, but continues up the road.

Jerk.

And then he slams on the brakes.

Phew! Thank you, Jesus.

The red, vintage looking tow truck slowly backs up as I stand there watching, wondering to myself if Linda sent a tow truck for me instead of coming to get me. I roll my eyes in frustration.

"Because I have all the money in the world to pay for a tow truck," I grumble to myself.

Trying not to look distressed, I patiently wait for the truck to back up enough for me to speak to the driver.

"Get in," he commands. His voice is rough and angry sounding. It stings my chest and for a moment I think about running away lest I be kidnapped and murdered, with my body thrown into the sound. I peek into the passenger door window and the driver punches the light above his head. My stomach flips upside down. Piercing gray eyes are staring at me…and then they're staring at the cleavage on display from my pink tank, before settling back on my face again.

"It's you," is all I can say.

"Get in," he repeats. His expression confuses me, scares me almost. He looks pissed off, and dare I say a little intimidating, but at the same time, the fired up look in his eye makes me feel things down below that definitely weren't on my mind a minute ago.

"You have a tow truck?" I ask bewildered. "You have a tow truck and you didn't tell me? God! You really must be truck whore." I stand at the passenger side window with my mouth hanging open in shock. Not just because Jacoby owns a tow truck but because this explains his reaction the other day when I said I had a sexual fantasy about tow trucks.

"KitKat, get in," he says one more time, not answering my question.

"Uh, okay," I say meekly as I open the passenger door and hoist myself up and into the cab. "My car…it won't start. I don't know what happened."

"I'll hook it up and we'll have a look." I watch as he swallows and takes a deep breath like he's trying to calm himself down-from what, I don't know. "Don't worry. I'll take care of you," he says quietly before hopping out of the truck with a pair of black work gloves. I watch in awe as his body turns and he hops down from the truck. He's wearing ripped jeans and a faded blue muscle shirt. Around his neck is a black leather cord necklace that has some sort of round coin-shaped charm hanging from it that I can't read without more light. Finally, his tattoo is clearly visible except that he moves too quickly from the truck to get a good look at it. I could be wrong but part of looked like…a cloud?

I grab my phone out of my pocket when he's gone and take a picture of where I am before sending it off to Linda.

Me: Never mind.
Jacoby is rescuing me…in his TOW TRUCK!
Who knew?

Linda: WTF?? LOL!!

Me: I'll explain later. Will call soon.
Thanks anyway.

Linda: Be safe. And by safe I mean use a condom!

"Oh give me a fucking break," I mutter as I roll my eyes. Jacoby may look like a steaming bowl of passion fruit tonight, but I didn't hop in this truck with sex on the brain. I'm pushing my phone back into the back pocket of my black work pants when Jacoby opens my door. "Thought you might want these. I'll need to pull the car up the ramp and we'll take her to the garage. I can fix it for you there."

"Thanks." I say when he hands me my purse and keys. "Um, okay. Yeah. Sounds good. Hey, thanks for uh…I don't know…being my white knight I guess." I shake my head, not really sure what to say. I mean how does he just show up in the right place at the right time?

Unless he was following me?

Impossible. I would've seen his truck.

Though I wasn't looking for a tow truck.

"I don't know that I'm as much a white knight than I am a dark horse. Let's go for a ride shall we?" The words…his words. They're not word vomit at all. They're more like stimulatingly seductive words that cause me to blush big time.

A dark horse?

Who wants to take me for a ride?

Dear God.

Yes, please.

Maybe I do have sex on the brain.

"Sooo how did you know I was here? On the side of the road I mean?" I question him as we pull back onto the road and head to who knows where.

"I didn't. I was just driving by."

"Oh. Well…ok. Thanks again then, for stopping. I didn't want to have to call my dad. He's a bit of an asshole."

Jacoby turns his head to look at me when I mention my father, his expression even more agitated. "Is he an asshole to you? Does he hurt you? Because I swear to God I will absolutely…"

"No!" I interrupt him. "No, I mean. It's fine. No, he doesn't hurt me. In all honesty, I don't know my father the way others know theirs. He was more like a sperm donor, so who knows if he's really an asshole. I just think he's an asshole because he decided to walk away from my mom and sister and me. I only call him if there's an emergency that my sister can't help me with."

"What about your mom?" he suggests.

"She's dead."

"Fuck." I hear him whisper to himself. "How?"

"How what?"

"How did your mom pass away?" he clips.

I look over at Jacoby as he drives. His gaze isn't on me. He's staring at the road in front of him, his left leg bouncing up and down beside him like he's nervous.

Or pissed.

I wonder who killed his cat.

"Cancer." I clear my throat. "She died of stage four cervical cancer."

I hear his sigh, but he doesn't say anything else. We drive in awkward silence for a few minutes, my anxiety wanting to get the better of me. I feel the urge to vomit all the words at him but clench my teeth in restraint. I don't even know what to say, anyway.

"I'm sorry about your Mom," he fumes.

"Thanks…?" I scowl at him a little confused as to his attitude. He doesn't sound to me like he's sorry at all. Why did he even ask then? I count to ten before speaking again. "Are you okay?" Clearly, he's not, but I don't have anything else to talk about.

"Yeah. Why?" he asks.

Now it's my turn to scoff. "Oh, I don't know. Maybe because you look like someone just fucked your girlfriend and you're ready to cut a bitch, but, you know, I could be wrong."

He roars with laughter, making me a little more at ease with him, though still a bit perplexed nonetheless. "Oh man. That was good, but no. Nobody has fucked my girlfriend or yeah, I *would* probably want to cut a bitch."

Damn.

He has a girlfriend.

Why is that even bothering me?

"Oh. Well, good then."

"But I would need to actually have a girlfriend for someone to fuck in order for me to turn into the Hulk, and since I don't..." He looks at me. "I guess we're both safe." I see the dimple in his cheek as he smiles briefly at me before sighing deeply and shaking his head. "Look, I'm sorry for my mood. You're not the only one with an asshole for a father. You just happened to show up when I was on my way home from mine."

Phew!

"No girlfriend and an asshole father! Score!"

Jacoby chuckles heartily. "Well I'm glad you approve, I guess."

My hand clamps over my mouth behind which I mutter "Oh my God, I said those words out loud, didn't I?"

Smiling, he nods. "Indeed, you did."

"Oh shit. I'm sorry. I don't mean to sound so forward. I'm not a slut, I promise. Sometimes I just lose control of my thoughts and just end up word-vomiting all over the damn place. I think it's a disease...like loquacitosis or something."

"I'm not sure that's a real word," he notes. "And I don't mind the forwardness at all."

I ignore his last comment, not really knowing how to react. "It's real. Trust me. Just Google it. I'm sure my name pops up somewhere on the screen. Sooo...what makes your dad such an asshole?" I inquire.

Tit for tat, pretty boy.

Jacoby blows out his breath and shakes his head disapprovingly. "Governor Malloy always has something to be pissed about or disappointed in. It may as well be me."

"Wait, your dad is Governor Malloy? Your name is Jacoby Malloy?"

"You didn't know that already?" he asks, perplexed.

I'm caught off guard by his question. I'm not sure what he expects me to say, so I opt for sheer honesty. "Uh, no. Before the other day I knew you as the hot guy who was a semi-regular in my store."

He's silent next to me.

"Plus," I continue. "I don't really give two shits about politics anyway. I've yet to see a sincere politician who really is 'for the people' as they say, and one who doesn't carry some sort of closet chocked full of skeletons."

Jacoby chuckles in a huff to himself. "You can say that again."

"So why is your dad disappointed in you? Did you do something bad?"

"Do I look like someone who does bad things?" he hints.

"No! Absolutely not. That's not what I was saying at all. I'm sorry if it came across that way," I apologize.

"I'll show you why," he says, nodding to the building in front of him as he turns off the road. As he does so he sighs what feels like a huge sigh of relief, like he's happy he made it home in one piece. Ahead of us is a large garage with a few cars parked outside along the building. Some of them are cars but most of them are trucks, classic trucks at that! They're beautiful. The sign on the top of the building says JACKED UP. Images of a gray t-shirt pop into my head.

"Really? They really call this place Jacked Up?"

"No. *I* call this place Jacked Up. It's mine. I own it." He winks before opening his door and walking around to my side of the truck. He opens the door and offers me a hand as I jump down from my seat. Immediately his demeanor has changed. He doesn't seem as pissed off as he was. I can tell his body is tense though, so whatever happened to him before he picked me up is still bothering him. Getting in this truck, I wasn't the least bit nervous, but now my knees feel like jelly. He holds my waist in his hands a little longer than what is probably appropriate for an innocent gesture, though I don't feel anything but safe. His eyes meet mine before gliding down my body and back up again. If I had about four beers in me I wouldn't think twice about jumping his bones right now…but that might be weird when I'm totally sober.

"So, you…repair cars?" I ask, almost stuttering.

"Yep. And restore classics."

"Huh. I would've never guessed."

"Oh yeah? And why is that?" he probes.

"Well, for one thing, your hands are never dirty. At least…I don't think they ever have been when I've seen you in the store…not that…you know, not that I spend a lot of time staring at your hands. I don't mean to sound like a creeper."

Shut up, Jenna.

Jacoby stares at me, running his hands through his hair as though he's unsure of what to say. He places his palm out in front of me, waiting for me to give him my keys. When I place my keys in his hand, his fingers immediately reach up and glide over the underside of my palm until he's holding onto my wrist, like he was planning that move the entire time. I stare at him as my breath hitches. He pulls me closer to him, his deliciously scented cologne pouring over my senses. My chest is now pressed firmly against his, our heartbeats rapidly growing as we stand here together. It's cliché to say I can feel how firm his body is, but holy crap on a cracker I can actually feel the ridges of his sixteen pack for crying out loud. His face inches toward mine, and my eyes relax like they do in that moment right before you kiss someone.

Oh my god, he's going to kiss me!

I lift my chin so that our lips can meet, and finally close my eyes in anticipation of what this kiss might feel like. His fingers are smooth as they reach behind my ear and weave into my hair. I resist the urge to moan. His breath on my ear is a shock to my body that sends tingles to my lady bits.

"Jenna?" His voice is magnetic, drawing me in, seducing me into a trance.

"Yes..." I draw out, waiting for his lips to brush mine.

"My hands are always clean because I wash them," he whispers provocatively before shifting back, waiting for me to open my eyes. When I do, he winks, turns away and walks back to the rear of the truck to unload my car off the tow truck.

Damn.

I just fell for that.

And now he knows.

Now he knows I'm interested.

Double damn damn.

I stand there in front of the truck and watch as he lowers my car back to the ground from where it was previously chained. He pops the hood and takes a look around. His hands move over several pieces under the hood as he checks lines, filters, fluid levels and I'm sure a barrage of other things, all the while not speaking to me. Nervously I bite at my fingernails, waiting for him to say anything that might change the subject from Jenna-thought-Jacoby-was-going-to-kiss-her-even-though-they've-only spent-ten-minutes-together.

Pull yourself together Jenna.

"Hmm…okay." I hear Jacoby say to himself. He walks over to the counter where several tools are sprawled in front of him, some hanging on hooks along the wall. I don't even recognize the ones he picks up, because I know absolutely nothing about cars, but he raises my car on his lift, grabs what he needs and kicks his skateboard-thingy towards my car before laying down on it and rolling underneath. When I watch his body slide underneath the car, his shirt rides up just enough for me to see the bottom of his abs and the waist band of his Calvin Klein boxers. I shouldn't even be paying attention to those details but dang…when they're right in front of me and he doesn't know I'm looking, how can I not?

"Is everything looking okay?" I ask after a few minutes of silent torture. He doesn't even know me, but somehow knows just how to mess with my brain.

"I think so," he mutters from under the car. After a few more minutes, he rolls out, catching me ogling his body as I stand near the front of the car. Why does he have to be so damn sexy? I swear I see one side of his lip rise up in a half smirk as he walks over to lower the lift back to the ground. He brushes himself off and steps in front of me with a heady look in his eye.

"So do you think you can fix the problem?" I ask him innocently, trying to not to make big deal of the fact that I feel hot enough standing in front of him that I may start sweating. Jacoby holds my stare for what feels like many long minutes-long enough to make my heart beat accelerate to uncomfortable levels. I wish I knew what was going through his head right now.

"Which problem would you liked fixed?"

Shit. It's bad.

There goes my savings.

Stupid fucking car.

"Well…can we start with the least expensive? Or maybe we should start with the most important. I don't know. I just - I have to have a car to get to work. I don't live close enough to walk, so whatever you think I sho…" Jacoby steps closer to me and places his index finger over my mouth. I think he's shushing me. This should be weird…except for some reason my insides are burning. Who knew a finger to my lips could be such a turn-on?

"You're doing it again." He grins.

"Doing what?"

"Word-vomiting." He chuckles. "Stop worrying. I can fix both problems." He places his left hand on my shoulder, making me jump, and immediately sending a million butterflies fluttering through my stomach. "If you want my professional opinion, I would tell you that the least expensive fix is also the most important."

"Okay."

"I would also tell you, in my professional opinion," he continues, "that you shouldn't stare at a guy when he's bent over or rolling out from under your car. Some guys may not have much restraint when you're standing there all sexy in your pink tank top, you know." He traces the shoulder strap on my tank top with his index finger, causing goose bumps to rise up on my arms.

"Oh," I say.

Shit. He's perceptive.

Or I was obvious.

"Uh…thanks? For the umm…the tip." My face is heating up. I can feel it. I probably have one of those embarrassing red blotches on my cheek. "So…" I clear my throat, trying to focus on the task at hand instead of the compulsion to kiss the hell out of him. I can't help but lick my lips though. All of this closeness is giving me a cotton mouth. "So, you can fix it then?"

"Yeah I can fix it. I just need another check under the hood first." His breathing is heavy, matching mine. I know we're standing here talking about my car, but it feels damn near like we're not talking about my car at all.

"Okay good, I'll just - I'll move out of your way." I answer, but when I go to move aside, his hand tightens, effectively trapping me between him and the car. My eyes snap up to his, slightly confused, but wanting oh so badly.

"Not that hood," he whispers. His places a hand around my waist as he raises his already dirty fingertips to my face, trailing sparks of desire down my cheeks, my neck, and my exposed shoulders. In a moment that can only be described as pure carnal need, Jacoby lifts me up before lowering me down to sit on top of my car. I don't even get a chance to say anything before his mouth crashes against mine, licking, tasting, taking all he wants and I unabashedly surrender to him. I'm not a girl to shy away from making out with a hot guy. If that makes me a slut, so be it. Hell, maybe he'll even fix my car for free.

Instinctively, my hands glide up his arms, grasping a firm hold on his biceps. A growling moan rises from the back of his throat as he forcefully pulls our bodies closer together, him standing between my open thighs. I can feel his erection pressing against his jeans. Holding me against him with his left hand, his right slides down my sternum to my breast. It feels so damn good, but when he squeezes me and pinches my nipple, I'm a goner.

"Oh God..." I moan as my head falls back, giving him easy access to my neck. He pulls my hair slightly with his left hand in order to lean in and lick behind my ear. I swear I almost come on the spot. I guess I like a man who isn't afraid to take command.

"I told you I need to check under the hood," he says, fluttering kisses down my neck and around my collar bone. "That okay? Do you trust me?"

"Yes. Yes," I answer in haste. I shouldn't trust him. I know. This is a guy that I just sort of met a few days ago, and know not much about, but right now, the pleasure ripping through my body isn't giving me any ability to think with my head. I've been alone with Jacoby for less than an hour between the café and tonight, but if he doesn't make me come soon, I might have to sprawl out on this car and provide a show for him because I now need to get off in the worst way.

Jacoby slides his hands under my shirt, his fingers brushing my naked skin underneath. Goosebumps meet his touch as my shirt is lifted above my head and thrown off. I don't even see where it goes, nor do I care. "You're beautiful," he says quietly, ogling my body with a desire I haven't seen in a man in a long time. I don't even notice where it comes from, but Jacoby takes the shirt he ripped off me and lays it out flat behind me on the hood of the car before pushing me back against it. Lucky for me, I wore my pink lace bra that opens in the front. Jacoby doesn't even look to see how it's done. His lips crash back to mine as I feel the quick tug and hear the pop that was my bra clasp.

Guess I'll be buying a new one of those.

Peppering kisses down my neck and chest, my body bucks instinctively into him, heavy pleasure blazing through my body. I try to reach up and touch him but he grabs my arms and holds them against the car on each side of me. His stare tells me he's in command

and all I can do in response is try to catch my breath. Jacoby takes one more look at my breasts, openly bared to him as I lay on the hood of my car, before pulling my nipple into his mouth, sucking, biting, licking. My body writhes underneath him as I scream out in ecstasy, not giving a shit who might hear us.

"You taste so good," he claims as he moves to the other side of my chest. "I've been wanting to taste you for a long time. Since the first day I saw you."

"There's more of me to taste," I answer.

Oh. My. God.

Did I just say that?

Out loud?

Jacoby's eyes snap to mine in delight, like I've just given him the most exciting Christmas gift. "Headlights…check." He growls. His response actually makes me laugh. I watch in wonder as he lifts his shirt over his head. He is glorious. Tanned skin, tight muscles, and I've now been introduced to more than one tattoo; the one is not a cloud like I originally thought. Instead, it's a black sheep. I want to spend time studying his body, the couple tattoos and the meanings behind them, the mark near his belly button that I assume is a birthmark, the nipple ring, which I noticed before, that I want to flick with my tongue, something I've never gotten to do. I want to run my fingers over him but he doesn't give me time. Smoothly he leans over me, tasting my lips, swirling his tongue around mine while his hands unbutton my black work pants. His right hand slides painstakingly slow down the path to wonderland. His tempo is slow enough that I secretly think back to the last time I trimmed the bushes and worry that he may be turned off by the shrubbery. My body tenses but when he looks up and catches my worried eyes his hand caresses me inside my pants. I mewl softly at his touch when his finger slowly moves in circles around me. I moan before panting like Meg Ryan in *When Harry Met Sally*.

"Dear God," he says in awe. "Lube, check."

Swiftly he pushes me up farther on the hood of the car before he grabs my pant legs and pulls. I'm sure there are much sexier ways to do this; in fact, I've been a part of sexier ways of undressing, but now, I'm not sure I could tame the beast even if I wanted to.

And I don't want to.

He lifts my legs so that they're sitting on each of his shoulders. Holy shit this is a compromising position and admittedly, one I've never been in before. Sex on a car, my legs in the air and…OH MY GOD how does he do that with his tongue? I scream out at the pleasure that is Jacoby's tongue on my exposed warm flesh. He moans forcefully with his mouth, covering my body, like he's devouring me. My body begins to tremble.

"Jacoby…" I cry out.

"Mmm." He moans again, moving his face slowly up and down as he feathers me with soft quick licks. The stubble on his face causes just the right amount of friction to the sensitivity causing a glorious explosion of all feeling throughout my body.

"I'm coming!" I shout in between panted breaths. "Jacoby, oh God! I'm coming!"

"I know, baby. It's fantastic. You're stunning." He smiles adoringly as my body pulses around his face.

Tenderly he lowers my legs back to the car before reaching for the buttons on his jeans.

"Fuck!" he exclaims.

"What is it?" I gasp. "Oh God, did my period start or something? It totally shouldn't have, it's not…"

"No." Jacoby shakes his head and laughs. "No baby, you're perfect. I just…I don't have a fucking condom."

"What?"

"I wasn't…I didn't pla…" he shakes his head again, annoyed with himself for giving himself a severe case of blue balls.

I grab his arm and squeeze, still coming down from my orgasm. "My purse. Inside pocket. Take your pick."

Jacoby's head tilts to the side as he looks at me, raising one eyebrow. "You carry condoms around with you?"

"Do you want to fuck me or not?" I argue.

A girl can never be too prepared.

"Shit," he mumbles. "Sorry. Be right back." I lay on the hood of my car trying to get my breathing under control and watch while Jacoby runs to my side of the truck, opens the door and grabs my purse.

"Inside pocket?" he confirms.

"Yes."

He grabs a foil packet out of my purse and drops the purse on the ground at his feet. He flips it over to look at it before ripping it open. His pants already unbuttoned, he pushes them down faster than Superman changing in a phone booth and slides the condom over himself, giving me an entertaining, yet arousing floor show. With his best smoldering look, he steps back in between my legs as I lay flat on the hood of the car. My breath hitches when he moistens the tip of his erection with my arousal.

"Wrap your legs around me baby," he says as he grabs a hold of my waist. "This might hurt a little." And with those words he pounds into me, making me scream at the fulfilling feeling.

"Yes!" he shouts. His voice, his desire, his pleasure, every part of him causes me to want to give him everything he wants, and take everything I want in return. "God, I need this," he says as he plunges inside me over and over again. His body against mine, thrusting into me, spreads a raging fire of hot desire straight to my core. I want him harder, faster, and for as long as he can last. I don't even care that he just told me that *he* needs this. I need this too, and since I have mad respect for the penis, I can justify all of my actions with no regrets.

"Yes! Jacoby! Please!" I clench around him, squeezing him as tight as I can, taking in every inch of him. Not knowing where to put my hands, I selfishly bring them up to my own breasts, pleasuring myself with my touch as Jacoby watches.

A fierce growl escapes him as his bats my hands away from my chest and replaces them with his own hands. "Mine!" he declares.

Damn. That's hot.

This is what I love. A man who knows what he wants and isn't afraid to take it. I don't need a dominant asshole. Straight up great sex is all this simple girl desires, and Jacoby can deliver. I can tell he's primed, pumped and ready to let go. His hands tense around my breasts and he squeezes my nipples between his fingers as his head falls back, his mouth open in ecstasy. He thrusts four more times, holding on to my breasts as if they were handlebars on a bike, as he reaches for his climax.

"Yes. Oh. Fuck. YES!"

The pulse, the heat, the feel of his balls as they hit me those last few times sends me spiraling over the edge once again as I shudder with euphoric bliss. We lay in this awkward position on the hood of my car for a few silent minutes before Jacoby breaks the silence.

"Are you okay?" he asks gently, peering into my eyes like I'm the love of his life.

"Yeah." I nod. "Yeah, I'm good. Better than good actually." I smile, slightly embarrassed to have even said that out loud.

"You carry condoms in your purse. Should I conclude something from that?" he asks. I notice he doesn't meet my eye when he speaks.

"Your condom-covered penis is still inside of me and you're asking me this question? Is this where we talk about our previous sexual partners?"

"No, I..." Whoa...he's speechless. "I'm sorry. I didn't mean to make it seem like I thought you were..."

"It's okay," I interrupt wherever the hell that was going to go. "I guess I would rather be prepared than not be prepared. I mean that's okay, right? I mean think about the consequences for you had I not been."

Jacoby raises his head to smile at me. "Fair point well made."

"Oil change...check." He says as he pulls out of me. I watch as he slides the condom off himself, wincing in the process. He blows out a satisfying breath when the condom is off and when I look at him, I see why.

Ring around the penis.

"Oh God. It was too small? The condom was too small? I'm sorry Jacoby. I didn't think..."

"KitKat, do me a favor and don't finish that sentence. Instead of having to hear you say you didn't think I would be that big, which would only bruise my ego about one hundred percent, allow me to bask in the satisfaction that I'm obviously the biggest you've had or else your condoms would come in a larger size."

Smiling, I nod my head in agreement. "It's a deal."

"Good." He leans down and kisses my forehead, an alarming display of affection that I didn't expect. "Are you really okay? Did I hurt you?"

"No." I shake my head. "I'm perfectly fine." I say that knowing full well that I'm certain there will be a few red spots on my back from the friction between my body and my car. What he doesn't know won't kill him.

"I'm sorry." His breath deflates. "I'm not usually so rough. I – I don't know what – I'm sorry."

"Jacoby?" I wait until his eyes meet mine. "I'm totally fine. Perfectly fine. I promise. Okay?"

He nods his head not sure if he wants to believe me or not. "Okay. Let's get you cleaned up." Jacoby stands up and pulls on his pants, buttoning them quickly before helping me up from my position on the car. Immediately I feel exposed and a bit insecure. I have no idea what one does after having sex on the top of a car...a car that's here to be fixed. I can't just run away, and at the moment, I'm stark naked.

"Here," Jacoby says, offering me his muscle shirt. Immediately I slide it on and take his hand as he helps me off the car. He holds my face in his hands, raising my chin so that our eyes meet. "You're a beautiful girl, Jenna. I could look at you all day." He places another soft kiss on the top of my head.

Sheepishly, I tuck a strand of hair behind my ear. I don't even know what to say. "Do you have a bathroom I could use?"

Good one Jenna.

That was so emphatically beautiful.

"Yeah." He smiles softly. "Right through that door on the right." He says, pointing to a door against the far wall of the garage.

"Thanks. I'll just be a minute." I take a few minutes to clean myself up but notice my panties are soaking wet. I roll my eyes and think of Linda and our girl's night conversations. We always see people having ridiculously hot sex in the movies, but nobody ever portrays the after-effects correctly. Nobody shows the girl running to the bathroom so she doesn't leak fluids all down her leg. The couples end up falling asleep in each other's arms but where is the huge puddle of cum on the sheets in the morning? Sex is messy. It's fantastic, yes, but messy nonetheless. Linda and I always laugh at how the best sex scenes end in cuddling or sleeping and never with the girl running to the bathroom to clean herself up.

Deciding to be bold and brave, I slide my work pants on over my bare ass and look around the bathroom quickly for a place to leave my panties as a souvenir for Jacoby. I open a drawer near the sink, and find a few bottles of Advil and Tylenol. Smirking to myself, I slip my panties in the drawer and slide it closed. Once I'm fully dressed again sans bra since it's now broken, I walk back to the garage where Jacoby is pouring something into my car.

"What is that?" I ask.

"Gas." He turns his head toward me with a shit-eating grin. "You were out of gas."

That's impossible. "My gas light didn't turn on."

"Well that might be another problem to fix then at some point," he says.

"Why didn't you just tell me I was out of gas earlier?"

The cat-ate-the-canary grin he wears gives him away. "Because I've been dying to be alone with you and I didn't want you to leave so soon." He finishes filling my tank – for the second time – and twists the cap back on to the red container and places it back on his shelf. I take a minute to look around the garage while he cleans up. Everything looks to be in place. It's a clean garage, and one that looks like it keeps him busy. I'm not sure I understand what he meant when he said his father is disappointed in him.

"What are you thinking about over there?" Jacoby asks me as he wipes down the front of my car. I never even thought about possible dents or scratches from our escapade.

"Nothing, really. Just…" I shrug. "I don't get it."

"Don't get what?" he asks.

"You made it sound earlier like your father views you as a disappointment. I look around this place and see nothing but evidence of a hard-working man," I explain.

Jacoby smiles softly, sticking his hands in the pockets of his jeans. "Well it's a far cry from a son walking in his father's footsteps, so there's that."

"You mean he expects you to become a politician."

"Yep. Like my older brother who is working his way up via a seat on the city council, and my younger sister who is my father's campaign manager."

"Oh. So, what drove you away from politics?" I ask him.

He laughs to himself and shakes his head. "You don't want to know."

"Well when you put it like that, now I really, really want to know," I tease.

He looks around the garage for a second before settling his eyes back on me. "A girl," he says quietly.

"A girl." I repeat, but not really asking for confirmation. So, there's a history there involving some girl. After what we just did, I'm not sure I want to know so I bite my tongue for now. Jacoby opens his mouth to say something when his cell phone rings in his back pocket. The ring tone isn't your usual ringer sound. It's the 007 theme song. I scowl in amusement when he curses at his phone.

"Shit. I'm sorry, but I have to take this. I should only be a minute." He says as he walks away from me answering his phone with a clipped "Yeah." I watch for a second until I hear him say "Yeah I have it, hold on.". He turns to me holding up his pointer finger signaling me to wait a minute. Without nodding to him I watch him walk through the same door I walked out of a few moments ago.

I'm now alone in his garage. All jacked up and no place to go. Actually, I have a lot of things I could be doing right now and playing naïve young girl with a crush on a guy who probably brings all the women back here for a quick lube, isn't really one of them. We'll both be better off if I just leave so we don't have to do that awkward what-do-we-do-after-a-one-night-stand thing. It's not like he would ask me to sleep over and I wouldn't anyway. And whatever history there is between him and this mystery girl, I don't want to be involved in the drama. Before he ends his phone call, I hastily look for my purse and car keys. My purse is on the floor where Jacoby left it and I find my keys in the ignition of the car. I get into the car as silently as I can and turn the engine. No matter how much or how little gas he put in here for me, I'm positive it'll be enough to get me down the road to a gas station. I put the car in reverse and turn smoothly out of the garage, down the driveway and onto the road.

This is what's best for both of us.

This way I won't word vomit all over him.

He had the best wiffy stick I've ever seen.

CHAPTER 4

007 Fail

Jacoby

I step quickly down the hall and into the house attached to my garage so that I can grab the info that James needs. I hate to leave Jenna out there alone, especially after I just mentioned another girl to her. What kind of guy talks about one girl after just fucking another? She must think I'm the biggest douchebag.

Lifting open my laptop, I click the file I need to answer James' questions. "Yeah. It's up to one hundred and four right now," I answer.

"Thousand? A hundred and four thousand?"

"Yep."

"Sounds promising. Good work. Everything going smoothly? Anything I can do to help?" James offers.

"Nah. I just need time and I know, I know, everything will be done in time." I roll my eyes. After four years of a working relationship I would've thought James would believe in me a little more than he seems to, instead of feeling the need to breathe down my neck all the time.

"No problem Jacoby. You still have a couple months. We're good. Oh, by the way, the *Today Show* called again. They really want to do an interview with you.

"Absolutely not. You know my stance on that. Look, James. I have company waiting on me right now so…" I start.

"Molly says it would be a fantastic shock and awe for fans."

Yeah, and my Dad.

Fuck me.

"And I said no, James." I'm kicking myself for not just having this quick conversation with James in the garage, so at least I could be with Jenna. Nothing about the conversation needs to be private.

"Alright, alright. I know. Just thought I would throw it out there again. Could be a great opportunity for sales growth. Hot guy…sex appeal. Anyway, I'll give you a call in a week or so and see where things stand."

"I have no doubt you will." I roll my eyes. "Talk to you later. And thanks."

"Sure thing." I hear him say before I quickly hit the button on my phone that ends our call. I push my laptop closed and exit the house back into the hallway that connects the house to the garage.

"I'm sorry, Jenna. I didn't mean to keep you…waiting." My voice trails off. She's not here. Neither is her car.

"Shit!" I curse to myself, kicking the tire of the tow truck now sitting alone in the garage.

Did she get pissed and leave?

Did she get a call and need to leave?

Did I scare her away?

I throw my hands into my hair, frustrated with myself for leaving her here alone in the first place. This is all my fucking fault. "I don't even have her phone number," I mumble. I can't call her. I can't explain anything to her. I can't even apologize because I have no way of communicating with her. I shouldn't even care except for some reason I can't get her out of my head. I haven't been able to get her out of my head for months, since the first time I saw her at The Hole Punch. She's so sweet to her customers, her laughter is like sunshine on a cloudy day, and her body…God, her body. She's not the skin and bones type that I can't stand. She has curves in all the right places. She's perfectly stunning and she's sassy and sarcastic and funny and…real.

"Facebook!" I shout to myself. My feet are carrying me back into the house before I can even think about stopping myself. As soon as I reach my office I throw myself into my chair and flip open my laptop. Facebook is already open in a window so I enlarge it and type in her name in the search bar at the top of the screen. As expected, about thirty Jennas come up. I slowly scroll through them all looking to see their locations and studying their profile pictures in hopes that she's easy to find. About ten of the profiles I see have profile pictures that aren't humans. One is a black puppy, one is a speedboat, one is a plate of cookies, one is a sexy pink piece of lingerie, one is a sunset on what looks like a beach and one is a little boy with cake on his face. None of those sounds like the Jenna I know, and I can't just send a private message to all of them.

"Oh hi, if you're the Jenna I just fucked in my garage, can you write me back?
If you're not her, just disregard this message. Thanks."

"Son of a bitch." I sigh in defeat. There's nothing I can do tonight. The Hole Punch is closed till morning. I have no choice but to wait until then. Dammit, I hate that I look like a complete prick who was just looking for a quick fuck. That's not who I am and I really need her to know that. I'm not sure what makes her stand out to me yet, and I sure as hell can't figure out why I can't keep her out of my mind.

Yes, you can, dumbass.

You like her.

I'm up at the crack of dawn Sunday morning sporting a woody that can only be explained in two words: Jenna induced. I went to bed thinking about her. The softness of her lips, the way she made those little noises when I touched her, the way her hands felt around my biceps, the smell of her hair and whatever the hell fruity shampoo she uses. She's my walking wet dream and I'm aching to experience something, anything, with her all over again. I have no choice but to rub one out while I'm in the shower. If I don't, I'll be walking around in tented pants all damn day. Knowing the Hole Punch won't open until noon on a Sunday, I busy myself in my office trying to get as much work done for James and Molly as I can. Sometimes I hate being on a deadline but at least this morning I know where I want this project to go.

By noon I'm taking the Studebaker for a ride into town, hoping above all hope that I'll be able to interest Jenna in a Sunday drive when she's done working. Though I don't want to come across as desperate, I would wait all day in the parking lot if she asked me to. When I pull into the parking lot of The Hole Punch I don't see Jenna's car anywhere. Praying that maybe some days she gets a ride to work I park the truck and walk inside the store, trying to be as nonchalant as possible. Like always, I walk back to the back of the store and grab a ream of paper, a few highlighters, and this time, some paperclips, all the while looking around for Jenna's face or listening for her voice. To my disappointment, I don't see her or hear her anywhere.

"Can I help you, Sir?" A young man smiles at me. His name tag says Adam.

"Uh, no, thank you. I think I got everything I was looking for," I tell him.

He responds with a friendly nod. "Let me know if I can help you with anything."

"Thanks." I continue forward, stopping suddenly and turning back toward the direction Adam was walking.

"Hey wait a sec. Is Jenna working this morning? I'm a…"

Shit! What do I say?

"I'm a friend of hers. Just thought I would say hello while I'm here." It's a half truth. That's justification enough.

"No, I'm sorry," Adam says. "She's off on Sundays. Spends the day with her sister usually. She'll be back tomorrow morning."

"Oh. Right. I forgot about Sundays." I pretend to know what he's talking about though I have no clue. "Thanks a lot."

"Sure thing."

Though I feel like dropping all the supplies that I'm carrying on the floor and crawling out of the store like a four-year old throwing a tantrum, I make my way to counter to check out. The girl at the register looks familiar, and by the way she's looking at me, perhaps the feeling is mutual. Her eyes narrow at me slightly when I lay my supplies on the counter in front of her. I look up enough to read that her nametag says Linda.

"Good morning," she says. "Did you find everyone…" She clears her throat. "I mean every*thing* you were looking for?"

Freudian slip?

I can't tell.

"Yeah." I nod. "Yeah, I did, thanks."

"Mmm-hmm." She says, her voice raising in pitch. I watch her ring up the paper and highlighters and paperclips. She smirks to herself and I instantly feel guilty, like I'm trying to hide something from this girl that I don't even know, like I'm trying to quickly buy a box of super XXL sized condoms without anyone noticing. I swipe my credit card in the machine and complete my transaction all the while purposely not making eye contact with Linda. She puts my receipt in my bag and hands it to me, continuing to watch me like she's trying to figure me out.

"Thanks." I nod.

"She opens tomorrow," Linda says, not making eye contact with me. My head snaps up in reaction to her words.

"Jenna" is all that comes out of my mouth.

Linda puts her hand on her hip, chewing the inside of her mouth for a second as she sizes me up. "But what I can't understand is why you're here, and she's not."

Shaking my head in confusion I wait for an explanation. "I'm sorry, I don't…"

"Well," she starts. "I mean I get that she's off today, but I know for a fact that she was with you last night. Either that or she's leading a secret life for which she is a damn good liar, and since I'm her best friend in the whole wide world, I know that's not true. So, if she was with you last night, and she's not with you this morning…*and* I haven't heard from her, that raises a red flag with me, Mr. Tall, Dark, and Handsome. So, maybe I shouldn't be telling you that she opens tomorrow, because maybe you were an asshole to her and she doesn't want to see you. And if you're here looking for her this morning, then she obviously didn't tell you she was off, which leads me to believe that you're either a creepy stalker or you did something you feel the need to apologize for, so which is it?"

My eyebrows rise at her lengthy yet spot on explanation, but I don't really want to lay my failures out on the counter in front of someone so close to the girl I'm sort of hot for. "Wow. Really I just came in for some paper and supplies." I try to play dumb but she's not buying it. Isn't the customer always supposed to be right?

"Well I'm pretty sure highlighters aren't a trending item on the black market so you can't be selling them on the street corner, so I can only assume you're a professional highlighter who sits at home highlighting notes for people all day since you seem to purchase them every time you're here. Either that, or maybe you're some sort of highlighter hoarder, and that's just…weird – I think." She smirks.

Fuck.

She's perceptive, this one.

Sighing in defeat and looking around to make sure other customers aren't standing around, I finally come clean. "Okay. You're right. I was with Jenna last night. I mean, I picked her up. She's…great…she's…" I can't even make the right words come out of my mouth. What the hell is my problem? "We had a great time – no." I shake my head disapprovingly. "That sounds stupid. I helped her out last night, fixed her car for her and…"

Had some of the best sex I've ever had and then she left me.

Linda's left eyebrow shoots up. "Uh huh…"

I close my eyes and inhale a deep breath before trying to let out a little bit of the truth. "And then I got an important phone call that I had to take and when I came back she was gone. I wanted to apologize to her for leaving her alone for a minute, but she left and I never got her cell phone number or an email or anything. I can't find her on Facebook and I have no idea where she lives, so yeah, I was hoping I might see her here today to let her know that I really enjoyed…uh…"

Don't say it Jacoby.

"I enjoyed her company."

"Her company," she reiterates.

Yeah, you're great with words, Jacoby.

I know. God, I sound like a lame ass idiot. "Yeah. Her company. Anyway, look, I'm not going to ask you for information about her. I understand the desire for privacy, but, you know, if you talk to her or see her," I pull out one of my Jacked Up business cards from my wallet and hand it to Linda. "Would you please tell her that I stopped by? Please?"

Linda holds up my card reading the info on both sides. "Jacked Up?" She chuckles. "Really? You have a place called 'Jacked Up'?"

"Yeah. Funny, Jenna said the exact same thing." I smile.

She looks at the card again before looking back to me. "Yeah, I'll tell her you stopped by. If she wants to talk to you, I'm sure you'll hear from her."

"Thanks. I really appreciate it." I grab my bag from the counter and head out the door. "Have a nice day," I say to Linda on the way out.

"Thanks, you as well." I hear her say.

Sulking as I enter my truck I pull my phone out of my back pocket and check for any missed messages, hoping that somehow, Jenna figured out a way to get in touch with me. The screen remains blank. The ball is in her court now I guess.

I wish it were my balls in her court.

I have no choice but to wait, and waiting sucks.

CHAPTER 5
Autocorrect

Jenna

"Hey thanks, Jen, for spending the day with me, and for dinner."

"Anytime, Babe," I answer my sister. "I know we both get busy, but I really love that we do this together, you know? I miss you, Bethy." I start to clean up the mess I have strewn all over the floor of the living room.

"Aww, I miss you too, Jen." She holds up two pieces in front of her. "And for the record, this peach one is my favorite. Straps and holes in all the right places." She smirks. We both giggle together as she lays my designs in the box next to me.

"Thanks," I tell her. "I need to drop them off tomorrow at some point. God willing, they'll all sell and I'll be up another thousand bucks for the week!"

Beth shakes her head in amazement. "I'm so proud of you Jen. You've got such an eye for design. You have so much talent. I wish I had what you had."

"You do. We're a team, Bethy. You know that. I couldn't do this without you. I need someone with a great eye and a savvy business sense. One day, maybe we'll be doing this full time. Our own place, our own line. We'll be like Mary Kate and Ashley Olsen." I wink at her.

Beth chuckles. "You know, John Stamos might be old enough to be my dad, but given the opportunity, I would bend over for him in a heartbeat."

"Hahaha, I don't doubt it with you, Beth." I laugh.

"So, what are you going to do about this guy from last night?" She asks me. "He sounds fun and…spontaneous?"

I try to wave her off so I don't have to discuss it. I'm really not sure what I want to do about Jacoby at all. "Probably nothing. You know me, I'm non-committal, and although the way he does a fourteen-point check on a car is maybe the hottest thing I've ever experienced, it was just a one-time thing."

"Uh huh." I hear Beth say, knowing damn well she thinks I'm lying through my teeth. A knock at the door saves me from delving further into our conversation. Walking over to the door, I check the peep hole before swinging it wide open.

"Girl, you have a key! What the hell are you doing knocking?" I ask Linda as she follows me into the living room.

"Yeah, I know, but I know it's Sunday, and – Hey Beth – I know you guys spend the day together working and I wouldn't want to walk in on one of you wearing something like…this." Linda picks up two pieces of black material adorned with beads and gemstones.

Beth laughs. "Hey Linda. Good to see you, and you just missed the modeling session. Had you been ten minutes earlier…"

"Damn! I wanted to see that purple one! Why didn't you call me Jizza?" She pouts.

"The purple one is a done deal. We worked on the peach one and the black one today, and then sketched out a few new ideas." I report, handing her my sketch book.

"Oooh that's…interesting…"

"Hahaha I had a feeling you would say that. Trust me, someone will want that. It's half the material and will sell for double the price!"

Linda's eyes grow large. "Whatever you say Jizz. You're an amazing bitch with some amazing talent," she says. "And speaking of fixing your car and keeping tall, dark, and handsome guys company…"

The smile on my face quickly fades to a deadpanned expression. "We weren't talking about those things at all." Oops, I forgot to call Linda last night and give her the run down. I didn't really feel like talking to anyone when I got home, so I climbed in bed still smelling Jacoby all over me, and fell asleep.

"Yeah that's my point, bitch! Why aren't we talking about hot guy, Jacoby, picking you up and helping fulfill all your sexual fantasies? Why weren't you with him when he came in this morning looking for you? Why did he even have to *come in* looking for you this morning? Why doesn't he have your phone number?"

Dang. What crawled into her pants?

"He came in looking for her?" Beth asks, her jaw practically on the floor. All I can do is look back and forth between Beth and Linda because I really have no idea what to say.

He was looking for me?

"Yes, he absolutely did. He told me he felt terrible for leaving you to take some kind of phone call, because when he came back you were gone. What the hell Jizza? What happened? Was he an asshole or something? Did he not like your bra and panty set or what?"

"How do you even know he saw my bra and panty set?" I retort.

She looks me dead in the eye, cocks her head to the side and says, "Tell me he didn't."

Shit.

I bow my head, twiddling my fingers. "I don't really know if he did. He ripped it off so fast I'm not sure he got a good look at it."

Both girls gasp simultaneously. When I look up they both share an excited-puppy-waiting-for-a-cookie expression. "What?" I ask, throwing my arms up.

"What do you fucking mean, 'what'? Jenna?" Beth yells. "You had sex and…"

Linda finishes Beth's sentence. "And you didn't talk about it afterwards!" She points straight at me. "You didn't even call me. I'm your best friend and you tell me everything from the amount of boob sweat you have to the amount of blood erupting from your vagicano during any given shark week, but THIS! You didn't call me about this, and that can only mean one thing."

Please don't say it.

"What?" I roll my eyes.

"You like him," Beth sings as she dances around the living room. "You like him, you like him, you like him!" Linda laughs and I cringe at the spectacle that is now my sister twerking in the living room.

"Spill it Jizza, what was he like? Did he cum in you like a wrecking ball? Did you invite him to the candy shop?" She winks as I burst out in laughter. "Is he everything you would expect him to be? Was he gentle and slow, or hard and fast? Come on babe, you have to give us something." Linda throws herself lazily on the couch next to me ready to hear all I'm willing to tell her. "Was it like a steamy scene in an Ashton Jacobs novel? Dear God, tell me it was like that!" She cries. I ponder the last several Ashton Jacobs novels I've read as of late, comparing them to my experience with Jacoby.

"Mmm…I guess it would depend on the novel. He didn't come across as an alpha-douchebag like in *Steam*, but he wasn't the gentle shy guy like in *Just Us*."

My normal behavior is to have a one-night stand with some guy I barely know. The sex is almost always abysmal or awkward, so I escape the situation as soon as I possibly can. I always end up calling Linda and/or Beth to tell them both how horrible everything was. We laugh it off like it's an everyday occurrence for me, and then move on to the next guy. This time though, this time it was all…

"Perfect. He was perfect."

"Details, bitch. Right now! Don't leave anything out." Linda growls. "Wait…I need a beer. Do you have any beer? We need beer." She stands up and stalks toward the kitchen. Beth giggles, following in her footsteps as I roll my eyes at the both of them again. Linda returns with a few bottles of Heineken, places them on the coffee table in front of us and then plops back down on the couch. Beth lays herself across the pile of pillows on the floor. Both of them wait expectedly for me to talk.

"Guys there really isn't much to say..." I start.

"Bullshit. There's tons to say. Start from the beginning," Linda demands.

I sigh as I think back to the very beginning of the evening. "Okay well, my car broke down and he showed up like my white night…except he referred to himself as a dark horse instead." I ponder that to myself, realizing I never talked to him about that.

"Oooooh…a bad boy eh? Those are my favorite." Linda winks at me again before taking a few more swigs of her beer.

"I didn't get the impression that he's a bad boy type, really. Misunderstood maybe? I just…I don't know…he was upset about something and seemed like he was in a bad mood, and I was already in a bad mood after spending my evening talking Crazy Larry off the ledge on the phone at work, and then my car breaking down. So yeah, he was driving by, saw me, picked me up, and took me to his garage…"

"Which is called 'Jacked Up' by the way." Linda cuts in. "Seriously…it's fucking brilliant!"

"How did you know that?" I ask her. She whips his card from her back pocket and throws it at me.

"Because he left this for you sweetheart. You ran out on him so damn fast he said he didn't know how to contact you. There's no way the sex was that bad if you're saying he was perfect and he's coming to the store looking for you. So, what the hell happened?"

"Nothing happened, I swear."

"Jenna, get real. You had sex with this guy and then ran out on him…but you're telling us he was perfect. None of that makes sense," Beth says.

"He was perfect." I recall the all-consuming thoughts that ran through me while I was with Jacoby. "His body is perfect. His penis is…." My breath flutters when I smirk. "So perfect. I mean, we're talking grade A super-sized hole punch." I practically drool talking about it which makes the girls laugh out loud. "His voice is perfect. His personality is ridiculously perfect, and I think about him constantly, so when he took his phone call, I did what I do best and I left. I didn't want him to think there were strings attached, like he had to ask me to stay or ask me out or anything, nor did I want to get attached to someone who's just going to hurt me in the long run. That's stupid. It was just sex. Yes, it was holy-shit-best-on-top-of-a-car-sex I've ever had but it was just that. Sex. It was a stress-relief for both of us. I'm sure I'm not the first girl he's taken back to his garage, and I sure as hell won't be the last. I don't have time for the drama of it all anyway." Was that convincing? As much as I like Jacoby and continue to think about him even now, I need to convince the girls, and myself that even thinking about getting involved is a bad idea.

"Yeah. Okay. You keep telling yourself that, you stupid slut." Linda rolls her eyes.

Apparently, I'm not as convincing as I had hoped.

"You had sex on top of a fucking car," Beth stresses.

"Yeah. I did. Aaaaand in a moment of freshly-fucked flirtations, I may have left my panties in one of his bathroom drawers," I say, slapping my hand over my face. "And now I realize what an embarrassment that is given the fact that I hopped in my car and drove away."

"Well…wet panties are, indeed, a far cry from a glass slipper," Linda states, chugging the rest of her beer. We all look to one another before busting into a fit of giggles. "Maybe you're just the modern-day Cinderella."

We sit around in silence for a few minutes after our giggle-fest. My thumb rubs against the business card I hold in my hand. I could so easily dial the number. I could text him, make up some sort of story about how I got an emergency call from Bethy and had to leave. I could just send a quick message telling him I enjoyed his company.

Lame, Jenna.

"So, are you going to call him?" Linda nods to the card in my hand that I keep rubbing my thumb over like I'm caressing the damn thing.

Shrugging like it's not important, I chew on my fingernail until it's ripped as low as it can go and still be considered a nail. "Probably not."

Linda sits straight up, shocked at my dull response. "What the fuck, Jizz? Why not? The guy clearly wants you! He is seeking you out and you're just…what…ignoring him? That's pretty ambitchous of you."

Beth laughs, but I'm not sure I get what exactly 'ambitchous' means…though I think I'm smart enough to figure it out. "Ambitchous?" I repeat.

"Yeah. You're working pretty hard to be a complete bitch to the guy. Dude, he's hot for you…and he's *hot* for Christ's sake. I mean if *you* don't want him, I'll…"

"Don't you fucking dare!" I point my finger at her. One of us going after a guy that the other has already laid claim to is against the bestie code. She knows it, and I know it, and we've never once broken that code. I know I haven't marked my territory by peeing on Jacoby or anything, but the fact that he gave me the fourteen-point check lube job yesterday means he's mine for all intents and purposes. Not that I plan on getting another oil change, I mean – you only do that once every three to five thousand miles anyway.

"Hehehe, I knew that would get your pretty pink panties in a twist. Text him, Jizza. There's no harm in a text message. Come on, Bethy and I will help you decide what to say." She smirks as she opens another beer and shoots it back. Clearly, she'll be sleeping here tonight.

"I'm not going to text him tonight. It's late." I shake my head. "I'll text him in the morning."

"Nope. Unacceptable," Linda states. "You'll be all work, work, work in the morning and you won't give him another thought. We're doing this. Right here, right now." I watch as she winks and nods to Beth, who lunges forward to grab my phone from the coffee table at the same time that Linda pulls the business card from my hand.

"What are you…" I watch as Beth throws the phone to Linda, who is already up and walking across the back of the living room. "Noooo, no, no, no, no!" I jump up to run after Linda, who is already quickly typing things into my phone.

Oh God.

This could be so bad.

"Linda don't!" I scream, but fear I'm too late. She's already giggling and holding up both hands in a touchdown stance, her sign of victory. With a proud cat-ate-the-canary smirk she hands me back my phone. Immediately I open my text messages to see what she wrote.

Me: Jason Derulo, Want to Want me <3 Jenna

I lean against the back wall sighing deeply, trying to calm myself down. What if he doesn't remember me? What if he doesn't even know that song? And God forbid, what if he's with another girl right now? There's no way this is going to end well for me. Maybe I can just send him a bunch of gibberish and then later apologize for drunk-texting. I could call and slur all my words so he thinks I'm a sloppy drunk, or I could just throw this phone in the dumpster at the store and tell him someone stole it.

But then I would be lying to him.

I'm not a good liar.

While I ponder that thought my phone dings in my hand. Swallowing the huge nervous lump of holy shit in my throat, I slowly bring my hand up to my face so I can see the text that I just received.

Jacoby: Wish You Were Here, Avril Lavigne– ps. I like this game.

"Oh My GOOOOOOD!" I scream and throw the phone out of my hands like it's on fire and slip into full blown panic mode. "He wrote back! Oh my God, girls, he wrote back! What the fuck do I do? I can't handle this! I don't know what to do. I can't do it." With my hand on my chest, I try to take a deep breath but another panic surges through me. "Oh God! Is he going to want to sext with me? I only know how to do the real thing. I like real penis. I can't talk about virtual penis. I don't know what to say. I can't talk dirty to him. Oh God, I can't breathe." I double over, holding my knees and trying to take a deep breath. I didn't expect him to write back.

"Well, what did he say?" Beth laughs.

"He sent me a song back." I throw my phone at Beth who looks at it before passing it to Linda.

"He likes Avril Lavigne?" She shrugs. "Huh. Well you can't stop now, Jizz! Keep talking to him!"

"I don't know what to say! What the hell do I say? Thanks for the fuck, sorry I left you? I can't do that!" I whine. My phone dings again in Linda's hand. She throws it back at me. "If you want to sound like a mega bitch you could. Just see where it goes, babe. You never know."

Jacoby: I went to the store looking for you today.

Me: I heard. I'm sorry I was off today.

Jacoby: I'm sorry you had to leave. I really enjoyed banging with you.
OMG hanging! Hanging with you!
I enjoyed hanging out with you.
Well it was nice knowing you.

I laugh at his string of texts and immediately feel like we're back at the café laughing over spilled mocha. He's just so easy to talk to when I'm around him, and I enjoy the conversation. That doesn't usually happen.

Me: LOL!
So are you saying you didn't enjoy banging me? ;)

Jacoby: I uh…um…are you flirting with me now or is this a trick question?

hahaha I enjoyed hanging with you too.

Good. Ok. That's good.

Sorry I left you. I don't even have a good excuse.

I left you first. We're even.

"Why are you so googly-eyed over there?" Beth asks, walking out of the kitchen with another beer.

"She's probably getting her sext on. Thatta girl, Jizza. You keep doin' what you're doin'!" Linda whispers loudly to me as if Jacoby can hear through texts.

"He's just being sweet. That's all. He's deflecting so I don't feel guilty for leaving him."

"As any gentleman would. Now tell him something sweet back." Beth has more experience in the relationship department than I do since I'm the usually the one-night-stand type. Contemplating what to say next, I decide complimenting him would give me a few bonus points.

Me: I should return your shirt to you
but it still smells like your colon.
I really like it.

Jacoby: You sure about that? ;)

"What?" I ask confused. I'm not sure what he means until I reread my text to him. "OH MY GOD!" I scream.

Me: FUCK!
Colon!
SHIT!
COLON
COLON
COLOGNE!
Fail. It was nice knowing YOU
...and your colon obviously.

Jacoby: HAHAHAHAHAHAHA
I'm sorry I'm laughing. You're adorable.

I wish I could blame alcohol
but I can't.

Can I see you again?

You will anyway.
You have an addiction to highlighters.

More like an addiction to you.
I meant something more like a date.

You don't have to explain anything from the other night. You didn't do anything I didn't want you to do.

Yes, I did. I was a douche.
Let me make it up to you, please.
I'm not a pump and dump kind of guy.

My insides cringe as he hits the nail on the all too familiar head when it comes to my life and my non-existent relationships. I'm a pump and dump kind of girl. The walking one-night-stand who fears commitment or anything close to a relationship. I went through a dry spell after my break-up with Chad, but in a night of drunken stupor I hit on some guy named Chris. I remember being caught up in the fact that his name started with a C-H just like Chad. I wanted to hate him, but he ended up showing me just how easy it was to get back up on the horse and damn, I enjoyed the ride. The next morning though, I remembered that his name was Chris that started with a C-H, like Chad, and that his name had four letters, like Chad – okay I know Chris has five letters but I was hung over, give me a break - so I slipped my clothes back on and left him before he ever woke up.

After Chris, there was Abe, the guy with the pubesplosion. Clearly, he didn't know anything about manscaping. I felt like I was finding those little curly hairs all over me for a week after that one. Stan was nice, but he made these really weird chirping noises when he would orgasm. He made me wonder if I was supposed to regurgitate my dinner and feed it back to him like some mother bird does to her babies. There was no way I could be with him again without laughing, so I left and never looked back. Wyatt was a biter in ways I could not appreciate. Marcus was a crier who thought I was the love of his life after spending forty minutes with him in a bar, and then doing the deed against the wall outside. And lastly there was Luke, the guy I met at the gym, who firmly believed dressing like Richard Simmons in the bedroom was a woman's wildest fantasy come true. Apparently, he knows nothing about tow trucks like Jacoby…which brings me back to Jacoby. Maybe he knows all about me. Maybe I've walked away from enough men that my name is now etched on the back of some bathroom stall somewhere. Being with him was different. He was kind, gentle but firm, and he wasn't turned off or disgusted by my klutzy behavior or my extreme word-vomiting habit.

It's just one date, right?

Jacoby: Jenna?

Me: Eat me out?
OH MY GOD!
I typed eating out! Not eat me out!
I hate this phone so fucking much!

"SHIT!" I shout. "I can't fucking text on this thing. God, he's going to think I'm some sort of nympho or something." Linda sweeps over and takes my phone from my hands to read my textversation with Jacoby. "This is priceless!" She snorts. I can't hold back the giggles this time either, at my stupid texting mistakes. My face is on fire and I'm grateful that Jacoby isn't standing here in my living room right now. I would be mortified.

Jacoby: Eating is good ;) Tomorrow?

Me: I work till 5

Pick you up at 6? Address?

43 Nantucket Dr.

I promise to only slightly stalk you now.
Can you keep your curtains open?

Har har. Good night, Jacoby.

See you tomorrow.

I push the button on my phone ending my texts with Jacoby, and lay my head back against the wall where I'm now seated. "What am I doing?" I mutter to myself.

"I don't know, but it sounds like you asked him to eat you out." Linda answers with a straighter face than I could ever have done if roles were reversed. "So, you tell us. What *are* you doing?"

"You did WHAT?" Bethy asks, choking on her beer.

"I'm going to eat out with him tomorrow night. EAT OUT…with Jacoby. You know, dinner."

"That's good!" Linda winks. Gasping suddenly, she looks at me raising her eyebrows up and down and says "You should wear that purple one."

"No way." I shake my head knowing exactly what she's implying.

"Come on. Beth, don't you think she should wear the purple one? He would love it!"

Beth looks up from the candies she's trying to crush on her phone. "Well yes, I do think he would like it, but I also know Jenna enough to know she'll never do it."

"Ugh! Why not?" Linda cries. "Live a little Jizz!"

"I am living a little, Linda! If I pretend that the other night was our first date, then that would make this our second date, and I've never done a second date with anyone. Not since…" Memories of a failed relationship float through my head.

"Chad was a dick anyway," Beth reassures me knowing full well what I was going to say.

"Anyway. No, I'm not wearing any of it," I assert.

Linda sighs in defeat. "Okay, okay. But do me a favor and never say never. Jacoby isn't Chad. Give the guy a chance. Just don't include the purple one in the stuff you drop off tomorrow. Save it for…a rainy day or something like that."

"Okay. I'll save it." I promise her.

"Great. Now let's go pick out your outfit and talk about how you're going to trim your bush."

CHAPTER 6

#Shitstorm

Jenna

I hate Mondays. I'm pretty sure every working person in the world hates Mondays. There isn't enough coffee in the world to change my mind about the start of the work week, but I'm trying very hard to be chipper and positive today. It's not every Monday that I have a date with an attractive guy. In fact, it's been quite a long time since I've been on a date at all. Thanks to Bethy and Linda, my nails are painted, my make-up is picked out, and my clothes are ready to go for tonight. I even took time to trim the bush, though I have no plans of showing off my landscaping this evening.

I've also tagged and laid out the pieces I want to drop off at the boutique after work, relieving me of that stress for the week. It'll be nice to have that all done so I can work on new designs. As I turn the key to open the building, I take a minute to remind myself that with any luck, I won't need this shitty retail job forever. Good things come to those who wait, and by God, I've waited long enough.

It takes me the first few hours of my day to complete the daily paperwork, check in on my inventory lists, and sit in on a conference call. I'm lucky to have Linda in my life on days like this. Not only is she my best friend, but she's also a kick-ass manager who doesn't take bullshit from anyone. She runs back and forth performing price overrides every time an associate asks for one, she deals with the bitchy customers who don't understand why we can't fix their computer while they wait when they can clearly see a line of six other computers on the table ahead of theirs, and she unloads freight off the truck when it comes like a boss. We're a great team and I love working with her.

"Jizz, you have got to come see this." I hear Linda through my ear piece as I exit the bathroom. She's not only laughing hysterically through her microphone, but I can hear her voice along with Frank, one of my asshats, carrying from the other side of the store.

"Be right there," I tell her, wondering what on earth could be so funny. These days I'm not at all surprised though, given the clientele we've been getting as of late. I walk over to the copy center where Linda and Frank are huddled in the corner holding their stomachs, they're laughing so hard.

Looking around to make sure there are no customers looking for help, I step over to see what has Frank and Linda so unbelievably captivated.

"OH. MY. GOD." I exclaim loudly before clapping a hand over my mouth.

"Shhh!" Linda widens her eyes at me. "I know, right? My eyes can't un-see this, yet I can't force myself to look away!"

"What the ever-loving fuck is this, and where the hell did you get it?"

Frank hands the pile of pictures to me. "It came through as a print order about ten minutes ago, I swear!" he says with his hands up in surrender.

"And you *printed* them?" Shocked isn't even the word for how I'm feeling right now.

"Well…I didn't remember there being a rule about not printing pornographic material so…yeah. I printed them. I mean the customer is going to show up here to pick them up, so what was I supposed to do? The customer is always right, right?" He asks innocently while trying to keep a straight face. The picture on the top of the pile as well as the rest of them that were printed are pictures of not just a couple going at it in their camper, they're pictures of an elderly couple going at it in their camper. They can't be younger than seventy years old. I'm pretty sure my eyes have just been burned.

Throwing my head back to stare at the ceiling, I take a deep breath and think of what I should do next.

Really, Monday?

"Was this the only thing they ordered? These prints?" I ask.

"Uh…no." Frank says. He turns to the counter where a sixteen by twenty foam board poster is laying upside down. He flips it over and immediately my eyes slam closed.

"Shit, Frank. I can't un-see this! Why do you insist on burning my eyes? For all that is right and holy will you please turn that back over?" Finally, I give in to the giggles that have been building up. "Seriously, who the hell takes sex pictures like this at that age? That's so gross! It's like looking at a picture of…Linda's parents!"

"Pffff!" Linda spits out the water she had just chugged. "BAHAHAHA Jizza! Ew! I will never be able to look at my parents the same way again!" Linda and I have always laughed about the fact that her parents are almost twenty years older than many parents of people our age.

"Okay, okay, Frank," I hand back the pictures in my hand and point to the poster lying on the counter. "Put those in a sealed manila envelope and make sure you can't see through it. Write the customer's name on it, and then good luck not reacting if and when they come to pick up their order. And dear God, let that be the oddest thing to happen today."

"Jenna, call on line four. Jenna, line four." My name is called over the loud speaker. I make my way over to the Customer Service desk, praying whoever is on the other end of the line isn't a dick.

"Hello, this is Jenna. How can I help you?"

"I TOLD you the government was watching me, and they're watching you too!" the male voice shouts into the phone.

Crazy Larry strikes again.

"Hello, Mr. Seymore." I greet him, rolling my eyes in annoyance, but grateful that he's not here to see my expression. I check the clock on the wall and tell myself I'll give him three minutes before I hang up and claim a lost connection.

"Those fucking idiots made my computer sick and I'm just done. I'm so fucking done," he shouts.

"Yes, I think you said that the other d…"

"Do you know what they did to me? I'm going to tell you what those fucking pigs did to me. I don't know why I need to tell you because I'm sure they're listening to this phone call and could just tell you their damn selves. But those fuckers hacked my computer and now it doesn't fucking work."

"Mr. Seymore, what exactly doesn't work?" Larry has been in our store no less than twenty-two times in the last forty days. There's always something wrong, someone is always spying on him, and it's always someone else's fault. Also, he uses the F-word more times than I can count on two hands in one conversation. The amount of times my tech guys have found porn on his computer, which explains the numerous viruses his computer gets infected with, is astronomical. The more and more I speak with him, the more I have a feeling his conspiracy theories are nothing more than guilt for spending all his time looking at the ridiculous things he studies online. The pictures I've seen coming from his Google searches brings a whole new meaning to the words hole punch. I'll never look at a wine bottle the same way…or a baseball bat.

"My interwebs don't work Ms. Zimmerman! Those bastards implanted viruses all through my computer while I was sleeping and now I can't search for anything without all these boxes popping up and this one keeps dinging like a goddamn siren. You fuckers are going to pay for what you've done! Do you hear me?" At this point I'm holding the phone receiver away from my ear to give Larry the opportunity to speak his peace to the government officials he insists are listening to his every call.

"Mr. Seymore, I would be happy to personally fix your computer if you want to bring it in and leave it with me. I can do a full virus wipe and maybe we should think about getting you some sort of virus protection so this doesn't keep happening."

"Virus protection? You've got to be kidding me! Those sons of bitches in the government can get through any kind of virus protection! What do you think is all over my computer? I'll tell you!

A shit ton of fucked up viruses and I need those gone because I have shit to do."

I nod my head, staring at my reflection in the store window. The droop in my eyes tells me that this day is wearing me out already. I'm in need of a nice long break.

"Ok Mr. Seymore. You bring your computer in to me and I'll see what I can do to help you."

"Well, I'll try but I can't promise that those pigs aren't going to follow me. If I don't show up there in the next hour you might want to check on me," he whispers. "I could be laying in a ditch somewhere with my computer shattered all around me!"

Oh good Lord.

"Okay Mr. Seymore. I'll see you soon." With that I don't even think about it before I hang up the phone. Now I just have to work myself up to being ready to deal with him personally when he gets here.

It's another couple hours before I'm able to sit down in the office for somewhat of a break and a few bites of my sandwich. Mr. Seymore's computer is being wiped of all viruses for the sixth time this month, yet he insists that he's not the one making this happen. At this point all I can do is try to laugh off this day and the absurdity of it with Linda while we take advantage of a slow afternoon.

"For real? A wine bottle?" Linda asks with a look of awe on her face. "I mean, I've heard of fisting and shit like that but who shoves an entire wine bottle up there?"

"Right?" I laugh. "Or a baseball bat for that matter. I mean I hope that's not a new meaning for 'homerun'."

"No way in hell," Linda says wiping her mouth with her napkin. "If anything, that would be a personal foul. Ew. So gross!" We both break out into laughter.

"It's amazing what some people shove up their ass holes. It's so wrong, but I shouldn't be surprised, though, with the shit I've seen from people's search engines." I shake my head as I take another bite of my lunch. "They bring their computers in here to have some mysterious virus removed, somehow not realizing that it's all the porn they look at that causes those viruses. "

"Hahaha like what? Tell me a good one."

I think back to some of my favorite tech clients and the laptops that have come across our tech desk. "Oh my gosh, this one man brought in his wife's laptop and said she kept getting this 'Garden Virus' he called it. I had no idea what he was talking about until I looked into it further and saw that she had quite the photo album saved on her computer from porn sites and sex toy shops online."

"What?!" Linda scrunches up her nose. "I can't even imagine what it could've possibly been!"

"Yeah you can." I laugh. "It was a variety of garden vegetable replica dildos! And I'm talking cucumbers, celery, and carrots that looked just like the real thing! I mean, who buys that shit?"

"Yeah," Linda agrees. "Like, why not just use the real thing?" She winks at me so I know she's not being serious.

"Well first of all, a real carrot doesn't vibrate, but secondly it could break off inside and then you're really screwed!" I explain.

Linda shrugs. "Meh. It's biodegradable. It wouldn't be up there long."

"Bahahahaha! You are so gross."

"Yep," she says before drinking the last of her water and throwing away the bottle. "And that's why you love me."

The next couple of hours go smoothly enough that I almost allow myself to get a little nervous about my upcoming date with Jacoby. I'm hanging ink and toner on the display wall when a lady approaches me with a completely disgusted look on her face.

"Excuse me, ma'am. Do you work here?" she asks. I drop the ink box into the basket holding all the product that needs shelved to turn to her.

No, I just wear this fugly cotton shirt with a nametag for the hell of it.

"Yes. I'm the manager on duty. What can I do for you?"

Her eyebrows shoot up and she crosses her arms over her chest. "Well for starters you can get someone in your women's restroom to clean up the mess someone left in there. It's the most atrocious thing I've ever seen in my life."

Frowning at her response I reply, "I'm sorry ma'am. The restrooms were cleaned after lunch. I hadn't heard of it needing attention again. I'll look into it right away."

"I should say so," the lady responds. "I had to use the men's room instead, and have my husband watch the door outside."

I hold back from rolling my eyes. There's probably a tampon floating in the toilet or toilet paper on the floor.

Some women are so damn afraid of a little pee on the seat.

Though why can't a bitch just wipe up after herself?

"Thank you for bringing it to my attention, I'll get…" I look around for an available associate to hand off the job to, but don't see one standing around anywhere. Everyone is busy either stocking shelves or helping customers. I sigh knowing that sometimes being a manager sucks ass. "I'll get it taken care of myself."

"Good idea," she says before walking away.

I tap my microphone lightly so that my asshats can hear me through their ear pieces. "I'll be cleaning the women's restroom for the next few minutes. If anyone needs an override, call for Linda."

Making my way to the supply closet, I grab a pair of rubber gloves and some Clorox cleaning spray. It's not until I push open the door to the women's restroom that I see just what the lady meant by the word atrocious. "Oh my God!" I cover my nose with my hand to try and mask the smell emanating from the room to no avail. My eyes are beginning to water and I gag slightly, praying that I don't vomit on the floor thus adding to the mess. This single occupancy bathroom looks like a war zone of pure shit.

What…?

How…?

I can't even begin to figure out how one person could've made this kind of a mess and still walk out of this store wearing clean pants. It seriously looks like someone was hovering – why they don't just sit their ass down on the damn seat is beyond me – but then had a surprise ass-plosion instead. There is shit everywhere. On the seat, on the back of the toilet, on the wall behind the toilet, on the bathroom sink, on the floor around the sink. Oh, and it looks like whoever did this tried to start to clean it up by wiping the toilet seat because that shit looks smudged all over the place. I stand there shaking my head in disgust, but also in total confusion.

How can one person…

I can't even…

"Where the hell do I even start? God, I hate this job," I mutter, backing out of the bathroom. I place the cleaning supplies I do have on the floor in front of the bathroom door and walk back to the closet to get a mask, the cleaning bucket and mop, and any other cleaning supplies I can possibly carry.

With the Clorox, I wage a war on the toilet with what seems like the entire bottle of spray. I grab a wet cloth from the bucket and lean over the toilet, ready to perform what will probably be the longest shit scrub of my life. I wipe down the wall, and the front of the toilet, but when I step to the side of the toilet, my foot slips in the puddle of excess Clorox spray dripping from the wall and I start to fall.

"Oommph!" I bang my head on the sink on the way down, landing on my side on a floor covered in exploded human feces.

"SHIT! No…FUCK!" The smell permeating my senses is too strong for my now woozy head. Flipping my body over just enough to be able to get myself up on my knees, I crawl myself to the door, my knees sliding through the crappy mess, wincing in pain every time my left hip moves. Just as I get to the door, it swings open, almost hitting me square in the forehead.

"OH! God!" Linda immediately covers her nose with her hand. "Are you okay? I heard you scream…as did the four customers standing just out by the tech center."

I look up at Linda with a pained and defeated expression. "Fuck this day, Linda. Please tell me what I did to deserve the shit I've put up with today."

Linda chuckles at my mention of shit. The irony isn't lost on me at all, but I'm no longer in any mood to laugh. In seconds the tears are falling out of my eyes. I raise my hand to wipe them from my cheeks when Linda shouts, "NOOOO DON'T! Jizz, your gloves! They have…well, they have shit all over them. Please don't touch your face. Come on, we need to get you out of here. It's after five anyway and you have a hot date. That will cheer you up."

Her reminder of my impending night with Jacoby raises my panic level to DEFCON 1. "I can't do it, Linda. There's no way. I'll smell like shit all night. It's in my nose. It's in my hair, it's…it's everywhere." I cry.

"You can do this Jizzy. You just need a long hot shower, and some brand new clothes. When you get home, you should just pitch these. Don't even try to wash them." She says with a slight chuckle that I can tell she's been trying to hold back. "In fact, you can take your work shirt off before you even leave and just throw it in the dumpster out back. I would tell you to take your pants off but that would be weird. Sooo…oooh I have an idea!"

I sigh in response, just standing in the back hallway waiting for her to explain her idea, which she doesn't do. She gives me a pitying nod before helping me take off my gloves and washing off my shoes as much as possible. I get my work shirt off, and with Linda's help, we ball it up in some plastic wrapping that was lying in our office.

"Aww you didn't tell me it was Care Bear day, Jizz." She says referring to my vintage Care Bear tank top with a huge Cheer Bear on the front – because life is supposed to be about rainbows and glitter, right? "I would've worn my slutty bear shirt today. You have to remind me of these things next time."

"Memo taken," I tell her.

"I'll meet you out by your car with your stuff. Don't worry. I've got this," she says.

I couldn't be happier to throw this damn work shirt away. I slam it in the dumpster and then carefully pull out my phone from my purse. There's no way I can do tonight. It'll take me hours of scrubbing myself to get this shit off me. I type out a quick text to Jacoby cancelling our night.

Me: I need to take a rain check for tonight. Very bad day. Long story. I'm sorry.

Slipping my phone back into my pocket, I head for my car where Linda is waiting, trash bag in hand.

"Linda, I can't take my pants off. I'm not driving home in a thong! That will be the one time I get pulled over."

"Nope. You don't have to. Look!" She holds up the bag to reveal two leg holes that she cut out of the bottom of the bag. "You can wear this to cover your pants so you don't stain your car interior. Think of it as a big ass bag of granny panty."

Taking a big breath, I release it in a huge smile. "You're a genius Linda! I never even thought about my car."

"I know. It's why you keep me around." She leans over, holding open the bag. "Now step in."

I lift up my left leg and carefully lower it down into and through the bag. After my right leg is through the hole, Linda pulls the bag up around my waist and pulls the red handles out of the sides to tighten the bag around me. "There. Perfect. I laid another bag on your seat and over your head rest just to be safe. You should make it home with no problem. Now go. Get a hot shower and drink a huge glass of wine before you see Jacoby. It'll take the edge off."

I don't bother telling her that I already cancelled our date. What she doesn't know won't kill her.

"Pretend I'm hugging you okay, Linda? I'm so glad you're my best friend."

"Haha. I love you, too, Jizz. Let me know when you make it home so I don't have to worry about rescuing your shitty self from the side of the road somewhere." She winks.

I start the car and shift into reverse. "Will do. Later Lindy."

CHAPTER 7
Schmidt Stain

Jacoby

I usually hate Mondays. Most of the time I spend my weekends knee deep in the engine of one of the classic vehicles I'm working on, and then hang out with a few buddies, either at the bar or on my boat. This past weekend though, I didn't do any of that. Instead, I spent Saturday morning finishing up work in my office, Saturday afternoon fighting with my father, and Saturday evening dick deep inside a girl that I would give anything to be inside of again. I don't consider myself the alpha-male type at all so I'm not sure what came over me when I had her here in my garage. I was pissed at my dad, testosterone was flowing freely, she looked and smelled like the sexiest breath of fresh air I've ever experienced and it all just…happened. I'm not sure what it says about her that she let me basically have my way with her, but her confidence was a hell of a turn-on. So yeah, I usually hate Mondays, but not today. Today is different. I get to see Jenna again, and something about that makes my insides stir and gives me all the adrenaline I need to make today a productive day until it's time to be with her again.

Since I finished my latest project and sent it off to James and Molly this morning, I decide to spend some time working on the fifty-eight Porsche Speedster that's been waiting on me for a while now. Finally having all the right parts shipped means I can get busy on my newest baby. The body is in perfect condition, but the engine is gutted. She'll need to be completely rebuilt before I can get her to purr again, but it's a challenge I've gladly accepted. Once I organize the parts on the tarp I've set up beside the car, I crank up my music playlist and get to work. Two hours or so into the job, I'm a greasy mess sitting on the ground deciphering the puzzle of car parts in front of me.

"Hey man! How's it going?" I look over to the entrance of my garage to see my best friend and old college roommate, Jack Schmidt, walking toward me.

"Hey Schmidt Stain!" His old nickname never gets old. "No clients to rip off today?" I smirk as I take in his attire that consists of khaki shorts, a blue polo shirt and casual loafer tennis shoes that I'm sure costs more than his entire outfit, including the leather wallet I know is in his back pocket.

"I had a deposition this morning but took the afternoon off. Missed you over the weekend. That's not like you. I thought I better swing by and see what's up."

Jack spends his days as a junior partner at the Pense & Marshall law firm in town. It's not lost on me that if and when Jack becomes a senior partner, the law firm will then become the PMS Attorneys at Law. I tease him a good bit, but Jack knows he's the brother I wish I could've had instead of the douchebag one I'm stuck with. Instead, Jack plays the part of my best friend and is also my personal lawyer when I need him.

"Ah. I see," I say wiping down the transmission and laying it back down on the ground. "I was uh…busy, over the weekend. Sorry, I didn't get to hang out."

His eyes narrow at me. "Busy huh? Meeting your deadline?"

"Yeah. That too." I nod.

"You got laid," he says matter-of-factly.

"What?" I ask, shocked. He's not buying anything that comes out of my mouth. Damn him for being a lawyer. He always knows when I'm lying or worse, just not telling the whole truth.

"Did I stutter, bro? I said, you got laid. I can see it in your face."

"There's nothing wrong with my face." Reaching a hand up I scratch the back of my neck.

"I didn't say there was anything wrong with it." He smiles. "It's just rare for you. Who is she?"

I take a minute to pretend I'm cleaning up my work so I can decide if I want to tell him all the info about something that could be nothing. "Her name is Jenna."

"Jenna…?" He probes.

"Umm, I uh…I don't know her last name." I wince.

Jack's eyebrows shoot up almost as though he's impressed. "You fucked her, and you don't even know her last name? Nice job J."

I shake my head. "No, it wasn't a nice job. Well, yeah, it was more than nice, but it was a dick move. Well, obviously, it was a dick move, but you know what I mean. She was here with me and I was pissed and she…fuck…she smelled so good. I just sort of, took her. God, I was like a feral animal and that's not me. You know that's not me."

But it sure was nice.

"Yeah. I get you. So, what's going on? What had you so pissed? And have you talked with this girl since…whenever it was you saw her last?" he asks.

"What else could it have been Schmidt? I saw my Dad Saturday afternoon. Got the run of the mill 'you're a failure of a son' treatment like always. Jenna just happened to show up in the right place at the right time so…you know."

"Jenna showed up here?"

"No. I picked her up." I shake my head. "It's a long story. I'll explain it all later."

"I still don't understand why you don't just tell your dad. I know love isn't about money, but if he knew how successful you really were, he may be a little prouder of you."

"That's not the fucking point." I can feel the rage build up just thinking about my always-politically-minded father. "A father should love his son no matter what path he chooses in life, no matter how successful or unsuccessful he is, and besides, if he knew, he would find some way to ruin the best thing I have going for me, and I love it too much to let the cat out of the bag."

Jack smiles endearingly. "For what it's worth, I'm proud of you, man. I mean who would've thought one college class would change your life forever?"

"Yeah," I mumble. "In more ways than one."

"So." Jack changes the subject to lighten our conversation. "How about a little boat cruise tonight? A few beers? You in?"

Shaking my head, I check my watch before I answer. "No can do, man. Jenna and I have a date tonight."

"No shit! You're serious about her huh?" he asks.

"It's just a first official date, but I'm serious enough to want to know her last name, yeah," I answer.

"Well good for you! I hope it goes well. Text me tomorrow, let's get together soon then alright?"

"Yeah, for sure." I tell him. "Hey Schmidt?"

"Yeah?" he says over his shoulder as he walks back to his car.

"Thanks. For checking up on me. I appreciate it."

"Anytime, Bro. Catch ya later."

"See ya."

My phone dings in my back pocket as I watch Jack pull down the driveway.

Jenna: I need to take a rain
check for tonight.
Very bad day.
I'm sorry.

"Shit." Disappointment flows through me at the thought of not getting to see her tonight. I can't shake the feeling that she just wants to be away from me because I walked away from her the other night. I may never forgive myself at this point. She didn't deserve that.

"I have to make it up to her," I whisper to myself.

I read her text over and over again, trying to discern whether or not she really doesn't want to hang out or if she's just trying to push me away. All the other times we were together, everything seemed so natural, so easy. And maybe I'm tooting my own horn but it sure seemed to me like she enjoyed what we did the other night.

I have to see her.

I make the decision to stop by her place to make sure she's okay. If she's had a bad day, maybe she'll just want to be alone, but maybe, just maybe, she'll want some company that a nice compassionate guy can provide. While packing up my tools and putting everything away, I come up with a plan that I hope can put a smile on Jenna's face. I owe that to her. Within the next hour, I'm showered and ready to go with a bag full of supplies and a short list of items to pick up along the way.

I pull up to her house just around a quarter till six, hoping she's home from work. My insides settle when I spot her car in the driveway, but that nervous feeling creeps up my neck.

What if she doesn't want me here?

Grow some balls Malloy.

Grabbing my two bags of groceries from the backseat, I walk up to the front door and press the button for the doorbell.

"Shit." I hear from inside the door. "Linda! I need to get out of this shit bag first!"

What-the?

"Uhh…it's not…I'm not Linda," I respond from the other side of the door. Immediately the door swings open, revealing Jenna with her hair swept up on top of her hair in one of those messy bun things, donning a Care Bear tank top that hugs her body just right and what looks to be a makeshift garbage bag…diaper?

"Oh God!" she exclaims before she slams the door shut in my face. I can hear her repeat "This is not happening. This is not happening. This is not happening."

Knocking lightly on the door, I try for a different approach. "Jenna? I'm sorry…I just…"

"Didn't you get my text?" She squeaks from the other side of the door.

"Yeah. I did actually, but I was worried about you and wanted to make sure you were okay."

"I'm okay!" she shouts.

She doesn't say anything after that, so I'm standing here at her front door unsure of what to do next. She knows I'm here but didn't invite me in. I know now that she's okay but don't want to invite myself in.

"Good. Okay…I'll just…go, then." I turn to head back down the walk but stop when she shouts again.

"NO! Don't go."

"Umm…okay. I'm here. Should I just, you know, stand out here for a while?"

"No. I'm going to open the door, but I need you to promise me you won't laugh." Her request brings a smile to my face.

"You know when someone asks that, it usually means there's something at least semi-funny happening, so I'm not sure I can promise that I won't laugh. But if you trust me, I'll at least promise to laugh with you and not at you."

I hear the click of the door knob and watch as her fingers appear on the edge of the door as she pulls it open. She's ridiculously cute standing there in her Care Bear shirt, but the expression on her face tugs at my heart. She looks defeated, exhausted, and on the verge of tears. I go to put down the bags I'm holding so that I can at the very least offer her a hug, but she steps back away from me.

"No. Don't touch me," she says holding up her hands. "I smell like shit."

"It's okay Jenna. It can happen to anyone," I try to console her.

"Nooooo." She chuckles lightly. "I didn't shit myself, I swear. I just…slipped and fell…on a floor covered in shit…and I wouldn't blame you one bit if you don't believe a word I just said." She sighs. "It's a long story, but I really just want to get this bag off me and get a long hot shower."

"Spaghetti or tacos?" I shoot her with the random question.

"What?"

"Which do you like better, spaghetti, or tacos?"

"Uhh…tacos, I guess? Why?"

"Because if it's okay with you, I would like to make you some dinner so you don't have to worry about feeding yourself after what looks like a long exhausting day," I explain.

She eyes my bag of groceries with narrowed eyes before looking back at me. Her beautiful brown eyes are soft and woeful. "You would be willing to do that? For me?"

I cock my head to the side watching her. "Would I be here if I wasn't? You said you had a bad day, so I thought the least I could do to help you feel better is make you dinner."

"How do I know you won't come into the bathroom and kill me like I'm in some sort of horror movie?" Her left eyebrow raises.

"First of all, I think you've seen *Psycho* one too many times. Secondly, I picked you up on the side of the road the other night, put you in my tow truck, and drove you to a garage out in the middle of nowhere. You weren't scared then. Are you scared now?" I ask her.

"No. Not at all." She shakes her head pushing the door open wide behind her. "I really need to get a long shower. And that's not an invitation to join me. I really stink," she tells me.

Feeling the blush creep up my face at the thought of showering with this beautiful girl, I remind myself to keep calm and stay in control. "I can smell you from here, so don't worry. I'm more than happy to cook dinner while you freshen up, besides, shit's not really my kind of aphrodisiac."

That gets her to laugh. "Is it anybody's?" She steps to the side and welcomes me in. I step past her and spot the kitchen right away. Heading that direction, I place my bags on the counter. "People are weird. I'm sure that kind of kink is out there somewhere."

"Well I, for one, can't wait to get this shit off so I'm going to hit the shower and then burn these clothes. Do you need anything? I mean, feel free to browse the cupboards for whatever you might need." She gestures around the kitchen.

I shake my head. "All taken care of. Enjoy your shower. Take your time."

"Thanks." She smiles. "I'll be back soon."

After watching her walk out of the kitchen and down the hall, I open a few cupboards and locate the pans I need to get started on dinner. I lay them on the stove top and pull out the vegetables that need chopped. Laying my cell phone on the counter, I pull up my favorite play list, and take a deep breath, enjoying that I'm in Jenna's house, doing something nice for a girl – something that hasn't happened in a while, and get to work.

CHAPTER 8
He Ate My Taco

Jenna

Part of me just wants to walk right into the shower wearing whatever I have on. I can't remember a time when I've ever felt this dirty. And the smell, ugh, I'm positive it'll be in my nose for a long time. Untying the garbage bag from around my waist, I pull it down my legs with the pants and undies I'm wearing. In one fell swoop I take it all off and ball it up, throwing it in an extra garbage bag I grabbed from the closet on the way to the bathroom. Reminding myself to hose off my shoes waiting for me by the back door of the house, I throw off my shirt and bra, and hastily get into the shower.

While standing under the hot water I look at each of the different soaps and scrubs I have lying around the tub. I'm a shameless addict of all things scrubby. I have body scrubs with fruity scents, beach scents, soothing scents and exhilarating scents. My dresser includes six different types of hand lotion and I love each of them. I might usually feel bad for hoarding all these products, but it also means I'm helping to support the young mom I bought them from who wants to grow her entrepreneurial skills. That's something I've been passionate about for several years now, so who would I be to say no? Trying to get the smell of human shit out of my nose, I open every canister of body scrub that I see around me. I don't even care if the scents mix weirdly. Anything would be better than the smell going through my senses right now.

After a few rounds of lathering my entire body in every soap I own, my mind starts to wander back to the guy who is presently about thirty yards away from me, maneuvering through my kitchen to make me dinner. I peek out of the shower curtain quickly to make certain that I locked the bathroom door. Once I confirm to myself that the door is indeed locked, I lean back on the shower wall smiling like a goofy crushing school girl. He's making me dinner!

Chad never made me dinner.

Thanking the Linda and Bethy gods that my bush is properly trimmed, I wash my hair no less than three times to make certain I am sparklingly clean from head to toe. When I turn the shower off a few minutes later, I open the curtain to grab my towel and hear music coming from the kitchen. It's some sort of rock music given the beat I can hear, but I can't make out what song it is. A smile graces my lips knowing that Jacoby is obviously making himself at home. I'm eager to join him to see what he's up to.

I step into my comfy gray cotton romper, throwing caution to the wind in terms of what I look like for the night. I'm comfy and I finally smell good and that's all that matters. What Jacoby sees is what he gets. I pull my wet hair up into a loose bun on the top of my head, not caring at all that a few strands didn't make it in. Slipping a few bangle bracelets onto my wrists I take one more look at myself in the mirror before stepping out of my room toward the kitchen.

Jacoby doesn't see or hear me standing in the doorway of the kitchen because he's facing the stove cooking the meat for our tacos. Not only is it a turn on to see a good-looking man in my kitchen cooking for me, but my insides flutter a little more as I listen to him singing along with Jimi Hendrix. I try so hard to stifle my giggle when he starts dancing like Garth Algar in one of my favorite *Wayne's World* scenes, but I fail miserably and erupt into a fit of laughter. Surprised but surprisingly not embarrassed, Jacoby turns toward me, using the wooded spoon in his hand as a microphone and continues to sing to me. I can't help but laugh each and every time his pelvis "schwings" in my direction.

A good-looking guy with a perfect penis, who can cook, and he's funny? SCHWING!

He makes his way to me before the end of the song and without hesitation, wraps his arm around me, pulling me closer to him. I'm a little taken aback because the gesture feels like one that happens when you've been with someone for a long time. Still though, his arms are comfortable and his torso feels like it was made to fit me as I lean into it. "Oh yeah." He sniffs the top of my head. "You smell delicious. Like raspberries and vanilla and…" He inhaless one more time. "Peaches?"

"Yeah that's probably about right," I answer him. "I used pretty much every type of soap or shampoo I own just to be sure I got clean enough."

"You look beautiful, by the way," he says as he steps back to look at me. "I mean you looked stunning in your garbage bag diaper, but this. I never get to see you in anything other than work clothes."

"Or nothing at all?" I tease him.

"Yeah well…it's your house, and you are more than welcome to walk around here in nothing at all if that's what you'd like. You won't hear a peep from me."

I laugh, not knowing for sure if he's being serious or not. "Well I think I'll keep my clothes on for now if that's okay. Now that I'm clean, I'm famished. Do you need any help?"

"Nope." He shakes his head. "Dinner is just about ready."

"Drinks? How about I get us some drinks? Do you like Corona?" I ask.

"Is today Monday?"

"Yeah."

"Then I like Corona." He winks at me. Oops. I totally missed the joke.

"Okay then. Coming right up." I spend the next few minutes setting the table and grabbing each of us a bottle of Corona, complete with lime wedge. Sitting at my seat I watch as Jacoby fills the table with all the fixings for tacos. He's got it all from Mexican rice to refried beans. Everything is as it would be if we were sitting at a Mexican restaurant. The color of the food alone fills me with a festive feeling.

"Jacoby, this looks fantastic. I can't believe you did all this."

"A fun dinner for a special girl. Dig in." He tells me as he hands me a hard taco shell.

Grabbing the spoon from the bowl in front of me, I fill three taco shells with meat, cheese, lettuce, tomato, sour cream and guacamole. My stomach rumbles in anticipation of the deliciousness that is this dinner in front of me.

"Mmm. This is so good," I tell Jacoby as pieces of my taco shell fall to my plate. "So, so, good." There really is no easy way to eat a hard taco.

He smiles as he watches me take a bite before filling up his own plate. We eat in silence for a few minutes, hearing nothing but the music coming from his phone in the kitchen accompanied by the crunch of our taco shells.

"So you like Classic Rock?" I ask him.

"Love it. I guess it's sort of what I grew up with so I just never changed," he says.

I respond with an agreeable nod. "What's your favorite song?"

Jacoby sits back in his seat. "My favorite classic rock song? Uhh…that's a good question. I guess I would say 'It's My Life', by Bon Jovi. I've always been a Bon Jovi fan."

"Interesting." I wipe my mouth with my napkin. "Why that song?"

Jacoby shrugs as he finishes off his first taco and grabs another off his plate. "I don't know. I guess it's sort of the song that feels the most like my life. Then and now."

Not remembering all of the lyrics to the song, I nod at his answer. I also make a mental note to Google it later. The reason behind why people like certain songs can be very telling. It's always been an interest of mine.

"What about you?" he asks.

"What about me?"

"You have a favorite song?" He pushes. Taking another bite of my taco, I allow my chewing to give me a reprieve from answering his question. "Nah, not really." I shake my head, looking down.

He watches me from across the table as I swallow my food and then lift my bottle to take a hefty chug of my Corona. His eyes narrow at me slightly when I finally look back at him. "I call bullshit. Everyone has a favorite song…but it's okay." He shrugs. "I'll give you a free pass on that one, but that means you have to answer another question."

Placing my bottle back on the table in front of me, I try not to smirk at him. "Oh. I didn't know this was a game. What if I don't want to tell you all there is to know about me?"

"You don't have to tell me anything if you don't want to. You're more than welcome to tell me to fuck off." He smiles. "I'm just making conversation. So, what's your very favorite Disney movie?"

"Disney movie? You mean like...the animated ones?" I ask.

"Yeah. Come on, everyone has a favorite Disney movie. Mine's *The Lion King*."

"Well that's easy, isn't it? My favorite is *Cinderella*." I tell him.

"Why is that an easy choice? Do you identify with Cinderella the most?"

"Not necessarily." I shrug. "I mean I think every girl wants to have the Cinderella life where the prince finds her and sweeps her off her feet to live happily ever after."

He nods, his brown eyes holding my gaze. "I can appreciate that. Okay next question."

Chewing up another bite of my taco I stop him. "Wait, wait, wait. Shouldn't it be my turn?"

"Not a chance." He winks. "Favorite ice cream flavor?"

"Moose Tracks," I say with my mouth full.

"Favorite alcoholic beverage?" He drills.

"Buttery nipple" slips off my tongue before I realize what I said. Watching Jacoby's speechless reaction with a narrowed eye, I raise an eyebrow. "Well I guess that makes it my turn then," I say, sitting up straighter.

"What's the last book you read? And no car magazines allowed."

"*Paper Towns,* by John Green," he responds. "You?"

"Uhh…I guess it must've been *Sea and Sky*, by Ashton Jacobs." I squint slightly knowing he's about to make fun of me.

Jacoby's eyebrows raise. "Isn't that one of those trashy romance novels? You're into those?"

I gasp at his accusation. "I don't see them as trashy romance novels at all, thank you very much! They're just – I don't know – good love stories."

"Uh huh." He teases. "And they're filled with sex, am I right?"

My face starts to flush, so I try to take the last bite of my taco to hide the pink embarrassment rising up my neck. Before I can respond, Jacoby sits back in his chair with a shit eating grin. "Is that where you get your moves? From the books you read?"

"WHAT?" I shout, half pissed, but half laughing. I grab a handful of shredded lettuce and throw it at the smart ass sitting across the table. "NO. For your information, it is NOT where I get my moves, but I'm happy to lend you my books sometime. Maybe you'll learn a few things you don't already know."

That gets him to laugh. "Thanks, but no thanks. I think I know enough. And I think you would probably agree with me." He winks.

I slide some of the loose strands of my hair behind my ear, attempting to once again cover up my embarrassment. I clear my throat before I say quietly, "I'm stuffed. Thank you for making dinner. I'll clean up since you cooked."

"You didn't eat your last taco," Jacoby says. "Was it okay?"

"Yeah, of course!" I make eye contact with him so he knows I'm being truthful. "It was delicious. I think my eyes were just bigger than my stomach. You should eat it. Otherwise it'll go to waste." I pick up my taco and hand it to Jacoby, who after looking at it for a few seconds, takes it from my hands, holding it up to admire it.

"So you're offering me your taco?" he asks.

"Yeah. I told you, you should eat it." I tell him again, standing up to begin clearing the table.

"So just to be clear…" He clears his throat and smiles wild enough that a dimple appears. "You're telling me to eat your taco?"

"Yes! Please, Jacoby, eat my taco for Pete's sake."

Chuckling softly, he responds "Careful Sweetstuff, you're turning me on."

"Seriously?" I ask grabbing a few platters and moving them to the kitchen counter. "Giving you permission to eat my taaaac-oooooooh." I exclaim, wide-eyed before buckling in laughter as I turn around to face him. "Oh my God! I can't believe that conversation just happened and it totally almost went over my head. I am so sorry! Hahahaha!"

While standing at the counter laughing so hard, I don't notice Jacoby rising from his seat until he's boxed me in between himself and the counter behind me. The look on his face humored, yet heated. "Your taco was delicious the first time and I'm pretty damn sure it would delight me a second time."

Hot – fucking – balls.

His comment sends jolts of pleasure through my body causing a gasp to escape my mouth. Without hesitation, Jacoby's lips are slamming against mine in a hungry pursuit. His hands are in my hair, and on the back of my neck, holding me while he devours all that I have to give. His tongue glides against mine, the taste of Corona on his lips. Allowing him to devour me, to take what he wants, feels freeing for the first time in - well, I can't remember how long. It's like with each pass of his tongue, he's licking away all my worries, my stresses, my demons. He doesn't come across as one of those alpha-type males I read about in books, nor am I the kind of girl who identifies with those who like to submit to their men, but for whatever reason, in this moment, I'm more than happy to let go and yield, even if just for a few minutes.

"Your lips are so soft," he whispers in between kisses. His hands slide smoothly up and down my arms, causing goosebumps to arise. My pulse already quickening, I grab on to Jacoby's t-shirt and pull him even closer to me than he already is, telling him that I'm okay with more. Like he's reading my mind, I feel his hands behind me pushing some of the dishes out of the way before he grabs my hips, lifts me up on the counter and stands in between my thighs.

"Jacoby." His name rolls off my tongue in a sweet moan of desire as his hands continue to roam up and down my body.

"You are so beautiful," he gasps as he kisses me once, twice, three more times before he sighs running his right hand through his dark hair. "I don't know what it is about you, Jenna, but I'm…I'm fucking captivated."

Damnit, why does he have to say such sweet things to me?

This isn't how I roll.

I don't deserve it.

A lone tear slides down my cheek catches Jacoby's attention before I can swipe it away. "Whoa, no, no, no, no." He shakes his head. "Why are you crying? I didn't mean to make you cry. Did I say something wrong?"

I shake my head back and forth as a few more tears defy me. "No. Jacoby, it's not you. You…" I sigh. "You never say anything wrong. I've just had a shitty day – literally and figuratively – and I don't feel like I deserve whatever this is and…"

"Shhhh. Jenna, listen to me." Jacoby takes my head in his hands and softly brushes away my tears. "I like you, okay? I really like you. I think I've made that pretty clear – at least – I hope I have. You're not like…any girl I've ever been with, but something about you has me wanting more and more and more."

"Jacoby," I breathe. "I think…"

"Shhh…" He says placing a finger over my mouth. "Don't think, Jenna. Just don't think any more tonight. Just feel." He kisses me again, softly, slowly, wrapping his tongue around mine in a sensual slow dance. Against all the alarms going off in my head reminding me that relationships are not my thing, my body melts into his, reveling in his warmth, in the comfort of his soft chest and his welcoming arms.

"Just relax and let me take care of you," he says before lifting and carrying me out of the kitchen.

Maybe relationships could be my thing again.

I pay no attention to where we're going, but instead, try to allow myself to do as he asked: to let go, to not think, to just feel. As he walks down the hall with me in his arms, I trail kisses up the side of his neck until I'm sucking on his earlobe. The grunt that comes from his throat is more than enough to let me know he likes it.

"Hooooly shit." I hear him say as he stops dead in his tracks. Opening my eyes, I turn my head to see where we are before closing them again as tightly as I can.

"Fuck!" I mutter as I wriggle myself from Jacoby's arms and clumsily run into my guest room which, right now, doubles as my office. I frantically grab material and ball it up in my arms.

"Shit! Shit! Shit! I'm sorry. You weren't – you weren't supposed to see any of this. God, I totally forgot about it and that was another thing I was supposed to do today and it didn't get done and SHIT! You weren't supposed to…."

"Whoa! Jenna, stop!" He steps in front of me, successfully blocking my flurry of activity around the room. "Just stop for a second." Looking around the room Jacoby eyes the piles of colored material. "What is all this?" he asks. My shoulders immediately droop.

History would've repeated itself anyway.

May as well just be honest.

"It's lingerie," I tell him.

"I can see that it's lingerie." His expression is like a kid in a candy shop. "I mean, I'm not complaining or anything, but wha-why is it here? Are you, um…" I watch as he slides his hand through his hair again, a clear sign of frustration? Confusion? Okay, maybe it's not so clear.

"Are you a dancer or something? I mean you're not like…you don't…are there cameras in here?"

Watching him try to ask me if I'm a porn star without offending me is almost cute. His question actually causes me to laugh. "No,

Jacoby. I'm not a porn star. These pieces are my designs. I design lingerie."

Jacoby's eyebrows shoot up. "*You* do this?" He asks, lifting one of the white teddies off my couch and admiring it. "You *created* this?"

I nod. "Yeah. My sister and I, we kind of have a side business. I design the clothing and she helps market it. Look," I shoo him away with the flick of my hand as I collect the remaining pieces and lay them gingerly into the box I should've packed them in last night. "It's really no big deal. I'm sorry you had to see it all."

"See it all? Are you kidding? I don't mind at all. I'm seriously impressed, but I would much rather see it *on*! You're going to model one of these for me, right?"

Images of a drunken asshole invade my mind.

Chad is laying in my bed, waiting for me, I want to walk out and surprise him. I'm so excited to show him what I've been working on. I picked my favorite one. It's red satin with sparkly little rhinestones and a flowing bow at the back that he will be able to untie. He can untie me like a present. I open the bathroom door and step out into my dimly lit room giving Chad my most seductive smile.

"What do you think?" I ask as I slowly turn for him to inspect his surprise package.

His eyebrow shoots up before he says, "I like your tits, baby. I don't need no piece of material trying to hide them from me. And your ass is too big for the back. Your cheeks spill out of the bottom. Just get it off and get in here. And turn out the lights before you come to bed." He lays back on his pillow with his arms behind his head like what he said didn't just tear me to shreds.

I step back into the bathroom, and gaze at my reflection in the mirror one more time before I fall to my knees, heart-broken by the man I love, the man I trust, the man I gave my virginity to. I do everything I can to make sure the tears don't escape down my face giving Chad more fodder to tell me how weak and useless I am. Quietly, I step out of my favorite red teddy before turning to open the drawer in front of me where I knew a pair of scissors are located. My hands shake as I open the scissors against the soft satin material.

I can't do it. I can't ruin my design, my very favorite design, the one I worked for hours on. The tears fall, and I let them as I mourn the loss of my dignity and my pride, alone on the bathroom floor.

"Absolutely not." I finally answer Jacoby's request with an easily deadpanned expression. "I never wear my own designs. Not anymore. I just – design them." My voice trails off.

"Jenna? What's wrong?" His concern is sweet, but I can't let him in. I've already let him in too far. It has to stop.

"Look, Jacoby. You need to understand something about me."

"Okay. What is it?" he asks gently.

"I don't do this. I can't do this."

"Do what?"

"This." I point back and forth between us. "Whatever this is between us, it can't happen. I'm sorry, but it just…can't. I can't." I make my way towards the living room, and the front door. Jacoby follows quietly behind me. When I stop at the door and turn around, I can see that Jacoby is confounded, and rightfully so.

Jacoby shakes his head, frowning. "I'm sorry, I don't understand."

"I'm not right for you, okay?" I shout. "I promise, I'm not good for you, and in the end, we'll both end up right back where we started."

"Jenna…"

"Thanks for dinner, Jacoby," I interrupt him. "It was really nice of you." I place my hand on the door knob. "But I think it would be best if we just ended the night. You should go."

I can't believe I'm doing this.

I don't want him to go.

I feel him watching me, so I try my best not to make eye contact. Eventually hearing his footsteps coming toward me, I finally look up as he stops in front of me and places his right hand against my cheek. I close my eyes at the contact, swallowing back the enormous knot in my throat. I want to lean into his hand so badly. He's been nothing but kind and compassionate to me, but I can't do this. I can't continue to give him what he wants.

"Who hurt you Jenna?" he whispers. His words slice through me to my core, exploding my emotions into a billion pieces. Tears spill from my eyes as I clutch my hand to my chest, the tightness feeling like I just completed a badly run marathon.

"Please," I beg. "Just go. I need you to go." I open the door, silently begging him to walk out and leave me alone. It takes him a minute, but before he walks out he leans forward and places a kiss on the top of my head.

"I'm sorry," he says before placing a second kiss on my forehead and walking out the door. I don't even watch him leave. I quietly shut the door before running to my bedroom and throwing myself on my bed, where I remain for the night, buried in my own sorrow.

Nope, relationships are definitely not my thing.

CHAPTER 9
The Jovi
Jacoby

"SHIT!" I punch the steering wheel with both of my fists once I'm alone in my car. "What the fuck was that?" One minute I have her in my arms and the next she's swallowing back tears. I can't get the image of her face when I asked her to model one of her pieces out of my head. Good Lord, her work…it's exquisite, and I have no doubt in my mind that she would look like a goddess wearing any one of the ones I saw today.

Her face though…

The tears…

Someone hurt her, I can feel it. She had it written all over her face and there was nothing I could do about it. I've never felt so damn helpless in my entire life. I haven't had this strong of an attraction to a girl since Sarah six years ago, and now? Now the girl I would love nothing more than to get to know is broken, and for reasons I can't explain, just erected a huge wall all around her that I don't know how to penetrate. The frustration drips off of me like a leaky faucet. Stealing another look at the house before I leave, I don't see her shadow in any of the windows. I wish I knew what was going through her head right now. I wish I could go back in there. I wish I knew the right words to say to make her feel better. I'm supposed to be good with words. Great with words, even, but this time, the words just aren't there.

Shifting the car into drive, I pull out onto the street and head to God knows where. I just drive in silence for miles. Around town, through town, along the coast, I must drive around for an hour alone with myself and my thoughts before I head to the one place that gives me complete solace, the one place I know that not one person will be able to bother me for the rest of the night. The Jovi.

It doesn't take too long to get to the Mystic Seaport Marina. It's muggier than I would like it to be, but since I have no control over the weather of Mystic, or anywhere else for that matter, I don't spend time being pissed about it. I park my car in its designated spot and head to the dock where The Jovi sits, waiting for me. The Heritage East Sundeck Yacht was a decision Jack Schmidt and I made together two years ago. We've both done ridiculously stupid things to impress a girl at one point or another and this was Jack's. The girl he was infatuated with at the time loved expensive things and she loved being on the water. He wanted to be able to take her there whenever she wanted. He didn't quite have the money to buy the used yacht outright himself, so with my help, we picked out something together that we could both be happy with. Aptly named *The Jovi,* after our favorite eighties rock band, our small yacht has brought us each a place for peace, a place for joy, a place for fun, and place for hiding out when we don't want to be bothered.

Jack mentioned earlier that he was thinking about a little cruising this evening, but since The Jovi is still docked, I'm guessing he must've changed his mind. That's good news for me. I now have the boat to myself, to drink away my thoughts of the beautiful girl I can't get my mind off of. Knowing that I plan on drinking whatever the hell is left in the cabin fridge, I make the responsible decision to not power up the boat and take her out to sea. I don't even turn on the lights inside before grabbing a couple beers out of the fridge, turning on the television, and laying back on the cabin chaise to drink the night away, alone, and embarrassingly devastated.

"Hey, Malloy! Bad night, I see, eh?" Jack's voice, along with the sound of heavily clanking bottles stirs me awake. My head throbs as I open my eyes to see Jack pitching several beer bottles into the nearby trash can. I flinch in pain with each bottle toss. "Son of a bitch, man!" Jack laughs. "Are you telling me you drank every last bottle in the fridge?"

"Mmm hmm. Probably," is all I can say.

"Probably? Jesus Christ, Malloy, there are over ten empty bottles in here. You want to tell me who bit your dick, or what? How long were you here? I thought you had a date last night?"

I take a minute to think through all the questions he just asked me. Rubbing my hands up and down my face I answer him. "Nobody. All night I guess. I did…and then I didn't. What time is it?" I ask, looking around for my phone.

"It's just after ten. I'm sorry I had to interrupt your stupor, but I'm taking some clients out later today. Just stopped in to make sure things are cleaned up and stocked." He shakes the trash can several times while trying to get the trash bag out to throw away. Each knock of the can on the floor is like thunder ringing through my hungover brain.

"Jesus, Schmidt Stain! Do you mind?" I wince and cover my ears from his banging around the cabin. When I look up at him from where I'm reclining he simply smirks.

"Oh. Sorry, is the noise bothering you?" He laughs. "Poor Jacoby had about seven too many beers last night, huh?" When he sees that I'm not laughing with him this time he sighs audibly before sitting in the chair across from me. "You want to talk about it?"

I shake my head, which only brings on more throbbing. "There's isn't much to talk about."

"Well what happened with the girl…what's her name again?"

"Jenna."

"Right. Jenna. What happened with Jenna?"

"I wish I knew." I slowly sit up and turn my legs to hang off the chaise. "One minute we were great and the next minute she was in tears, and I swear I didn't do a damn thing. Something's wrong and she didn't let me stick around long enough to figure out what it is.

Some douchebag had to have hurt her at some point in her past or something."

"What makes you think that?"

"I don't know. I asked her a question and she immediately clammed up and shut me out. I don't know what I said or why it affected her so much but she asked me to leave. After what I witnessed, I wasn't about to fight her on it. She no longer felt safe with me there. I wasn't going to be another guy who hurts her." I bow my head. "Just when I meet someone I think..." I sigh. "I think I could've really liked her."

"Liked her?" Jack asks.

"Yeah."

"No," he answers me, catching my attention. "Not *liked* her. You still like her or else this wouldn't have your dick in a twist. I mean, look at yourself Malloy. When was the last time you got yourself shit-faced and passed out over a girl?"

He's right. It's been a long time. Six years to be exact.

"Yeah I know. Sarah."

"Yeah, Sarah," he answers. "Stop comparing one to the other. It was a long time ago. Times are different. People are different. If you really like this girl, then get off your drunk ass, sober up, and do something about it!"

"Like what Jack-ass?" I shout, wincing at the sound of my own voice. "She doesn't want me. She kicked me out. How am I supposed to hurdle the wall she's built up around herself?"

Jack smiles the all-knowing smile that tells me he knows the answer and isn't going to tell me. "You're Jacoby Malloy, dude. I have all the faith in the world that you'll figure it out. You tell me shit like that all the time. Remember the crap I went through with Veronica? You were always telling me to do what I had to do."

"Yeah but you're not together anymore, so maybe that advice was bogus," I argue.

"That's bullshit and you know it. Veronica was so not the right one for me. She would've been better off with your brother."

"Watch it, Schmidt Stain," I mumble as I give him the evil eye.

"Ooh," he says with a smirk. "Too soon?" When I don't answer, he changes the subject. "What do you have going on tonight?"

I reach for my back pocket where I keep my phone, but find the pocket empty.

"Shit," I mumble. "I left my phone at Jenna's house last night." I left it sitting on the kitchen counter, forgetting I used it to play music while cooking dinner.

"Well, I guess I know what you'll be doing today then." He slaps me on the shoulder before getting up to do a quick check around the rest of the cabin. "I'm going to get rid of this trash and then I need to head out to restock the fridge. You going to be okay?"

"Yeah." I nod. "I'll be alright. Give me a few minutes and I'll be out of here and out of your way."

"No problem man. I'll catch you later," he says before taking the steps up to the deck. "And good luck!"

Slumping back into my seat, I close my eyes and desperately try to come up with a genius plan, but one never comes. There's no way in hell I can just show up at Jenna's house and get my phone. After last night, I don't want to look like a stalker. I'll have to eventually, because now that she has my phone, she can't just text me to get it back to me. Deciding not to worry about my phone for now, I get up from my seat and splash some water on my face in the bathroom in hopes that my body will wake up a little faster. I should just go home, shower, and get to work on something to keep my mind off of what I want to be thinking about. At least with no phone, it's one less stress off my back that nobody can reach me today. Maybe I'll get something productive done.

Sheer personal masochism has me driving by The Hole Punch on my way home, even though my conscience is screaming at me to just drive the other way. I just want to see if her car is in the parking lot. I want to know that she's at least okay enough to go to work. I would hate myself if I found out later that she spent the entire night stewing by herself over something that is clearly still raw for her.

Maybe it's not our time.

"No. Screw that, Jacoby," I tell myself. "You're good for her. You can be good for her. You've wanted her for so long. Do something about it before it's too late."

As I finally drive past the Hole Punch parking lot I spot Jenna's blue Ford Fusion parked at the side of the building. Immediately ideas start swimming through my head of things I could do to at least let her know I'm still here. I know I'll have to see her again eventually to get my phone back, but until that happens, and I can maybe talk to her, face to face, I need to keep things light. Remembering one of our first conversations, an idea pops into my mind that could be perfect. Making a right-hand turn at the next light, I head back towards the middle of town to pick up the things I need before making my last stop at Mystic Florals. It's time to see a guy about a girl.

CHAPTER 10
Hole-Punched Heart

Jenna

"You really kicked him out?" Linda asks as she takes a bite of her salad. She was all too eager to get to our lunch break this afternoon so she could hear all about last night.

I nod, taking a bite of my sandwich. "Yeah. I did. I didn't want to, I just…reacted."

"Why, Jizz? You said he made you a fantastic dinner and he kissed you and…"

"And then asked me to model a piece of lingerie I had left out. Well, I had left it all out, actually, because I was supposed to drop it off at the boutique after work yesterday and forgot about it after the shit storm we had here."

Linda bows her head to the side. "Sweetie, he didn't know. He was just being a guy, you know?"

"Yeah I know. I really do, but it all came back right then. That night with Chad? What he said? How I felt? I didn't take the time to explain it to Jacoby because I had just reacted. By then, I had ruined the night anyway. It was best for both of us for the night to just be over."

"Awww Jizza, I'm sorry that all happened," Linda says.

"Yeah well, I have to see him again at some point, because he left his phone at my place," I point to the phone plugged into the charger in the corner of the room. "Actually, I'm a little surprised he didn't come right back in for it," I explain. "Though I suppose, even I didn't see it until I was making breakfast this morning. I brought it with me so I could charge it for him."

"So how are you going to get it to him? You can't text him. You can't call him."

"Well, I assume he'll be in at some point this afternoon. He knows what my car looks like, obviously. If he sees it parked outside, he'll come in and ask about it. Then we're on neutral ground and I won't have time for awkward conversation, you know?"

Linda nods slowly watching me with narrowed eyes. "Yeah, I guess. Soooo you don't want to patch things up with Jacoby even a little bit?"

Exasperated I scowl at Linda like she's on my last nerve. "Even if I did, Linda, what good would it do? I don't need another guy telling me that I'm not good enough, because dammit, I *am* good enough. I'm a catch and one day, the right guy will come along and he'll see that. He'll see that I'm a girl with drive and ambition and passion about the things I do."

"Uh huh…" Linda says. When I look over at her, she stands up to throw her empty salad carton away. "And he'll be a sweet guy who cooks you dinner when you slip in shit at work, or maybe, maybe he'll even give you the shirt off his back when you spill iced mocha all over your damn self. So tell me Jizz, when will *you* see it for real? When will you see that you really are good enough and that just maybe this guy cares for you?" I watch as she sympathetically smiles at me before stepping out of the break room.

Sometimes she's a bitch.

Except I know she's right.

The afternoon is sweltering hot which, of course, means I'm stuck in the warehouse unloading a truck full of freight and moving pallets around, sweating like a damn pig. I'm counting down the ninety minutes before I get to leave this place for the day, go home and shower and then drop off my pieces at the boutique. The only down side of this day is that Jacoby hasn't come in yet since his cell phone is still in my pocket. At some point I'm going to have to face him. I can't just keep his phone; he knows I have it.

I just have no idea what to say.

"Jenna you're needed at the Customer Service Desk." I hear one of my ass-hats say through my ear piece.

Wiping the sweat from my face, I roll my eyes and push the button for my microphone. "Seriously? I mean I'm sort of busy back here. Can it wait? Or can Linda get it?"

"Get your pretty little ass up here biotch," Linda says into my ear piece. "You're needed at the Customer Service desk."

Shit!

Jacoby's here.

The sweat I just wiped from my face returns immediately, but this time it's a nervous clammy sweat. Good Lord, will I ever be in front of this man when I'm not covered in frozen liquid, shit, or my own sweat? Why me? I have the worst case of nerves as I make my way through the warehouse doors and down the aisle toward the front of the store. What if Jacoby is pissed? What if I start to cry? How can I even look at him again after what I did? I don't want to do this here in the front of the whole store. Maybe I can walk him out and talk there for a few minutes. That's the plan I have myself talked into until I get to the front of the store and don't see Jacoby anywhere.

"What's up? What did you need?" I ask Julie at the Customer Service desk.

"Oh, Linda has a special delivery for you." She smiles. "It's in the office now."

"Uh, okay." I turn and head into the office, praying that Jacoby isn't in there with her. Lucky for me, my prayers are answered when I step into the office and see Linda standing in front of our desk with a huge smile on her face.

"What's going on?" I ask her. She shuffles to the side revealing a massive bouquet of – surprisingly - not flowers. "Are those candy bars?"

"Yeah, they are, Jizz! Check it out!" She squeals. "Have you ever seen such a thing? I mean who would think to use Kit Kats?"

A smile graces my lips as I pull the white envelope from the center of the chocolate bouquet knowing full well who they're from. I have to give credit where it's due, this is the most imaginative gift I've ever been given.

And he remembered.

These would've been dessert. I'm sorry about last night.
I thought these might brighten your day.
- Jacoby

I can't not smile at his note, or at the thought that he did this for me, even after the way I treated him last night.

"Did Jacoby deliver these himself? Why didn't he stay?" I ask her, looking out the window for his car. The pang of disappointment hits my heart. Even though I've been telling myself the opposite, I sort of, kind of, really wanted to see him.

She shakes her head. "No. It wasn't him. They came from Mystic Florals. Some delivery guy in a van."

"Huh." I shrug, gazing at the bouquet again. "I didn't even know they did anything like this. This is pretty impressive."

"Almost like you're worth it, huh?" Linda winks.

"Watch it," I tease her.

Linda continues. "I mean the guy gives you the shirt off his back, fixes your car, eats you out, fucks you senseless, makes you dinner, and delivers a chocolate bouquet to your place of employment, basically telling the entire store that he likes you, and for some reason you think he doesn't care enough? Or that you're not good enough? What's a guy got to do to get your attention Jizz?"

"Okay, Okay! I hear you." I surrender. "I'll…go see him, I guess. I have to get his phone back to him somehow anyway."

Linda wraps me in a big hug. "That's my girl! You got this, Jizz. You can do it. You're good enough, and from the looks and sounds of things, he is too. Give him a chance okay? And stop looking back. You're not going that way."

"Yeah. I'll try." I don't make her any promises.

"That's all I ask," she says.

By five-thirty I'm home, showered, and ready to get these new pieces dropped off at Chic Boutique. Hopefully, Leslie, the owner of the beautifully trendy little shop, won't be too upset that I'm a day late with my delivery. Loading the last hanging garment bag into the car, I make sure that Jacoby's phone is safely tucked away in my pocket before heading into town. I plan to stop at his garage on the way home to see if he's there.

"Hey Leslie!" I say cheerfully, carrying my garment bags into the Chic Boutique. From the back I hear her squeal followed by the click-clack of her heels rushing up to the front of the store.

"Jenna! I'm so excited you're here! I have great news for you, are you ready?" she exclaims.

"I'm always ready for good news, girl. Hit me!"

"Your stock is sold out. Like, completely sold out! I don't even have one piece left for myself! Girl, your designs are in high demand! I sold the last four of them online this morning!" She claps her hand and bounces up and down in pure excitement, not only for her shop sales, but for my personal success as well. My partnership with Leslie has always been so great and this just makes it one hundred percent better.

"Are you kidding me?" My jaw falls in disbelief. "Are you sure? Like, *all* of them? Even the yellow one with the red tassels?"

Leslie laughs at me. "Yes! In fact, I got a message online today to ask if that one was sold in any other color schemes! She thought the tassels were genius! You're on fire, Jenna! I'm so glad you brought me some new pieces!" She opens her arms in welcome, gesturing toward the back counter. "Let's see what you got this time!"

We spend the next thirty minutes or so looking over the twenty-five pieces I brought in with me today…five more than I usually bring. I give her the rundown on how some of them need to be worn and even removed. I like to think outside the box when it comes to lingerie, so sometimes getting them on and off can look a lot more confusing than it really is. There are almost always extra straps, buttons, hooks, gems etc. Leslie loves the uniqueness of each one. Apparently, her clientele do as well.

"Oh my God, I'm setting this one aside for myself right now! It's gorgeous!" Leslie holds up the white garment that Jacoby had in his hands last night. My face flushes slightly thinking about his excitement and his curiosity. I nod in appreciation. I'm just grateful that she loves my designs and is willing to sell them for me here.

"I'm sure you would look great in that one," I agree with her.

"I'm sure Todd will be singing your praises tonight, my friend."

"Umm, let's hope he's singing *your* praises," I emphasize. "I'm totally okay if he never mentions my name."

We both laugh as she takes the lingerie to the back to be tagged before being set out for sale in the morning. We head back to the front where she pulls my latest commission check from her file and hands it to me.

"Thank you, so much Jenna. Your pieces are exquisite and I can't tell you how much traffic you bring to this store. I'll be thanking you for the rest of my life. One day, you're going to end up New York City. I can just tell."

"Nah, probably not. But I really do appreciate everything you do for me, allowing me to bring my designs here to sell. It really is a dream come true. I should get going though. I have one more stop to make before I get home."

"Okay. I'll give you a call toward the end of the week and let you know how sales are going," Leslie tells me.

"Sounds good. Thanks. I'll see you soon." I wave goodbye and walk a few feet down the street to where my car is parked. I hit the button on my key fab to unlock the car and get in. As I move to turn the ignition, the cell phone in my pocket vibrates and dings.

Jacoby's cell phone.

It's the first time today I've heard anything from his phone, so instinctively I pull it out of my back pocket. Assuming the screen is locked I push the center button knowing I'll be able to at least see who was contacting him. The text on his screen isn't from someone I recognize, obviously, but what does catch my eye is that my name is included in the text.

Jack: How did things go with Jenna today?

Oh my God.

Who is Jack?

He's talking about me.

That means Jacoby has talked about me.

"How did things go with Jenna today?" I reread the text out loud to myself. This text implies that Jacoby had some sort of plan to see me today. My stomach flips when I think about the fact that Jacoby has talked about me to someone. I don't know why I'm that surprised by the thought. It's not like I haven't talked about Jacoby with Linda and Bethy. I just never expected him to really…care.

Maybe he doesn't.

I have to try to keep my head clear. It's possible that he lamented to a friend last night, but it's also entirely possible that he vented to a friend about what a bitch I was. Either way, I guess I'll be finding out soon enough. Laying Jacoby's cell phone on the seat next to me, I put the name of his garage into my GPS and follow the directions out of town until I'm on the long winding road I recognize from the other night. I take a deep breath as I turn on my turn signal and pull into the dirt parking lot of Jacked Up. My heart begins to race and the butterflies in my stomach flutter nervously when I see that the garage door is open and there are lights on. I swallow the lump in my throat, and turn off the ignition.

"Don't look back, Jenna. You're not going that way." I whisper to myself before grabbing Jacoby's phone and opening my car door.

CHAPTER 11

What's the Difference?

Jenna

Music.

Loud music.

Loud music that I recognize.

Yesterday he asked if I had a favorite song.

I told him no.

I was lying, of course.

This is my favorite song. The one that just so happens to be blaring in Jacoby's garage as I walk in. 'Creep', by Radiohead. At the very least, it's the one I seem to identify with the most. He can't see me, but I can see him. The music must be loud enough that he didn't hear me drive up. Leaning underneath the open hood of a car without a shirt on, and in a pair of ripped up jeans filled with grease stains, my breath hitches as I watch his ab muscles expand and contract. The black sheep tattoo that I once thought was a cloud moves as he flexes his arms.

He sees himself as a black sheep?

Sweat glistens on his back and shoulders and he wears an old red baseball cap backwards to hold his hair back from his face. He's obviously been at this for a while. I almost wish he wasn't so easy on the eyes. It would make things a hell of a lot easier for me. I don't mean to look like I'm hiding behind the wall, but since I'm here, I take the opportunity to watch him while listening to the words about having a perfect body and a perfect soul.

I do wish I was special to someone.

But I have to admit, I am a bit of a weirdo. I regularly vomit all the words, I work retail at a store called The Hole Punch, which I know, sounds an awful lot like some sort of brothel and speaking of brothels, I design unusually artistic lingerie in my spare time.

"Jenna?"

I hear my name before my eyes focus on the sexy beast staring at me. I didn't even hear him turn down the music and I certainly didn't notice him walking toward me. Startling out of my trance, words begin to spill out of me before I even think about what I want to say. "Does this song speak to you because of your dad? I mean, you said - at least I think it was you who told me - that he views you as a disappointment, so I just wondered if maybe this song speaks to you like it speaks..." My voice fades as I run out of breath. "To...me."

A soft smile smooths over Jacoby's face. He wipes his hands on the rag hanging from his pocket. I'm sure he doesn't know how to react to my question.

"Something like that," he says softly, watching me. "Hi."

"Hi." I try to smile but I'm positive my lips just flip all over the place resulting in more of a sneer, or that look you get when someone tells you to smile for a picture and catches you off guard so you just look like someone who walked out of a dentist's office with half of a numbed face.

"What are you doing here?" He prods, cocking his head to the side. My somewhat-of-a- smile fades immediately.

Oh God, I was right.

He doesn't want me here.

"Umm…"

Words, Jenna! Words!

"I umm…I just…" With a shaky hand, I hold out his phone for him to see. "You left this. At my house, I mean. You left it last night and then you didn't show up at the store today, so I figured I should stop by and see if you were here, which you are, so I should give this back to you, because it's yours and you need it, so here." I hand Jacoby his phone, which he takes from my hand without ever looking down at our hands as they touch. I don't understand how he can't look down when the spark between our touch shoots through me all the way to my toes.

Maybe he doesn't feel it.

"Why is your hand shaking?" He notices without ever looking down. He's been holding my stare the entire time so how did he even notice my hand was shaking? "Do I scare you? Are you afraid of me, Jenna?"

"No!" I shake my head ridiculously too many times. "I'm not scared of you."

I like you.

"Look, I didn't mean to interrupt you…" I start.

I'm just too scared to say it out loud.

"I just wanted to make sure you got your phone back…"

I'm not scared of you. I'm just scared because I like you.

"I know how busy you are and if you miss a call that could be bad, especially if someone needs a tow truck, you know? So, I should go." God, I know how to ramble.

"No," he says adamantly, still watching my every move with the utmost attention.

"What?" The word flies out. I don't even know why.

"Please don't go, Jenna. I'm glad you're here. I – uh – I want to show you something. Take a walk with me?"

"I…I don't know." I shake my head.

He holds his hand out for me to take. "Please. I know I'm a dirty mess right now, but if I go wash up and change, I risk you leaving me again and I don't want that to happen, so please. Will you just walk with me? Please?"

Without ever blinking I watch him talk to me, and for the first time, I can feel the sincerity in his voice, see it in the way he moves. Actually, I'm sure it's been there all along, I've just been too caught up in my own fears to see it. I reach out my hand and place it in his. "Okay." I say as his fingers softly wrap around my hand, watching as his thumb strokes the top from side to side.

"Come on, it's this way." He gently tugs my hand as he leads me back through the garage and in through the same doorway I've been through before. One of the doors off the interior hallway leads to a bathroom that I used the last time I was here. I wonder to myself if my panties are still in the drawer I hid them in, and then it hits me. What if he's already found them?

"Oh, God. You found them! I'm sorry! I totally forgot I put them there and I should've told you..."

"What? Found what?" Jacoby asks.

"My...umm..." Ugh, don't make me say it. "My panties. I was just trying to be cute. I didn't mean to upset you. I'm so..."

"Whoa, whoa, whoa. What about your panties?" He raises his eyebrows in surprise. I shake my head once realizing he has no idea what I'm talking about.

"Uhh...I..." All I can do is shake my head, unsure of what to say next. "Never mind. It's nothing."

"It's definitely not nothing." Jacoby replies. "But whatever it is you think I want to show you, I promise you that's not it. Come on." We continue walking until we reach the door at the end of the hallway.

"This is where I live," Jacoby says, turning the knob and opening the door for me to enter. I'm a little caught off guard. I had no idea there was anything other than maybe a few offices or something attached to this garage. I certainly couldn't see another part of the building from the street. But when I step inside, it seems as though I just walked into one of those beautiful homes that HGTV gives away. Three feet inside and I'm standing in an expansive kitchen surrounded in dark mahogany cabinetry, gray granite countertops and stainless steel appliances. It's a dream kitchen if I ever saw one.

"You? You live here?" I try to hide the shock in my voice but I'm sure I failed if the dimple in Jacoby's cheek has anything to say.

"You like it?" he asks.

"Like it? It's every woman's dream kitchen." I say, gliding my fingertips across the countertops. "You live here? By yourself?"

"Yeah."

"Did you build this house?" I ask.

"No. Actually, I bought this house a few years ago, and then built the garage onto the back."

"Wait, so your house doesn't face the street? Isn't that…I don't know, weird? Most houses face the street, don't they?" Is it weird that I'm even asking this?

"That's a good question," he responds as he walks over to the sink to wash his greasy hands. "I'll show you around eventually, but this house was actually built before that road was." He hitches his thumb behind him to motion towards the road I came in on. "There's a long gravel driveway at the front of the house that leads to one of the back country roads. You can't see the house from that road either. That's why I fell in love with this place when the realtor showed it to me."

"You don't like to be seen?"

I mean he's in The Hole Punch twice a week at least.

"I don't mind being seen. I just like my privacy," he says.

I nod, completely understanding that statement.

"But the kitchen isn't what I want to show you." He dries his hands on the towel lying next to the sink. I follow him through the kitchen, into what looks like a family room of sorts and over to a wall of book shelves.

"This is what I wanted to show you," he says, suddenly reserved. My eyes flitter around the book shelves, reading title after title. Some of them are books I've read, mysteries, adventure, science fiction, epic novels, and old standards; his collection is impressive.

"Wow! I didn't know you were such a reader!" I exclaim.

"Yeah," he says. "But I'm not just a reader." I watch as he pulls out a handle that's hidden in the wood of the bookshelf so that the bookshelf now becomes a door that he pulls open for me. Like a kid seeing a magic trick for the first time, I gasp in excitement and enter the small room behind the bookshelf. I'm only slightly disappointed when I step in and see that it's just a small hidden office, until I see the books that line the shelves in this room.

Ashton Jacobs romance novels.

All of them.

More than one of all of them.

Every one she's ever written. Even different versions that I've never seen before. Titles in other languages.

I take a minute to look around the room. Two walls are lined with bookshelves full of Ashton Jacobs novels. One blue wall holds a desk with a laptop, and other miscellaneous electronics, and the along the other wall is a brown leather sofa complete with light blue throw blanket and decorative pillows.

"Wait a minute," I say smirking. "The other night you teased me about reading these quote-un-quote 'trashy' love stories, and now you're showing me that you read them all too? In fact, from the look of things, you're a little obsessed. I had no idea you liked her writing."

"No, Jenna." Jacoby shakes his head. "I'm not an obsessed reader." He reaches to his back pocket and pulls out his wallet. Confused, I watch as he pulls his driver's license out and hands it to me.

"Read it," he commands.

I hold up his license so I can read it. "Jacoby Ashton Malloy." I look up to him for an answer to a question I obviously haven't asked yet.

"Ashton Jacobs…" he says. "'She' is me, Jenna. I'm Ashton Jacobs and I wrote all of these books."

Not sure how I should be reacting, I feel my eyes narrow in suspicion. I turn around and grab a book off the shelf immediately fleeting to the back of the book. I turn through the last couple pages looking for the author's bio, but when I come to it, there is no picture. I look back to Jacoby.

"No picture. Because how could I possibly come up with one?" he asks, shrugging as he watches me for a reaction.

"Is this a joke? Are you teasing me about the other day?" I ask one more time, watching his expression just to be sure, even though I know that no matter what he says, I still won't be sure.

"Would I fill a small office with book shelves filled with all versions of Ashton Jacobs books just to tease you? Especially if I had no idea you would be stopping by?"

"Well…" I consider his comment. "I suppose not, but I don't understand. Ashton Jacobs is huge, Jacoby. I mean…she's huge! Everyone loves her books. They fly off the shelves when new ones are released. There are Facebook groups galore! People are dying for signed copies."

"And now you see why they can't get them in person. I can't do book signings, Jenna. My agent has been trying to get me to reveal who I am because they see the demand for signings and interviews and all the shit that comes with a high-profile job. In fact, the other night, when you were here. The phone call I had to take?"

"Yeah."

"It was my agent, James."

007…I remember the ringtone.

"Sly ring tone, sir." I wink.

"Yeah, I guess." He's staring at me again with a trusting look in his eye.

"Wow. I can't believe she is you. This is all so unbelievable! Ashton Jacobs is a guy?" I'm amazed. I walk around the room, taking mental notes of everything I see. The pictures around the room, the clean lines of the walls and shelves, the spotless desk, the huge stack of paper reams on the floor next to a large box of pens, highlighters, and post-it notes.

"Wait…" I point to the paper and box of supplies on the floor.

"Yeah," Jacoby answers my unasked question. "I had to have a reason for coming into the store. It's not like I could walk in and just stand there watching you all day."

"Wait, wait, wait. What?" I ask. "You did all this…" I say motioning to the pile again. "For me?"

Jacoby nods sheepishly. "The first time I saw you there I thought you were a breath of fresh air. You were laughing and being so nice to your customers." He shrugs. "I just watched you…until someone asked me if they could help me find something…so I had to make up a list of things I needed."

"Jacoby, this is a lot of pens and highlighters and…paper." I tell him.

"Well, the paper I'll use. Maybe I can donate some of the pens and highlighters." He watches me with a thoughtful eye before he speaks again.

"Hmph. And you call me a stalker." I smirk.

He answers me with a sheepish smile and slides his hands into the pockets of jeans. "Touché. I guess I'm the only stalker here. So, umm, I need to tell you something." He cringes slightly.

"Oh. Okay," I say. I watch his face for any sign of surprise.

"There are only four people in my life who know this secret about me. You're now the fifth."

"What?" I panic. "No, no, no, I'm not good with secrets, Jacoby! Why the hell did you tell me? Oh my God, Jacoby! I vomit words out of my mouth on a regular basis, especially around you, and you're trusting me with information like this?"

"Yes. I am." He nods, seriously.

"Your Dad? He knows?" I ask.

Jacoby chuckles. "Hell no, he doesn't know. I can only imagine what he would say if he found out that the son he wanted to have follow in his political footsteps actually makes his money writing erotic romance novels."

"So why do you do it then? Why do you write these books?" I motion to the bookshelf beside me.

All Jacoby does is tilt his head and smile as if I'm supposed to already know the answer. "Why do you make lingerie?"

I'm thrown off guard by his question, though I think now I understand his point. "Because it's something I love doing, and I'm pretty good at it."

Jacoby nods his head slowly. "Exactly. And I'm good at writing. You say so yourself, as do thousands of my fans and because of that, I've grown to love doing it. I don't give a damn that it isn't what I set out to do. It certainly wasn't my dream growing up, but because of my hard work and determination, I can live my dream any way I want now."

"So then why not just tell your dad? I mean, if you don't seem to care what anyone thinks..."

Jacoby sighs. "To be honest? I don't know." He shrugs. "I guess all these years I've been so pissed about the way he treats me. All because I didn't choose the path most traveled in my family. He wouldn't understand. He has no idea how much money I make or how I choose to spend it because I don't need his money like my siblings do. I don't ask for anything, ever. He can't control the way I live my life and I like it that way. I'm free and I'm not tied up in political family scandals."

"But to have all this – freedom, as you say – you've basically had to give up your family?"

"Not entirely. My brother and sister still keep in touch with me and I make sure to go visit my mom. Most of the time Dad is too busy to even be around. Those are the best days to visit, because there's no tension between the rest of us. My brother can be an asshole sometimes, but for the most part, he's okay. I think my siblings sort of envy my ability to stand up to my father and live my own life. It's only when he's around that the tension grows until it explodes somehow and I end up leaving in a pissy mood."

"Sounds like fun," I say, hoping he gets my sarcasm.

"Always."

I stuff my hands in my back pockets and look around his office a little more, not sure of where the conversation should go next, not sure of what he expects from me, not sure of my own feelings. "Soooo why are you doing this? Why now? Why tonight? Why me at all? I mean, I kicked you out of my house yesterday, and now you're trusting me with your life secrets. I don't really get it. I certainly don't deserve it after the way I acted last night."

Jacoby takes my hand and leads me to the leather couch against the wall. He sits facing me, still holding my hand, as he begins to explain. "Jenna last night I obviously said something that hurt you, and I'm so sorry for that, because the very last thing I would ever want to do is hurt someone I care about."

"You care about me?" I ask naively.

"Isn't it obvious?" He laughs. "Jenna, I like you." His thumb glides across the top of my hand. "I like you a lot. I feel like I'm some sort of fifteen-year-old boy with a high- school crush. It's exhilarating and awkward all at the same time. I'm sorry about last night. Please know that whatever happened, whatever I said, whoever hurt you before we met – if that is, in fact, what happened - it gutted me that you were hurting in the end because of something I said. I didn't want to leave you alone. I would've slept outside on your front door steps to make sure you felt safe if I didn't think someone might call the cops on me."

Taking a deep breath, I whisper, "It wasn't your fault, Jacoby. I just…I overreacted. I'm sorry too for…being a big baby. I didn't want to push you away. It was just a gut reaction to protect myself."

"From what?"

"From…" I can feel the heat rise in my cheeks as I shake my head back and forth. "From jerks, and assholes, and pain, and heartache, and…I don't know, my past, I guess. I'm not very good with relationships and you seem like a really nice guy. You don't deserve to be treated the way I've treated guys in my past, the way I fear I'll end up treating you."

Jacoby tenderly rubs his hand up and down my thigh, a small sign of compassionate affection, but also one that causes the heat to rise in places I'm not ready to be thinking about right now. "I can appreciate your fears, but I can also assure you I'm not like most guys. I mean, how many erotic romance novel writers have you dated?" He winks, causing a smile to cross my face.

"Touché." I laugh.

"I can also guarantee you that I've never dated anyone with even close to a talent like yours."

His words calm my heart. "Really?"

"Really. How you come up with so many words to vomit out of your mouth at one time..." He shakes his head back and forth, smirking. "There has to be a world record in there for you somewhere."

My mouth pops open when I click my tongue at him before smiling and playfully nudging him. For once, I can appreciate the teasing. "Thanks a lot, I think. Maybe I'll consider holding a master class someday."

"Or you could just..." his hand reaches up to smooth a few stray strands of my hair from my face. "Give me private lessons." My breath hitches slightly when his hand doesn't leave the back of my head. Instead he slowly pulls my head toward him all the while staring at my lips. "Because I like listening to you talk," he whispers. Instinctively, I lick my lips, an innocent gesture, and one I probably do so many times a day without ever thinking about it, but this time it's different. This time I watch Jacoby lick his lips as well as he continues to pull my head toward him.

"Jenna?" He breathes.

"Yeah?"

"I really want to kiss you, but I don't want to kiss you if it's going to hurt you or scare you in any way." Our foreheads touch and for a moment we stay in this position on his couch, in his office. The quiet calm surrounds us, yet the beating of my heart, and the accelerated pumping of my blood sounds like an epic fireworks display going off in my head.

"Then don't bite my lip," I challenge.

Our foreheads still touching, I see his smile grow as he nuzzles my nose with his in the sweetest Eskimo kiss. His lips separate just enough to cover mine as he places a few fingers under my chin. I feel the softness of his tongue glide along my bottom lip in a kiss so tender, soft, and emotional. His hands reach up to frame my face as we continue this blissful pampering of our mouths. As if I can taste his feelings pouring into me through his kiss, I feel a tear escape down my cheek.

"Why are you crying?" Jacoby asks. "Are you alright?"

I nod quickly. "Yeah, fine. I'm good. Better than good, even. I'm…your kisses…they take my breath away every time. I swear I didn't tell my eyes to leak. They just have a mind of their own. I wish I could explain it."

"KitKat, you don't have to explain anything to me. Ever," he assures me as he gently wipes my stray tear away with his thumb.

I stare at him for a moment, contemplating the enigma that is Jacoby.

What is it about Jacoby that makes this feel different from every other guy I've been with?

"Kissing you gives me a feeling of contentment that I haven't experienced in a long time." I explain as I wring my fingers together. "Maybe even ever. It's comforting, it's healing. It's fucking sexy and it makes me want to believe in fairy tales again." I chuckle half-heartedly to myself. "That probably sounds stupid, doesn't it?"

"Stay with me tonight." His response catches me off guard.

"What?"

"I don't want you to leave," he says. "I just really like being around you and now that you're here, and now that I've kissed you, I don't want to stop kissing you. I know we've only really known each for like…three or four days, but I believe in fairy tales, Jenna. I believe in the power of a kiss, and your..." He shakes his head in wonderment. "Your kiss… It's the magic I write about in my books and for the first time in a very long time, I feel it with you, so I don't want you to go. Please. Stay with me?"

The difference is, he's different.

Like me.

CHAPTER 12
First Time for Everything

Jenna

"I don't have anything to wear. I didn't plan for this, so I don't have any of my things." I'm not saying no, but maybe I am trying to talk myself into a yes.

"You don't need anything. You can wear something of mine to sleep in or you can wear nothing at all. My woody and I will even sleep on the couch if that's the case." His admittance to getting a hard on if I were to sleep naked makes me laugh. He's nothing if he's not honest.

I like that.

"I don't want to make you uncomfortable. I just want…" He sighs. "I just want you. Here. With me." He leans over just enough to kiss me again, this time a little more forceful, needy, tempting. A groan escapes from the back of his throat that lights my libido on fire.

Day-um!

What is it about hearing a man's pleasure groan? Whatever the magic is, it turns me into a cougar and makes me brave. Throwing caution to the wind, I take his heavenly man noises as my sign of approval to take what I want from him, and God, do I want him. My lips never leaving his, I shuffle myself over his lap. His hands grab my ass enough to pull me over his legs until I'm straddling him, my knees on either side of his hips. Pulling me tighter against him, I have contact with his skin and his chest, for the first time since the first time. He still smells of grease and gasoline, but his skin is warm, so I don't care. He moans again when my hands touch his shoulders and slide down his chest, causing butterflies to chaotically flutter around in my stomach, but I try to ignore them as best I can. This just feels too good to worry about anything else right now.

"Is that a yes?" Jacoby asks in between kisses.

"Mmm hmm," I moan into his mouth. "Yes."

Slowly, Jacoby ends our kiss with another nuzzle to my nose. He slaps my ass making me squeal and gets up off the couch, carrying me right along with him. "Good. Now that that's all settled. I need sustenance," he proclaims in his most Thor-like voice as he moves towards the kitchen. "Tell me woman, would you like pizza or Chinese?" He plops me down, giggling, on the cold granite countertop.

"Umm…I haven't had Chinese in a while." I tell him.

"Chinese it is, then. Do you like General Tso's?"

"Uh, is the Pope Catholic?" I ask.

"Last time I checked."

"Then YES! I love General Tso's. I would love a vegetable egg roll too, if you don't mind."

His eyebrows raise when he smiles. "Ah, a woman after my own heart. I could eat egg rolls all day. Well, when I'm not sucking your face, that is."

He's cute when he's happy.

"So, I'm going to call this in to be delivered and then I should really hop in the shower. I don't want to smell like the garage all night. Is that okay? I mean, you won't leave, will you?"

Guilt washes over me when he brings up what happened the last time I was here. "I promise I won't. I'll just spend my time in your hidden office taking picture after picture and posting how excited I am all over social media."

Jacoby stops in his tracks and turns back to me. "Hmm, on second thought." He bends over to lift me over his shoulder.

"Hey!" I giggle. "What are you doing?"

"Maybe you should just shower with me so I can keep an eye on you." He slaps my butt playfully as he walks down the hall to – I'm guessing – his bedroom.

"I was kidding!" I laugh. "Totally kidding, Jacoby! You can put me down. I swear I was only kidding!"

Jacoby throws me onto his bed which feels like a puffy cloud compared to my mattress.

Dang. A girl could get used to this.

Pouncing on the bed like a lion attacking his prey, he pulls my arms up over my head, holding on to both of my hands. The look in his eye is a playful one, so I'm not the least bit worried. He places a light kiss on my forehead. "I was too." He winks. "But you are welcome to stay here, in my room, if you want." He picks up the remote control from the bed stand, and hands it to me. "The bed is comfortable and the TV is huge so relax if you want. I'll only be a few minutes."

"You're right about the bed being comfortable, so don't be surprised if you come back out here and your guest is fast asleep," I warn him, but he just laughs.

"Well that would be a first," he says as he walks over to his dresser.

"What would be a first?" I ask.

"I've never had a woman fall asleep in my bed before," he says, his body turned away from me.

"Oh. So you're the splurge and purge type? Duly note…"

"No." Jacoby swings his body quickly around and stares seriously at me, contemplating what to say next. "Yes…" He sighs. "No…" He squints like what he's thinking is painful for him. "Look, I've had relationships before, Jenna. They've just been – I don't know – semi-one sided? I think, in the end, they wanted more than I was ready to give. I knew I couldn't bring a woman here and try to keep what I do a secret, so I just…never brought anyone here."

Wait, what?

I frown at his comment. "Hold up, you mean this isn't just the first time that a woman might fall asleep in your bed. This is the first time a woman has ever been *on* or *in* your bed?"

He nods solemnly. "In my bed, in my kitchen, in my office, in my house." He gestures around the room. "This has always been my oasis. Mine. Not my dad's, or my brother's or anyone else's. Mine. I've always wanted to keep it that way."

My eyes shift down so that I'm not looking at him. I can feel the pink rise in my cheeks, not knowing for sure if he really wanted me here, or if I'm here because I invited myself. I'm the one who showed up unannounced.

"Until you came along, Jenna."

"Huh?" I look up, biting my lower lip.

Jacoby sits on the edge of the bed next to me. "Something was different about you from the first time I met you. And then definitely the second and third time." He chuckles. "You're unique and you don't care what people think. You're strong-willed and hard-working and passionate. I love all of those characteristics. You wear them well. It's very attractive, and it makes me want to be around you all the time, so wipe the look off of your face that tells me you're wondering if I really want you here. If I didn't, you wouldn't be. Okay? You certainly wouldn't have seen my office and absolutely wouldn't be in my bedroom, on your back, in my bed."

His last comment makes me blush. "Well if it's any consolation, I like being on my back in your bed."

"Jesus, Jenna," he says painfully. "I may have to take a damn *cold* shower now. Thanks a lot."

"You're welcome. Now go." I playfully shove him off the bed. "Get clean. And don't forget, it's slippery when wet, so be careful."

He shakes his head, chuckling as he shuffles into the bathroom attached to his room. "Woody and I will be back soon." He sighs.

"Did you get enough to eat?" Jacoby asks as he stuffs the last part of his egg roll into his mouth.

Leaning back in my chair with my hands on my stomach, I let out a huge breath. "Oh my gosh, yes. I couldn't eat another bite if I tried. What is it about Chinese food that makes it so filling?"

"HA!" Jacoby exclaims. "Well, where should I begin? High sodium content, MSG, carbohydrates…"

"Yeah, yeah, smart-ass. I get it. It just tastes so freaking good! It's like crack. Not that I know what crack tastes like, because I don't, but if I had to guess, I'm sure it tastes a lot like General Tso's Chicken."

"Yeah. Maybe," he agrees.

"So, now that you've showed me your secrets Mr. Malloy, tell me how you got started. What on earth made you want to start writing romance novels? And not just mediocre romance novels, mind you, fantastically hot read-them-multiple-times-in-a-row romance novels."

"You really want to know?" He raises one eyebrow.

"Of course. I know the what, now I want to know the why," I reply.

"I did it for a girl," he says, looking a bit disappointed.

My eyes roll before my brain can tell them not to. "A girl? Seriously? What, you wanted to get in her pants so you wrote the whole scene out for her? That's presumptuous, if not even a little narcissistic, wouldn't you say?"

Jacoby smiles and nods his head. "Yeah, I probably would say, but that's not what I mean. I didn't write the book for the girl. I took a class in college to woo a girl. Romance Lit. The girl was hot, and I wanted to date her so I signed up for the same class as her once I found out what she had registered for. I figured it was perfect, you know? Read a few stupid romance novels, talk about how sweet they are, sweep the girl off her feet and get my happily ever after."

"Well? How'd that work out for you?

Jacoby takes a quick swig of his beer, swallowing before he answers. "I took her for coffee one evening after a group project she and I were involved in."

"And…" I wait for him to continue.

"Her name was Sarah. We dated for almost a year," he says. He doesn't look at me, but instead, scratches the label off of his beer bottle until it rips enough that he can pull it off. I sit quietly with the feeling that he's not done talking. He inhales a deep breath and continues. "And then one night I saw her making out with some douchebag from the Sigma Alphas on the quad while I was walking back to my dorm."

"Ouch!" I say, feeling for him.

"Tell me about it. She tried to tell me she got drunk and made a mistake but I don't settle for sloppy seconds. At the time, I knew the last thing my father needed while running for office were pictures of his ivy league son partying with some sort of cheating drunk. He would shove pictures of Prince Harry in my face and say 'don't ever disappoint me like this, son.' He didn't like that I was dating anyone at the time anyway. He was always telling me to keep my eyes on the prize and I would end up a successful man like him someday." Jacoby shakes his head. "He just doesn't get it."

"I'm sorry it didn't work out," I tell him.

He shrugs. "I'm not. Turns out my father was right about one thing."

"Oh? What was that?"

"My Romance Lit. professor loved my work, so when I had to write a short romance novella for a final project, she edited it, and encouraged me to self-publish it. Under a pen name of course, so my father wouldn't know. I made close to ten grand within the first couple months of the book's release, so she encouraged me to continue writing and change my major. I kept my Poli-Sci major, lest my father stop paying for my education, but I wrote another book that summer while interning for him – don't tell him I did that." He winks. "During the following school year, Doctor Sling sent it off to a publisher she knew in New York. They picked it up close to Christmas that year, and wanted to publish it. Offered me a pretty shiny penny, too…and I guess the rest is history – or – future?"

"Wow." I shake my head, stunned. "You did all of that without your father ever knowing?"

"Absolutely. He would try to shut me down quicker than he could piss if he knew. It's bad enough I have a political science degree and didn't choose to go on to law. To him, I'm a disappointment. Just a washed-up nobody who spends his days covered in car grease."

"But…you're so successful, Jacoby. I mean, the money..."

He scoffs silently.

Shit. That's not what I meant.

"Jacoby, I don't give a shit about your money. Please know that's not why I'm bringing this up, but you have to be making a shit load. How does he not see that?"

"Easy. I don't show him. He's seen this house, but I've worked hard to keep it modest. It's just me here anyway. He sees me drive a tow-truck or my pick-up truck. He has no idea that I own a boat."

"You own a boat?" I exclaim.

Jacoby smiles. "Yeah. A small one. Actually I own half a boat. My buddy, Jack Schmidt, and I own it together. He was my college roommate, and best friend growing up. He's my confidant when it comes to my writing. He's one of the five that know."

"What does Jack do?"

Jacoby grins. "Oddly enough, he's a lawyer. Used to work for my dad. He's a great guy with a great story. I hope to introduce you to him someday soon." He chucks back the rest of his beer and places his empty bottle on the counter in front of us. "But enough about me. I want to know about you."

I shrug. "I work at The Hole Punch, an office supply store that sounds like a sex act. There really isn't much more to me."

"Not true." He laughs. "I know the what – that you design lingerie – and now I want to know the why."

"Ooh touché." I crinkle my nose, smiling at him. "Umm…well, I guess for me it's pretty cut and dry. I spent two years at Drexel University in Philadelphia working towards my fashion and merchandising degree. I went to this fashion show during my first year that showcased intimate apparel, but I wasn't at all impressed."

"Oh? Why not?" Jacoby asks.

"The girl was trying way too hard to be like Victoria's Secret. All pink and frilly with lots of sparkly bling. I mean, some of that isn't a bad thing, in my opinion, but there was no flare. There was nothing that set her apart from what you see in department stores every day."

"Could it be that guys like pink and frilly and all that shit? I mean isn't the sole purpose of lingerie to turn on your sexual partner?"

What?

I tilt my head, puzzled. "Is the sole purpose of your book to put a woman in the mood for sex via your erotic sex scenes?"

"No. Not at all," he responds.

"Exactly. In my opinion, and my end goal in each of my designs, is to make a woman feel like she's the most stunning person on the earth at that moment. That she's unique, and that no matter what her body type, there is something in my collection that can make her feel exceptional." I continue. "Now, does a woman's confidence rise when she feels beautiful? Yes. Does a woman's mind lean towards sexual ideas when she sees or wears lingerie? Most likely. She doesn't need a sexual partner to objectify her while she wears it. You can't buy and wear lingerie in the hopes that your sexual partner will like what they see. I mean, I guess many do it that way, but what *I* hope is that more women will wear my designs because they are *unique* and because of the way that piece makes them *feel* when they're wearing it."

Jacoby is quiet, silently watching me and not responding one way or another to all that I've just said. I take a drink of my beer, thinking that the pause in conversation will motivate him to say something.

But it doesn't.

"What are you thinking?" I finally ask.

He's hesitant to respond. "You want women to feel good wearing your designs, but you won't wear them yourself."

Fuck.

I inhale a deep breath before trying to answer him. "It's not that I..."

"No. Don't answer that." Jacoby lays his hand over mine. "I'm sorry. That was out of line. It's none of my business, and I shouldn't have said that. I'm sorry."

Solemnly I look at him, not sure of what to say. I want to tell him the truth. I want to put it out there so he gets me, but I don't want his pity. And I certainly don't want my insecurities to make him think he needs to tell me all the time how pretty I am. It's better if he doesn't know.

"You said you were at Drexel for two years."

I clear my throat before answering. "Yeah."

"Did you transfer after that?" he asks.

"Well, yes. You could say that. I transferred home. That's when Mom got sick. She had nobody else since my dad was never around, and I wasn't about to make Bethy, my sister, handle it all herself, so I dropped out of school and came home to live with my mom. She needed someone to be there for her. Take her to chemo, clean her up when she was sick…" Thoughts of my mom float through my mind, happier times of us singing in the house or in the car, eating pizza in bed while watching chick flicks. I'm hit with a pang of sadness knowing I can't have those experiences with her anymore.

You never really ever get over losing your mom.

"I'm sorry," Jacoby says. "For your loss, I mean. And…for all that you and your sister had to go through. I can't even imagine."

"Nobody can until they're faced with it." I release a deep breath. "You live, you get cancer, you die. That seems to be the circle of life these days."

"Do you have happy memories of your mom?"

"Oh yeah. Tons of them. She was a fantastic mom for Bethy and me, and believe me, we didn't make it easy on her."

Jacoby chuckles. "No, I'm sure you didn't, and I'm sure deep down, you know your mom loves you and is so proud of the person you've become. Passionate. Compassionate. Kind. Witty…."

"Yeah," I murmur, half smiling. I feel him squeeze my hand. Feeling him next to me is definitely comforting.

"Okay, so that went deep for a while." I stand up from my seat and carry my dinner plate to the kitchen sink. "So, what do you do to entertain yourself around here huh?"

Jacoby smiles as he follows me into the kitchen with his plate and a handful of garbage to be thrown out.

"I don't usually do much entertaining of myself really. I'm either working on a car or writing, but if you're feeling brave enough I have something we could play."

I turn around from the garbage can to peer at him. "Uh…when you say play…you don't mean like, red room of pain or anything do you?"

Please say no. Please say no. Please say no.

I watch as one of Jacoby's eyebrows raises up as he grins. "Well now that I know what your hard limits are…" he jokes. "You'll be happy to know, that no, I don't have a red room of pain."

I release my deep breath. "Phew. Ok, then I'm game for…"

"It's a light yellow room of pain actually," he interrupts.

My smile falters. "I'm sorry. What?"

"My yellow room of pain. It's downstairs. I'm happy to show you if you want to see it."

I shake my head vigorously. I have zero interest in that kind of sexual activity. "Noooo. I don't. It's okay. We can stay up here. I'm perfectly fine with that." My hand flies up to my neck as the room starts to feel stifling. I should've known this was too good to be true. He's into kinky sex. Of course he is. That's why he likes the idea of my lingerie line.

"Jenna?" he says against my ear. I flinch at his nearness, having not paid attention to the fact that he moved closer to me.

"Yeah." My voice is scratchy.

"My yellow room of pain is a gym."

His comment catches me off guard. "Huh?"

"It's a gym. My personal gym. You know like, a treadmill, weightlifting bench, barbells, elliptical machine? It's a room of pain. The walls are yellow because yellow is an energetic color."

I watch as he says the words and give myself a moment for them to sink in. "I promise my yellow room is not sexual by any means. I'm not into BDSM – although I should tell you in honesty – I do own a few things you might find in a room like that, but only for book research purposes. I've never actually used them. I'm a far cry from a dominant."

"Ooooh thank God." I exclaim. "I admit. You got me. Here I was wondering how I was going to get out of this." I laugh nervously. "Never do that to me again!"

"Hahaha! Sorry. You kind of walked right into that one. I couldn't resist." He grabs my hand. "Come on, I was thinking more along the lines of some Xbox fun. You game?"

My eyes grow wide in excitement. "Video game ass-kicking? I'm totally in! Let's do it!"

Jacoby takes me to the entertainment room that's set up almost like a small theater with darker gray walls and plush black leather reclining chairs. There's a huge television hanging on the wall and three different game consoles.

"Wow. You must love your video games." I tell him as I ogle the Nintendo Wii, the Playstation, and the Xbox, all complete with their own games. "I thought you said you don't do much to entertain yourself."

"I don't," he replies. "I mean, I live alone, so once I solve a game I don't usually play it anymore. But I haven't gotten to play a multi-player game in ages, and since you're here and you're willing…"

I gasp in excitement as I pull a game off the shelf. "You have 007 Night Fire??? I LOVED this game during my college days!"

Jacoby looks at me, perplexed. "You played 007 in college?"

"Yeah I did! Well, the guys in the dorm did so I would always join them. One of them had a classic Xbox and this very same game. God, it was so much fun." I smile remembering all those nights I kicked their asses.

"You want to play?" Jacoby asks.

"Hell yeah I do! Let's do it, but beware…I can be pretty good with a gun."

Jacoby chuckles. "Point taken. I'll watch my back."

"What are you doing?" I ask innocently as Jacoby opens a closet door next to the bathroom and pulls out an extra blanket and pillow. Our amazing evening of Xbox kick-assery was the best time I've had just letting loose in a long time. The swear words that came out of my mouth while jutting around the screen with a gun in my hand could single handedly create an entirely new dictionary, but it was so much fun letting down my walls. Dressed in a pair of Jacoby's boxers and one of his t-shirts, I'm lying in his bed snuggled under his warm duvet and loving that I'm cocooned in his smell. Who cares if it's the middle of summer when you have blankets this soft and a smell this enticing.

"I'm just grabbing a blanket and pillow for myself. That's all. I want you to sleep comfortably and I promised you no funny business," he says nonchalantly. "So, I'm going to sleep on the couch."

"Absolutely not. That's unacceptable," I declare.

Jacoby chuckles at my pointed declaration. "I'm sorry?"

"I didn't agree to stay here with you only to not be staying *with you*," I tell him.

"Oh," he says quietly. "Well, I just…"

"No," I interrupt. "No. No. No. If I'm staying here, you're staying here with me, in your own bed. I mean, do you really want to explain to your friend, Jack what's-his-name, that you finally had a female sleeping in your bed and you didn't sleep next to her? I mean, how lame is that?"

"It's really lame." He nods.

"Yeah it is. So, what are you going to do about it?" I stare at him with my eyebrows raised. I have nervous butterflies in my stomach, but as far as I can tell, they're good butterflies. I want to lay next to him. I wouldn't turn away a cuddle...or a little more than a cuddle. I feel good when I'm with him. I want to be with him.

Jacoby drops the blanket and pillow he was holding. "I sleep in my underwear," he says, making me chuckle. He's so damn cute.

I shake my head, shrugging. "I don't care."

Watching me, he slowly pulls down his sweatpants revealing the sexiest body in the sexiest pair of Calvin Klein boxer briefs. I can see the outline of the grade-A hole punch I experienced not too long ago through his briefs, and immediately have to stifle the need to experience it all again tonight. "You sure you're okay with this? Because if I come into that bed with you, I can't promise you that I won't at least try to kiss you."

"I'm counting on it," I reply.

"I may try to cop a feel." He goads me with a raise of his eyebrows.

"I'm looking forward to it." I lick my bottom lip.

"I may not let go of you for hours," he warns.

"Please don't," I whisper. He's easily got me hot and bothered enough that if he tries anything, I'm not sure I'll be strong enough to say no. I'm not even sure I want to say no. His body, his voice, his warmth, his honesty – it draws me in like a moth to a flame. He turns off the overhead light, and climbs into bed, nestling himself next to me. I can feel his eyes on me even though it's dark enough in here that I can barely see him.

We lay here in bed, beside each other, for a couple minutes without ever saying a word. My eyes roam up and down what I can see of his face as if I'm studying every facial feature I can find in the darkened room. I crave his touch, but I know he's trying to be good. He's trying to be respectful of me.

But what if I have needs?

What if I have desires?

I scoot a little closer to Jacoby's warm body as if we weren't close enough already. I can feel the flex of the hole punch I was just admiring a moment ago, and it takes everything in me to not reach my hand down and grasp it tightly. I can imagine the madness that would ensue if I did and it makes me hotter than a jacked off mountain lion on a hot tin roof.

"Jenna," Jacoby whispers.

"Yes?"

"I really need to kiss you."

I smile even though he probably can't see it. "Then shut up and kiss mmmmm…" I don't even have time to finish my sentence before his lips crash gently against mine. My body melts into his, inviting his touch. His legs entwine with mine as his hands desperately cling to my face, my cheek, my hair. In a moment of brave seduction, I slow the frenzy of our tongues so that I'm practically licking the inside of his mouth. He tastes of cool mint toothpaste.

Jacoby's right hand slides down my neck and shoulder, grazing my skin with his fingertips between kisses. Down my arm, and back up again fueling my desire for so much more. Why does he affect me this way? Why are there happy butterflies in my stomach? Why am I feeling anything at all? I don't usually feel at all when this happens, but there's something about Jacoby's touch, his kiss, the feel of his pulse against mine. He draws out my feelings like an author writing a perfectly timed romance.

Ironic.

Stretching my body enough so that my chest firmly pushes into his, my head rolls back giving his lips access to my neck.

"KitKat…" He groans.

"Yeah," I whimper.

"If we keep this up I can't promise I'm going to be able to restrain myself."

"Restrain yourself from what?" I pant.

"Touching you. Your body, up against mine, in my bed…" He breathes. "You're like the forbidden fruit that I shouldn't taste but is so damn irresistible."

Whatever kind of string is tied around my heart, I just felt it tighten. "Touch me Jacoby. Please," I beg weakly. "I know you want to be respectful and I love that about you, but I want you to touch me. I want you to, Jacoby. Please."

Ours bodies stop moving together as I feel his hand slide down my shoulder, down my chest until he reaches the peak he's looking for. I cry out when his hand squeezes me with a heated pressure. Shamelessly, I tug at the hem of the t-shirt I'm wearing so that he helps me pull it up and over my head. My back arches as he lifts me to help with my shirt and I gasp loudly as his tongue licks against my right nipple.

"Oh, my God, Jacoby!" I cry.

"You like that?"

I can't even make words to answer him right now. His body on mine, parts of me in his mouth. His tongue worshiping my skin, it's overwhelming and so addictive all at the same time.

"We can go as far as you want KitKat. Or not at all. Either way I'm bound to have a wet dream." Jacoby squeezes one breast as he licks the other, sending me into an oblivion that I never want to end.

"Please, Jacoby."

"Please what, Baby?"

"I need you." I stroke my fingers down his soft exposed chest, taking in every inch of him that I can put to memory. Feeling his breathing quicken, I trail my fingers to the band of his briefs, innocently gliding over the steely hole-punch hiding underneath.

"Mmm…" He grunts, flexing his body toward me.

I can't believe I'm doing this.

He was okay with no sex.

I'm the temptress tonight.

And I don't even care.

"Take my pants off, Jacoby."

"Yes ma'am," he murmurs as he sits back on his legs. I lift my hips just enough for him to easily maneuver my boxers and panties down my legs. He lays them on the floor next to the bed as he stands up. I hear the wrestling of clothes and can only assume he's removing his briefs as well.

"Jenna." He breathes as he enters the bed, wrapping his body around mine. "Your body is so warm." We writhe together finding a rhythm that makes us both hungry. Showering my body with kisses, Jacoby makes his way on top of me. My legs stretch open for him, welcoming what I know is about to come.

"I need to grab a condom. I'll just be a min…"

"No." I pant. "Pill. I'm on the pill. I've been on the pill for years. It's okay."

"Are you sure? I don't mind." He assures me. I thrust my hips into him, grabbing his flesh, and guiding him to me, silently screaming for him to be inside me. "Yes. I'm sure, Jacoby. I want you like this."

"Hold on, baby." he says as he squeezes my breasts and slides effortlessly into me. It only takes a few thrusts before I come apart completely, and only a few more before Jacoby finds his finale. The scent of sweat and sex permeates the air around us, as does a sense of euphoria that I don't think I've ever felt before.

I like this feeling.

I want to experience this feeling again.

And again.

And again.

With him.

Once we're both cleaned up and snuggled back into bed, Jacoby wraps his arms around me, holding me against his chest. He lightly slides his fingers up and down my arms, a move that a while ago was intoxicatingly erotic, but is now calming, and easily lulling me to sleep.

"Jacoby?" I say, half asleep.

"Yeah?"

"My ex-boyfriend…" I yawn. "He was an abusive dick, and he's the reason I never wear my lingerie."

Silence surrounds us and I think Jacoby has fallen asleep beside me, except that I can feel a twitching in his arm that tells me he's still awake.

"He didn't deserve you, KitKat. And if I ever meet the guy, I'll chop off his balls and feed them to him for dinner."

I smile to myself knowing that he probably means every word he just said, and because it's Jacoby, I'm totally okay with that.

"I'll never hurt you." Those are the last words I hear from Jacoby's mouth before I drift off into the deepest sleep I've had in months.

CHAPTER 13

Angry Vagina Box

Jacoby

The sunlight seeps through the windows alerting me to the fact that it's morning. I'm not ready for my night to end though. For the first time since I moved into this house, I have a girl in my arms, snuggled up next to me in my bed, and she feels like heaven. Writing is a very lonely life for me. It's a life I love, except for the part where I have to keep it all a secret lest my father ruin everything for me. But, after last night, having Jenna here with me, I finally feel like a small portion of the weight of the world has chipped and fallen off my shoulders. I don't feel so alone. I can trust her with my secret, and I want to be a support system for her as well. I want this girl. I want to fall in love with her and I want to keep her and I want to never let her go. She's a sight for sore eyes laying in my bed, dressed in my clothes. She didn't say last night if she has to work today, but if she does, I wish she could call off and stay here with me all day.

You still don't know her last name, Malloy.

I cringe to myself knowing that I've now had sex with this girl twice and I never even asked her last name. What kind of douchebag does that? I roll over to my back sighing, staring at the ceiling, wondering how on Earth this girl isn't going to want to kick me in the balls when I ask her last name.

I could go find her wallet. There has to be a driver's license in there somewhere. But that would mean letting go of her body and I'm too warm and relaxed to let her go. It takes a few minutes, but eventually Jenna's body stretches against me and she rolls over to face me. Her big brown eyes open, and when they do, a smile travels across her face.

Fuck me, I make her smile.

"Good mornin'." She yawns.

"What's your last name?" I cringe again, waiting for her to slap me. God, I deserve to be slapped.

She rises up on her elbows to focus on me and what I just asked her. "What?"

"Your last name." I sigh heavily as I run my hand up and down my face.

"I…we…ugh!" This is so unbelievably embarrassing that I even have to ask. I roll over toward her so that her body is almost under my own. I smooth away her hair from her face and kiss her on her forehead. "I'm a complete douchebag who has had sex with you twice now and never even bothered to ask you your last name."

She laughs.

She laughs?

Thank God, she laughs.

She grabs a hold of my worried face and plants a sweet kiss on my cheek. "It's Zimmerman. Thanks for asking." She winks at me playfully. I can't help but release a huge sigh of relief that she's not pissed.

"Jenna Zimmerman." I smile. "It's a beautiful name…for a beautiful girl."

She grins at me with a quizzical look in her eye that makes me chuckle. I bury my head in her neck. "I really thought you would be offended," I say, kissing her neck softly. "Thank God you're laughing."

"Jacoby, you may very well be the first guy in a long time that I've told my last name to. That should tell you something about my past…uh…behaviors."

"Hmm…fuck and run?" I ask her.

Her smile grows wide. "I'm not running now, am I?"

I moan as I put my arms underneath her and roll us both over so that she's straddling me. She squeals at my surprise move and holds on to my biceps to steady herself. She sits up on me and I can't help it that Woody takes notice.

"I'm glad you didn't run. Thank you, for not running. Did you sleep okay?" I'll feel guilty for asking her to stay here if she didn't sleep well.

"I slept better than I have in months actually." She says excitedly before cringing sadly. "And it sucks that I have to go to work today. I'm sorry I can't just stay here with you all day…not that you asked me to stay here with you, I shouldn't have assumed that. I just meant if you were to want me to, I wish I could but…" She takes a huge breath after all the rambling. "I can't."

"What time do you work today?" I ask her.

"I need to be there by ten. Aaaand I should probably stop at home and get some new clothes so I'm not wearing the same underwear to work that I wore yesterday."

"Can I drive you to work?"

"Well…" She nods her head toward the door. "My car is outside."

"I know. Leave it here. I'll have Jack help me drop it off at the store later."

"Why don't you just pick me up in it this evening and then come to my place. I'm off tomorrow, so we can just figure it out then."

Did she just invite me for a sleepover?

She wants me to stay?

"You want me to stay?" Please say yes. Please say yes. Please say yes.

"I mean," she shrugs. "If you want to. I wouldn't mind the company. I do need to get a few things done after work with my product line so I can be ready for next week's drop-off."

"So, I would get to watch you work?" I'm intrigued.

She smiles at me as she smooths herself over my body, resting her arms and chin on my bare chest. "Yeah I guess you would. Is that okay?"

"Yeah it's great," I tell her. "Maybe I'll bring my laptop so I can get some work done before I make you stop so we can play for the night."

"Play?" Her eyebrows raise at my words. "What kind of playing do you have in mind?"

It only takes a quick flex of my pelvis underneath her for her to get the picture. She gasps and then giggles. Damn her eyes. Those big, brown, excited eyes of hers draw me in and make me want her in the worst way. I love it when she smiles. There's nothing more attractive than a happy woman.

"Hmmm..." Her voice is soft like velvet. "I think I could be talked in to that kind of playtime."

I kiss her softly on her forehead. "Good. How about I make us some coffee while you get yourself ready? We'll stop at your place to get your things before taking you to work."

"That sounds great. Thank you." She rolls herself off of me, but kisses my cheek before leaving my side. Instantly the bed is cold without her next to me. It feels foreign to me now, enough so that I don't want to be in it any longer. I hop out of bed and grab a pair of shorts and a t-shirt to put on before making my way to the kitchen to make coffee. For the first time in weeks, since I first laid eyes on Jenna, a feeling of contentment finally washes over me. I don't know why I've suddenly been hit by Cupid's infatuation arrow, when I've spent these last few years having no real relationship. Do men have biological clocks? Maybe mine is ticking. Maybe I'm ready to give my focus and energy to something else in my life, I don't know. For whatever reason though, having Jenna in my life right now is what my soul hungers for, and I sure as hell hope to keep feeding it.

As we pull into the parking lot of The Hole Punch, Jenna's friend – Linda, if memory serves me right – is also just arriving. Spotting Jenna in my car, she stops and waits before entering the building.

"Good morning, Jizza!" I hear her call out while walking her to the door. I don't know why I'm walking her to the door. We're not in high school and this isn't her parents' house, but I didn't want to just drop her from my car.

"Jizza?" I repeat quietly. "Why does she call you Jizza? That sounds an awful lot like jizz." I can't help but chuckle. I'm a guy and I just said jizz.

"Yeah…she calls me Jizz all the time," Jenna says.

"Why?"

She sighs heavily and rolls her eyes. "My initials. My full name is Jenna Irene Zimmerman sooo...J-I-Z"

"Ahhh. Got it." I smile, trying not to laugh too much. Obviously, she knows it's humorous but my guess is she's heard it her entire life.

"Yeah. Linda's good at making sure I never forget it. What a bestie, huh?" she asks, as we approach Linda.

"She obviously loves you." I wink.

"Who loves who in the what now?" Linda asks as we approach her.

Jenna smiles shaking her head. "Linds, this is Jacoby." She says gesturing to me. "Jacoby, this is my best friend in the whole wide world, and also world's greatest bitch, Linda."

I reach out to shake Linda's hand. "It's very nice to meet you formally." She moves a shoebox-sized box underneath her other arm so she can shake my hand. It only catches my attention because it's a shoebox with sharks all over it.

She gives me a sly approving nod. "The pleasure's all mine, Jacoby."

Nodding to the box under her arm, I ask her, "What's in the box?"

Jenna laughs and reaches out to pat my arm. "You don't want to know what's in the box."

"My angry vagina box?" Linda asks.

"Uh…I'm sorry?" Maybe I didn't hear her right.

"It's my angry vagina box," she repeats.

"Okay, so I didn't hear you wrong. I thought that's what you said. What's an angry vagina box and what does that have to do with sharks?"

"Well, Jacoby," Linda smirks. "Since you asked so sincerely, let me tell you all about my box. In fact, here, I'll just let you look for yourself." Linda looks to Jenna, maniacally laughing as she holds out the box for me.

An angry vagina box?

This has to be good.

I take the box, decorated with sharks of all shapes and size, from Linda's hands and lift the lid slowly. Inside is a chaotic mess of what looks to be different feminine products and a few of those bite sized chocolate bars. Drawn on the inside of the lid with a sharpie marker is an open shark's mouth with sharp pointy teeth.

"Uh…okay." I mutter as I close the box and hand it back to Linda.

"It's shark week Jacoby. The vagicano is erupting hot messy lava, and that means my angry vagina box comes to work with me, because my vagina is angry. No, she's not angry, she's downright pissed!"

I try not to smile too much as Jenna laughs next to me whispering, "You asked for it."

"I'm uh…" I chuckle just a little bit. "I'm sorry to hear that. Really, I am."

"Yeah well, it's like a crime scene in my pants right now," Linda continues. "And I don't have any caution tape so I just bring my angry vagina box to work, put it in the break room, and then the asshats know to leave me the hell alone until the angry vagina box is gone."

"Asshats?" I whisper to Jenna.

"Associates," she tells me quickly. "We call them our asshats. Long story."

"Got it."

"And if they're going to piss me off royally," Linda explains. "Then they know they better bring me chocolate as a sacrifice."

Well this has been educational.

"Okay." I nod. "I think I got this. Shark week equals angry vagina box and lots of chocolate. Do you need a uterus massage while you're at it?"

Immediately Linda's face softens. Her angry, irritated expression turns into a pitiful kitten needing a cuddle. "O.M.G. Jenna, your hot man friend here speaks my language. I think I approve." She turns to me. "And if you could find an easy way to make that happen, that would be fantastic."

I smile and nod, because that's what you do when a woman is in heat, right? "I'll do some research and see what I can do."

"You're the best, Jacoby." Linda smiles and links arms with Jenna, who turns to me smiling sincerely, a look that I know is thanking me for making her friend smile before going into work.

"I'll see you later then?" she asks.

"Count on it. I'll pick you up tonight. Just text me when you're about ready." Not knowing how comfortable she is kissing me in front of Linda, I lean over to kiss her temple. "See you soon." I murmur.

"Okay. And thank you – for the ride." She responds grabbing my hand with a gentle squeeze, a wink, and a smile.

It was a hell of a ride.

"My pleasure." Jenna and Linda enter the building together as I head back to the car. I run through my list of to-dos and check my messages before getting myself in the mindset of work for the day. It's hard to focus on anything other than the smell of Jenna, the feel of Jenna in my arms, the taste of her kisses, the feel of her body against mine. Damn if it doesn't turn me on just thinking about it. Fortunately, knowing that I get to see her again tonight allows me the ability to at least want to be productive today. Getting shit done will make the day go faster for me anyway.

My phone rings in my office. Looking over to see the word MOM on the screen, I turn down the music playing as I work so that I can answer the call. She usually tries to check in with me at least every other day, so I know she'll continue to call if I don't answer. I think it's actually been three days now.

I pick up my phone and slide right. "Hi, Mom."

"Hey sweetheart. I didn't hear from you yesterday. How are you?" she asks.

"Just fine, Mom. Sorry, I've been pretty busy. What are you up to?" Mom has no idea that I write for a living and I'm not about to be the one to tell her. I'm sure she would love to know that her sweet little boy writes erotic romantic fiction novels. Mom has always been a classy lady more so, I think, because she's had to be with a husband in the spotlight. I always felt bad for her growing up. Everything she did was scrutinized by the soccer moms of the world. If they only knew that all she probably ever wanted to be was a soccer mom driving a mini-van. Instead she's a Stepford wife who, luckily for her, is aging gracefully. She reminds me so much of Helen Mirren, but without the British accent.

"Oh I was just talking to Sarah about little Charlie's birthday party. You'll be coming, right?"

Shit. I forgot all about my nephew having a birthday coming up. "Sure, Mom. When is it again?" I grab my planner that sits next to me.

"We're getting together on the twenty-third of August. That's a Sunday. He'll start Kindergarten after Labor Day, so we'll give him one big five-year-old celebration."

"The twenty-third." I repeat writing the birthday party down in my calendar so I don't forget. "Sounds good, we'll be there."

There's a silence on the other line before Mom says anything. "We'll be there?"

"Shit. No. I mean I'll be there. I'll be there, Mom. Don't worry."

"Who's this *we* you're talking about, Jacoby?" She gasps. "Do you have a lady friend? Oh sweetheart, I'm so happy for you. When do we get to meet her? Oh you simply have to bring her to the party. I'm sure Charlie would love to meet her."

"Mom." I say rubbing my free hand up and down my face. "No. I don't know. Yes, I met a girl, but I don't know what's going to happen between now and then. I'm not so sure meeting the family right now is a good idea. I mean, meeting Andy and Sarah and Charlie is one thing, but Dad…"

"Your father won't even be here, sweetheart, so you don't need to worry. He has a campaign strategy meeting and won't be home for most of the day."

"Oh," I say quietly. I take a few minutes to breathe, letting thoughts of Jenna invade my head for a minute.

Would she want to come with me?

Is she even ready for that?

Are we even ready for that?

"Look, Mom, I don't know if Jenna will come or not, okay? We've only just started…"

Fucking.

"Dating," I continue. "I don't want to make her uncomfortable, so we'll see. I'll talk to her okay?"

"Jenna sounds like a beautiful name and I'm sure she's as sweet as pie. I, for one, am so happy you've met someone."

My heart smiles just a little. It is nice to know my mom cares about what goes on with me even though my dad could give a shit. "Thanks, Mom."

"Okay, sweetheart, well I'll let you go. You just keep in touch with me and let me know what you're planning alright? We can't wait to see you."

"Yeah. Sure Mom. I'll talk to you later."

"Goodbye sweetheart."

"Bye, Mom."

I put my phone back down on my desk and take a deep breath. I knew this day would eventually come, when I would meet a girl and my mother would want to meet her. I know if there's any chance at a future, she has to meet my family, but I also feel the incredible need to protect her from them. Or maybe I'm just feeling the need to protect myself.

After several hours of writing and deleting, and writing more and deleting more, I give up. I can't focus with so much on my mind. Not able to take the tension building in my shoulders anymore, I decide that maybe getting a quick workout in before picking up Jenna would be good for me. Maybe that'll help clear my head, because all I want to be thinking about when I pull into that parking lot is her.

I make quick work of the gym, feeling the tension lift away with every lift of the weights, every push-up, every sit-up and every minute spent on the elliptical. After jumping in the shower to clean myself up, I'm ready to head out to pick up my girl. An idea hits me as I leave my driveway that brings a smart-ass grin to my face. Assuming she worked the same shift as Jenna, I think a quick stop is in order before I face the exploding vagicano again. She's likely to be tired and grumpy and in need of a sacrifice.

CHAPTER 14
Red Hots

Jenna

"Hey Jizza! Loverboy awaits!" Linda says to me through her microphone. I roll my eyes even though she can't see me but feel the silly grin form on my face knowing that Jacoby did, indeed, show up to pick me up from work. My stomach growls and I wonder if he thought ahead to pick up food. I should've warned him I would be on the verge of hangry by the time I was done working.

"Be right there!" I answer Linda before ripping off my ear piece and microphone, leaving it on my desk, and grabbing my things to head out. It feels so good to be done with a work day, especially when I have more to look forward to before the night is over, and even more especially because I have the day off tomorrow. Linda and I both walk out together where we see Jacoby leaning on his dark blue pick-up truck, waiting patiently.

Linda whistles as we walk across the parking lot. "Well hey there, hot stuff! How's it hangin'?" I slap her in the arm, but she only winces slightly and laughs.

"It's hangin' pretty comfortably right now, thanks." Jacoby replies once we're within a safe distance. He smiles at Linda but winks at me as we approach.

"Hey." He nods, opening his arm for a welcoming embrace which I gladly accept. The small kiss on the top of my head doesn't go unnoticed either.

"Hey yourself," I tell him. "Thanks for coming to get me."

"My pleasure." He smiles.

Linda nods her chin toward Jacoby. "What's in the bag hot stuff? Did you buy me presents?" She's nothing if not a shameless flirt. She's lucky she my bestie or I might want to kill her sometimes.

"Actually, yeah, I did." Jacoby hands the bag he's holding over to Jenna. "A little something for the sacrifice to the Red Goddess."

I turn my head to look up at him but he only smirks and winks again as he pulls me against him a little tighter. What a tease he is, to both of us. We both watch as Linda excitedly takes the bag. The girl loves presents. Come to think of it, I suppose any girl loves presents, but it melts my heart a little bit that the guy I'm with tries to make nice with my friends as well.

"Hahahaha! You turd!" Linda shouts at Jacoby. For a moment, my eyes widen and pangs of anxiety rise as I wonder what could possibly be in the bag to cause that type of a reaction. I hope it's not too embarrassing.

"Seriously? Pop Rocks and Red Hots? That's so…thoughtful, and weird…but only in a mildly creepy way." She shakes her head. "I totally love it! Thank you!"

"You're welcome. I thought it would make a nice addition to your angry vagina box."

"You have a sick mind, Jacoby." Linda shakes her head, thankfully, smiling. "And you're the only guy in my life to buy me such a creative present, so thank you."

"My pleasure." Jacoby nods to her before he gives me another small squeeze around my shoulder. "You ready to go?"

"Yeah absolutely." I wave to Linda as I walk to my side of the truck. "I'm off tomorrow, but I'll call you, okay?"

"Sure thing. He's a keeper," she mouths to me. "Later Jizz!" She waves back before getting into her car and pulling out of the parking lot.

"Hungry?" Jacoby asks as I buckle my seatbelt.

"Starving!" I respond.

"Do you want to go out or get take-out? Or I'm happy to cook something," he suggests.

"No, I don't want to wait for cooking, even though I'm positive it would be mouth-watering. How about something fast and unhealthy, like a burger or something?"

"How about Five Guys? It's close," he says.

"Yes! That's perfect! I haven't been there in forever, so that sounds great."

Jacoby puts the car in reverse and steps on the gas. "Burger and fries, or the unhealthiest cheese dog you can imagine, coming right up."

"So you design all these pieces and your sister helps you sell them? Is that how this all works?" Jacoby sits on the couch, half working on his own stuff, and half watching me record inventory around my living room.

"Well, sort of. I come up with the designs, and Bethy and I both spend Sundays plus any other nights we need, sewing everything together. Some will take longer to finish than just the one day, especially if they're more intricate. Or sometimes we'll tag-team. I'll sew and she'll add the beading or any of the other important parts of each piece. Then yeah, Bethy spends a lot of time on marketing, trying to get us into bigger stores."

"Where do you sell these now?" he asks.

"I deliver inventory weekly up town to the Chic Boutique. The owner there does a great job spotlighting them for me. I mean, I can get maybe twenty to twenty-five pieces up there each week, but they're almost all gone by my next delivery. I almost can't keep up with the demand." I stop what I'm doing to remember to look up and talk to Jacoby, especially since he seems to be sincerely interested in what I do.

"Sounds like you guys keep pretty busy then. Your success is fantastic." His excitement for me is contagious.

"Well," I smile. "I'm no New York Times best-selling author, and this can get very overwhelming at times. February and December are both terrible months for us - in a good way. We make a killing, but lingerie is in demand for Valentine's Day and Christmas, so we're busy from sun up to sun down many days. And through it all, we both have full time jobs."

"I can see where that might stress you out," he adds.

"Don't get me wrong, we love it! The work, the excitement around the holidays, the high demand – it keeps us moving forward. I really enjoy the process of building this business from the ground up. And this fall we're participating in the fashion show portion of the huge Mystic Bridal Show that happens every year, so we're getting really excited about that," I explain.

"I'm impressed, Jenna. Really. It's amazing what you guys have started. I'm excited for you and your sister," he says. "Come here." He opens his arms for me to join him on the couch which I do without hesitation.

"Do I get to come watch the fashion show?" he asks. I'm drawn into the sultry sound of his voice, or maybe I'm just horny now that I'm straddling his lap on my couch thinking of all the different positions we could find for the two of us here. He leans forward just enough to kiss my lips softly, not giving me the chance to respond right away.

"That depends." I finally answer in between kisses. Jacoby wraps his arms around me, pulling tighter against him as he peppers kisses down my neck.

"On what?"

"Well – umm – are we officially a thing? Not that I'm telling you we have to be because we don't. I just – I wouldn't take just anyone to an event like this, but I might take my steady boyfriend – you know – if I had..."

"You have one." He squeezes me tighter, stealing my breath with the force of his arms. "Jenna Irene Zimmerman," he bows his head just enough for our foreheads to touch. "You have one." He kisses me again. "If you'll have me by your side, I'll be your biggest cheerleader. I don't have eyes for anyone else in my life but you."

It's really hard to kiss someone sentimentally when you're smiling too much. I can't wipe the happy grin off of my face, so instead, I sit back and hold Jacoby's face in my hands. "You're serious? I mean I continuously vomit words out my mouth, I drop things more often than I can count, I slip in human feces and then wear trash bag diapers home from work. And my initials spell JIZ for Pete's sake. I would understand if you didn't want to get involved."

Jacoby laughs. "I think I can live just fine with all those endearing side-effects of dating you. Thanks, though, for the reminder of how unbelievably cute you are."

I kiss him first on his forehead, and then both of his cheeks, before finally feeling my lips connect to his. "Then yes. I would love it if you came with me to the fashion show. I don't know what I'm getting into just yet; I may have to put you to work."

"It's a deal," he says before his lips meet mine once again.

The passing final weeks of summer are like a blur of busy happiness for me. Work has been insane with back-to-school season, and Jacoby has been spending a lot of time going through edits of his latest novel. Bethy has been putting in extra hours behind the sewing machine while I'm at work to prepare us for the fall fashion show and to also keep our inventory in check. Supply and demand is quickly becoming overwhelming which wears on me after a while, but I refuse to let it get me down. These are all good problems to have.

On those nights when I do get to see Jacoby, which is least every other night and the past few Saturdays before or after work, I feel like I'm far enough away from home, even when he's with me at my place, that I can let my stresses melt away. He makes me smile and laugh and step outside of my busy life to do fun things like fishing, playing video games, cruising on the Jovi, watching Netflix and then not watching Netflix at the same time. The not watching Netflix part is probably my favorite. I'm sure it's his too, but tonight, as we sit around his living room watching episodes of *Orange is the New Black*, something about him just feels off. I've been looking forward to spending the weekend with him. After a long week, there's nobody else I want to spend my Friday night with, but something about him tonight makes me wonder if maybe he's not feeling the same way. He's not usually this distant.

"Jacoby?" I ask while lying in his arms on the couch.

"Mmm?"

"Are you alright?" I swallow my fear praying to all the gods that I haven't done something to turn him off.

"I have the girl of my dreams relaxed in my arms. Why wouldn't I be alright?" he asks me.

"Well, I may be relaxed, but I'm not so certain that you are. The tension has been rolling off of you all evening, and I can't figure out what I've done to upset you."

Don't cry Jenna.

Don't you dare cry.

Don't be a baby.

Jacoby is quiet for a moment which only heightens my fear of what he might say. I feel him take a deep breath trying to release it as slowly as possible. Calmly, I sit up and turn around so I can see his face. May as well just get this over with. Rip off the band aid.

"I'm sorry if I've been tense. It's really not my intention," he says.

"Well, do you want to talk about it? Is it about the book? Is it work related? Have I done something to bother you?" I choke back the knot in my throat.

"No! God," He breathes and takes a hold of my face. "No, no, no. It's not you, Babe." His lips gently touch mine before he kisses my forehead and then wraps me up in his arms.

"Then what is it?" My voice is muffled with my mouth buried in his chest. "You can talk to me. You can always talk to me."

I feel his body tense as he inhales another deep breath. "I need to know if you want to go to a birthday party with me?"

Leaning back out of his embrace a little bit, I look at his pained face. "A birthday party?"

"Yeah. My nephew, Charlie. He's turning five and my family is doing this big party for him on Sunday before he goes to school, and I said I would go, and I may have accidentally said *we* instead of *I*. And now my mom knows that there's someone in my life, and so she wants to meet you, but it's my family, and I wouldn't be at all disappointed if you said you didn't want to go. There's a lot I haven't told you about them, and I know you're really busy on Sunday's with…"

"Whoa, whoa, whoa." I place a finger to his mouth to shush him. "I'm the one who does the word vomiting, okay?"

He nods silently. The puppy dog eyes kill me.

"If you're asking me to come with you because you want me to meet your family, then of course I would love to come with you. It means a lot to me that you would even think of including me in your family events."

He smooths a few hairs away from my face. "You are my family, Jenna. You're the one I…"

"But if you want me to say no," I interrupt him. "Because you're not ready for that step, the meet-my-family step, then that's okay too. I'll do whatever makes you happy because what I don't like is the tension I can feel in your body even when you're laying with me on the couch. This has obviously been weighing heavily on your mind."

"It's not because I don't want you to come. Seriously. Everyone's family is a little bit screwed up and I've told you about my Dad, but my sister and brother…" He shakes his head.

"I get it. It's okay. You don't owe me any explanations," I reassure him.

"I didn't mean to scare you. I'm sorry." He looks at me for a few seconds, studying my face, and my hair. "Is it too soon to be saying things like I want to be where you are, and I want you to be where I am all the time? I don't sound like an obsessed creeper when I say that do I?" he asks.

"Umm, I'm going to say no only because I really, really, like being around you too. I've just never met the family of the guy I'm sleeping with. This is all new territory for me."

"For me too. I mean, I knew my high school girlfriend's parents, but I don't count that."

"Me neither. I'm just sorry I don't really have a family to introduce you to. You met Bethy a couple weeks ago, and Linda. Other than them, around here, that's it."

"Then I think you have a spectacular family," he whispers.

"So, did you buy him a gift yet?" I ask.

"Who? Charlie? Uh, no. Actually, I didn't yet." Jacoby looks around his living room searching, I think, for ideas.

"All I got is a case of beer and a box of condoms." He shrugs.

"Uhhh…" I laugh. "I'm not so sure that's the right kind of gift. Maybe we should make a quick stop on our way out in the morning. What kinds of things does he like to do?"

"Well he's always playing with Legos, and like any other kid, he loves his video games. He's probably a little young for Golden Eye though." He winks.

"Let me guess." I raise my hand to stop him. "Mario Brothers?"

"Haha. Yeah. That's his favorite. How did you know?"

"He's a boy and he's five." I shrug. Jacoby tilts his head, perplexed. "Aaaaand, one of the asshats at work has little kids and he's always talking about his son's obsession with all things Mario Brothers."

"Ahh, I see. Yeah I guess it's a boy thing. We'll stop at the store tomorrow and see what we can find. It'll be fun."

"Sounds good to me." I reach over and kiss Jacoby's cheek. "Thank you for asking me to come with you, Jacoby."

"Thank you for saying yes."

CHAPTER 15

Secrets, Secrets, Are No Fun

Jenna

Jacoby told me that the party would just be a summer casual event, except I have no idea what summer casual means when you're the governor's family. I've spent time imagining the men of the family in khaki pants and expensive polo shirts while the girls are all dressed like the Real Housewives of New Jersey, complete with eight hundred dollar sunglasses and very sparkly jewelry. None of that is me though, so I'm going for a more comfortable look. It's a kid's birthday party after all. My ripped skinny jeans and a teal tunic should be just fine. I grab my brown beaded sandals, throw on a complementing necklace and some longer earrings and I'm good to go.

"Does this look okay?" I ask Jacoby upon walking into the kitchen.

"No," he says quickly without even looking. "You're wearing too many clothes. Go take something off."

Laughing at his boyish behavior, I stand there until he looks up at me. "Seriously, though. Is everyone going to be way more dressed up than this?"

"KitKat, you look sexy as hell. Trust me. What you're wearing is just fine. Come on," he says as he grabs a pair of keys off the hook by the door. "Let's go."

When we enter the garage, I look past Jacoby's tow truck and head for his pick-up a few feet away. It's the car we almost always take when we go somewhere, but this time Jacoby tugs my arm in the opposite direction. "I know you have a tow truck fantasy and all," Jacoby teases. "But I thought we would take a different ride today."

"Oh? What does that mean? You want to saddle up the horses?"

"Horses? No," he answers. "Horse power? Yes." As we enter the garage he nods his head in the direction of a few sporty looking cars parked beside each other. The black one, he tells me, is a nineteen sixty-three vintage Ferrari and the red one, a nineteen fifty-eight Corvette, but neither of those is my favorite. Every time I'm here I eye the last car sitting in the corner. A yellow nineteen fifty-five Thunderbird, or so Jacoby says. I know nothing about cars except that they're pretty, and this one is the most beautiful car I've ever seen. Knowing that Jacoby was able to fully restore the once old clunker into this piece of art makes it even that much more special. Jacoby walks over to the very car I'm gawking over and opens the passenger door.

"Your chariot awaits."

"Oh, my Gosh! We're taking this one? It's my favorite!" I exclaim.

"I could tell, so yeah, let's take her for a spin. It's a nice day. The world needs a little more yellow." He smiles.

I watch in excitement as Jacoby puts the key in the ignition and turns his hand. The old car roars to life, sending vibrations through the car all the way to the parts of me that have no business being turned on right now. As he pulls out of the garage and onto the road, the car settles into a beautiful purr. I can't control the smile that forms on my face as I lean my head back against the head rest. It's going to be a beautiful day.

"Isn't the Governor's Mansion in Hartford?" I ask Jacoby on our way to his family's home. Picking out Charlie's birthday present was quick and easy, especially since every boy likes Legos and video games. Jacoby insists on getting him something educational every year as well, so we found a cool child's microscope that he can use to look at things like dirt, and rocks, and probably his own boogers.

"Yeah it is. It's only an hour from here. My Dad spends a lot of time there throughout the week since most of his business needs to happen around there anyway, but my Mom didn't want to let go of our childhood home. She usually comes down here anytime the family is going to be together. She doesn't like to be way from her grandkids."

"How many does she have?"

"Three. My sister has two kids and my brother has one. Mom's friends are here too. I know she has her passions that she keeps busy with in Hartford, but she likes to be able to invite the ladies over to play cards or gossip about the latest scandal. She's smart enough to know that one day my dad won't be the governor anymore and when they retire back here, she'll still want to have friends."

"Smart lady," I say.

"Yeah."

"So, who am I meeting today?" I ask as we pull into an estate with a locked gate. Jacoby rolls the window down to enter the security code. When he does so, the black wrought iron gate opens and we drive through. He's silent for a moment as we pull up the driveway and swing the car around the circle.

"Well, my dad isn't supposed to be here today, thank God." He sighs. "You don't need to see that shit storm. But anyway, my mom should be here, and my sister Erica and her husband, Tom. Little Charlie, he's the birthday boy. He can be a handful and loves to have fun, but he's a little teddy bear too." Jacoby smiles.

"Is Charlie your brother's kid or sister's kid?" I ask him.

Before he answers I swear I see a slight twinge in his cheek. "Charlie is my brother's kid. My brother's name is Andy and his wife's name is…"

"UNCLE JACOBYYYYY!" We here a little voice shout as the front door swings open and a small little boy jolts out and around the car. "WOW! You drived this here?"

Jacoby laughs. "Hey buddy! Yeah, I did. Do you like it?"

"Yeah I do." Charlie nods. "Yellow is my favorite color 'cause Minions are yellow too! Will you take me for a ride?" he asks, jumping up and down.

"Well, how about we go inside for a few minutes so I can hello to Nana and Mommy and Daddy okay?"

"And Uncle Jack!" Charlie exclaims.

I see Jacoby's head swing around and smile as his eyebrows shoot up. "Even better! Jack is here."

"Jack?" I whisper to him as we step out of the car.

"Jack Schmidt. I should've known he would be invited. Come on, let's go say hi and see who I should introduce you to." He takes my hand and leads me into the house to meet his family.

"Uncle Jacoby, who is that?" Charlie says pointing to me. Oops. Busted.

Jacoby crouches down to his height and holds out one of his gift bags. "Her name is Jenna. She's one of my friends, so I invited her to come with me today, is that okay?"

"Yeah, 'cause she's pretty and you guys brought me a present and that's what happens when you go to a party. You bring presents, and I like presents so she can stay."

Jacoby and I both share in a laugh. "Thank you very much, Charlie," I tell him. "I'm very excited to be at your party."

"Come on! I want to show you my cake. It's HUUUUUUGE!"

"Jenna, I should tell you something," Jacoby says quietly, but Charlie has my hand and is tugging me into the house.

As soon as we step inside the house, there's a flurry of activity. There's a child crying somewhere in the house and a woman's voice trying to calm her down. Someone is shouting for Charlie, but when I turn around to where he just was walking in with us, he's not there. Dang, kids are fast and stealthy when they want to be. Flying by us before Jacoby can snatch him up, another little boy comes running through the entryway and into the next room.

"That would be Miles," Jacoby tells me. "He just turned six not too long ago. Belongs to my sister."

I nod trying to mentally take notes so I don't feel too much like a goof. Finally, we make our way into the back portion of the house where, it seems, the party is in full swing. Judging by the striped decorations, the games around the yard, and the massive three-tiered topsy-turvy cake in the middle of the table in the kitchen, it looks like we're celebrating circus themed birthday party, Pinterest-style. This family certainly spares no expense on birthday parties. Quickly my eyes dart around the yard, but I don't see what I'm expecting to see.

"Are you looking for something?" a guy holding a beer says to me. I'm caught off guard, because I never saw him coming toward me. Jacoby squeezes my hand and when I look at him all I can say is "Elephants."

The guy holding the beer laughs quietly and fist pumps Jacoby. "You must be Jenna." He holds out his hand that isn't holding onto a beer. "I'm Jack, Jacoby's…"

"Brother from another mother. Yeah, he told me all about you. It's a pleasure to meet you, Jack," I respond, shaking his hand.

"Something like that." He chuckles. "The pleasure is all mine Jenna. I hope he didn't bore you with too much information about me. Would you like a beer?"

"Uh, sure. Thanks."

"No problem," he says. "Jacoby I'll grab you one too."

"Thanks, man." Jacoby shakes his head playfully back and forth and repeats "Elephants?"

"Yeah well, it looks like a circus, doesn't it? It's like the perfect Pinterest post out here," I say, looking around the back yard. "I just assumed there would be elephants somewhere."

Jacoby pulls me toward him and puts his arm around my waist. "I'm sorry you may be disappointed then. Look I should tell you…"

"Jacoby! I'm so glad you're here!" A classy woman, who looks remarkably like Helen Mirren, strides up to us. Jacoby gives her a kiss on the cheek before letting go of me to hug her.

"Mom, this is Jenna. Jenna, this is my mom, Debbie." Jacoby says.

I nod offering her my hand. "It's a pleasure to meet you, Mrs. Malloy."

"Oh, no need for the formalities dear." She wraps me up in a hug. "We're all family here. Call me Debbie. I'm so very happy to meet you."

"Oh, well thank you." I smile. "I'm very happy to be here. Thanks for the invitation."

"Anytime, dear. Come, come, let's have you meet the rest of the family." Mrs. Malloy links her arm with mine, an act that immediately makes me miss my mom, as we stroll across the yard to where the other adults are mingling.

There are several words of greeting between Jacoby and the other adults hanging out around the food as the kids play. "Jenna," Jacoby motions his way around the circle. "This is my sister, Erica, and her husband, Tom." They both nod to me and smile. "Miles and Maddie belong to them."

"It's very nice to meet you." I nod, trying once again to remember the facts.

Jacoby looks at another couple standing around with the adults. "I'm sorry, I don't know you." He smiles and extends his hand in greeting. "I'm Uncle Jacoby. This is my girlfriend, Jenna."

"Pleasure to meet you." The female says. "I'm Crystal. This is my husband, Nate. We're Kyle's parents. He and Charlie are great friends."

"Great to meet you as well." Jacoby says clearing his throat before continuing around the circle. "And this is my brother, Andy, and his wife, Sarah." I look at the last couple standing around the table. My first impression of Andy is that he looks like a smaller, almost just as ugly version of Donald Trump. Dressed in what I'm sure is a designer pair of khaki pants and a Tommy Hilfiger polo shirt, he looks the part of the flaunting rich man with the perfect trophy wife on his arm. Her petite figure and huge store-bought tits rub up against her husband in a way that should be embarrassing to everyone else standing around us. At least it is to me. I have to look away after giving them both a quick smile and hello. Sarah and Mrs. Malloy step away to tend to Charlie and his friends, but when I make eye contact again, Andy gives me a creepy smirk and then licks his lips like I'm his next meal. Ew.

"So, little brother," Andy says before taking a swig of the beer in his hand. "How long do you think it would take me to get her on her back?" He looks at me and winks, like I'm supposed to think what he just said is funny.

Is he talking about his wife?

Or me?

"Fuck you," Jacoby says as he squeezes my hand.

Shit. He was definitely talking about me.

"Excuse me?" I ask, giving Andy my best stink eye.

"Andy cut it out. You're drunk," Erica says as she brings her hand to her forehead. Crystal and Nate both look at him, clearly embarrassed by his remarks.

"Oh, he hasn't told you yet?" Andy goads.

"Told me what?"

"Drop it Andy." Jacoby tenses up beside me.

"He hasn't told you that he used to be in love with my gorgeous wife, but he just couldn't get her done?" he says, gesturing with his pelvis a few times. "So being the helpful big brother that I am, I had to step in and help a girl out." I start to respond but feel the squeeze of Jacoby's hand.

Don't react.

He's clearly drunk.

He's purposely pushing Jacoby's buttons.

But does he still love her?

"Of course, he told me," I lie. "Do you honestly think he would bring me here and introduce me to your lovely wife if I didn't already know? Sorry to burst your bubble, but Jacoby has more class than that."

"Here you go." Jack arrives just in time with a beer for both Jacoby and me.

"Thanks, man," Jacoby says quietly. He leans over and kisses my cheek.

"Let's go check out some of the games?" He poses the question, but I know it's more like a let's-get-the-hell-out-of-here.

"Yeah. Sure. Excuse us," I say to the group, making damn sure my stare penetrates the asshole that is Jacoby's brother. Anger flows through me at not only the fact that what Andy just told me must be true or everyone would be denying it, but that I had to learn it from the asshole first. Erica and Tom nod understandingly. Jacoby gestures to Jack, who follows us over to where the ring-toss game is set up.

"Why did you do that?" Jacoby wonders as we walk across the lawn.

"Do what?"

"Lie. For me," he says.

I take a deep breath knowing full well why I lied for him. "Well, number one, he's clearly intoxicated."

"Whatever gave you that idea?" Jack says, his words dripping with sarcasm.

"I wasn't about to let him disrespect you right in front of me the very first time we met. And number two…" I can't even bring myself to ask the question. I don't really want to know the answer. "I mean, this is weird, you know?" I look to Jack for confirmation. "It's weird, right? It's true? The girl he once loved marries his brother?"

Jack chuckles a little, nodding affirmatively. I appreciate that he sees the awkward humor. "Truth. And yeah, it's a little weird, but not as weird as it was all those years ago."

"Look," Jacoby starts. "You have to understand…"

"Oh, I understand just fine!" I huff quietly so we don't make a scene. I even bend over to pick up a few rings to toss so it looks like we're happily playing the party games placed around the yard. Tossing the first ring forward, it misses the stake in the ground. "You brought me to a family event where you knew I would meet…what's her name again?"

"Sarah," Jack and Jacoby say together.

"Right. Sarah. The girl with the rack. The girl with the perfect body and stunning face." I point my finger at Jacoby. "The girl who was your muse for so long! The girl who was the reason you started writing for Pete's sake."

Jack chokes on his drink. "Dude, you told her?" he asks Jacoby.

"Of course, I told her," Jacoby answers. "I don't want to hide anything from her."

"Do you trust her?" Jack mumbles.

"Hello!! I'm standing right here!" I shout. Quickly, I look around, hoping nobody heard my outburst, but the yard isn't that huge. "It's your turn!" I shout again to help cover up our conversation. Handing Jacoby a ring to toss, I step out of the way muttering, "And you sure as hell did a good job at hiding this!"

"I wasn't trying to hide anything from you, Jenna. I swear. I tried to tell you three times today, but I kept getting interrupted. I tried to tell you in the car. I tried to tell you in the kitchen. I tried to tell you before we even crossed the fucking lawn, but my mom wouldn't leave you alone." He sighs. "I'm sorry, okay? I'm sorry I didn't try harder to tell you earlier. I didn't know what the hell to say or how to say it, and then I waited too long and then…."

"Do you love her?" I interrupt. My stomach twists just hearing myself ask him that question. I don't even want to know the answer.

"Do I…what? NO!" he loudly whispers. "I would never do that to you."

I don't make eye contact because I don't know what to say. I'm not in a place where I can just walk off to be alone to think, so instead, I pick up another ring and throw it at the next stake in the ground without saying a word. To my dismay, it hits the stake and bounces off making a loud clanging noise.

"Jenna, look at me."

Begrudgingly, I lift my eyes.

"I'm really sorry I didn't tell you before today. It's part of my past, I can't do anything about it now, but my double dog douchebag of a brother likes to rub my face in all of his successes. I should've known he would do something like that. I should've warned you."

"Why does he rub your face in his successes? Because you're not successful enough?" I roll my eyes.

"No, it's not that. It's just that he gets off on thinking he's one-upping me. There's too much of my dad in him."

"Why don't you just set him straight? Set your whole family straight? I don't get it," I tell him.

"I've been asking him that for years." Jack chimes in.

"Because then I would be just like them," he says before downing the rest of his beer. "And I'm not just like them at all. My life isn't about making a shit ton of money. My life is about doing something I love doing, so that at the end of the day, I'm happy." He shrugs. "It just so happens that I'm even luckier because doing something that I love doing, brings in enough money that I can enjoy doing some of the other things I like to do."

"Jacoby!" Mrs. Malloy shouts from the back porch. "Sweetheart, can you give me a hand with something inside?" Jacoby looks to me, and then back to his mom, and then back to me again, clearly having an internal battle over where he needs to be at this moment.

"Go." I tell him. "I'm fine. It's fine. We're fine. I really…don't want this to be a big deal."

"I'll just be a minute, ok?" He steps toward me, holding tenderly onto my upper arm, and kisses the side of my head. "I'll be right back," he whispers before he turns and says, "Sure, Mom. Be right there." I watch him walk to the other end of the yard and into the house realizing I probably look like a love-sick child with a school-girl crush.

"You like him a lot," Jack says, then shoots back his beer.

"I love him." The words spring out of my mouth before I can stop them. Instinctively my hand flies over my mouth as if I had just called my best friend a twatzilla.

Jack chokes on his drink, coughing a few times before he pleads, "Come again?" Like a deer in the headlights I turn to look at Jack's face, hand-covered-mouth and all. I try to say something, anything, to him, but words just don't seem to want to form in my head.

"I…"

Don't take it back, Jenna.

That's even worse.

"I…"

"Oh my God, you *do* love him." Jack gasps, but gives me a goofy appreciative grin.

"I don't know," I admit, still wide-eyed. "I'm not sure I know what love is, really."

"You do know. You said the words." Jack confirms. "You said them without being asked. That's how you know, you know?"

I shake my head like a scared child. "Jack I…I haven't…"

"You haven't told him yet?" he asks.

I shake my head. "No. I…I didn't know I was going to say that. I'm sorry, I'm not sure I'm ready to say it again, and I'm really not sure he's ready to hear it anyway. Jack, you don't know me, and you certainly don't owe me anything, but you would be doing me a huge favor if you just didn't tell him what I said, okay?"

"Because you think you don't mean it or because you think you do mean it, but you're too scared of what might happen if you say it again?"

Dang.

Am I that much of an open book?

Surprisingly, I'm rewarded by Jack's sincere smile and nod of understanding. He gestures to me that what I said is safe with him as he zips his lips and tosses the key. "Relax. I won't say a word, but for what it's worth, if what you say is true, and you do really love him, then *I* owe *you* the world, because that guy deserves only the best things in life." He explains. "Seeing the way he looks at you, and knowing what he's gone through with that gold-digging bitch over there, and with his father…" Jack inhales a deep breath as he looks around the yard. The kids are playing in the ball pit, the adults are chatting and laughing. "He deserves to finally be happy."

"How did you guys meet? You've been friends for a long time?" I ask, trying to gently change the subject. We walk along the yard a little more, stopping in an alcove where we can see the harbor. The water sparkles in the sunshine, and the flurry of activity on the water brings a calm smile to my face. I don't get out on the water much, but I've always enjoyed spending time in an area where not many people can bother me.

"Since middle school, yeah," Jack answers. "I moved here when I was in eighth grade. I was a pretty scrawny kid without many friends, but for whatever reason, Jacoby and I became inseparable. It's been that way ever since."

"I see. Jacoby tells me you're a lawyer? Do you restore old cars too?"

Jack laughs. "No. I can probably change a tire and maybe a car battery or two if I tried, but that's Jacoby's expertise. The firm keeps me busy most days.

"Oh," I say.

"And obviously, I represent Jacoby anytime he needs it. Not that I'm saying he needs it a lot, I'm just saying…for those times that he needs legal advice when it comes to his other job." He winks.

"Got it." I nod.

"And speaking of his other job, I need you to understand something," he says.

"Okay."

"Jacoby doesn't tell just anyone about what he does. In fact, I'm pretty sure only four or five of us know."

I try to reassure Jack. "Yeah. He told me that the night he showed his office."

"I'm sure you know that his father doesn't know but even Sarah…wait, did you just say he showed you his office?"

Perplexed at his surprise I nod my head. "Yeah. The hidden writing room on the other side of his book shelves?"

Jack's eyebrows raise. "So, you've obviously been in his house."

I have to laugh. "I'm beginning to think maybe you guys aren't the besties that you say you are. Is Jacoby that private of a person that he doesn't tell his best friend when he brings a girl to his house?"

"Ooh touché." He laughs with me. "You're right. It's just…he's never allowed a girl in his house. So yeah, I guess to an extent, he is a private person, but the fact that he's so easily let you in should tell you a few things."

I watch Jack for a moment, waiting for him to clarify his statement, but clarification never comes. I decide to try and change the subject so I can get myself out of the hot seat. "What about you, Jack? Is there a special person in your life?"

"Me? Nah, not right now. To be honest I don't always have the best luck with women, so I keep busy with work. One day maybe the right girl will come along. We'll see." He shrugs.

Maybe I should set him up with Linda. She deserves a nice guy – hahaha - this one may be too nice for her amount of sass. I'll have to remember to ask Jacoby more about him. We both look back to the house to see Jacoby carrying Charlie's ridiculously large, most likely exorbitantly expensive birthday cake out to the party table.

"Cake and presents!" We hear Charlie squeal as the kids sprint towards the back deck.

"Come on," he says. "Let's go get another beer and watch Charlie open his presents."

CHAPTER 16
I Just Needed to Pee!

Jenna

Legos and microscopes and even video games be damned when a six-year-old boy gets a new bike for his birthday. And not just any bike, a red, white, and blue, Captain America themed bike complete with the shield decoration and bike helmet to match the famed Avenger. Charlie won't be leaving the parking lot-sized driveway for quite some time. Cake will have to wait. The adults all disperse back around to the deck while the kids watch Charlie try out his new wheels.

"Can you tell me where the bathroom is?" I ask Jacoby discreetly. I've had too many drinks throughout the afternoon and I'm ready to burst.

"Yeah. Right inside the house, down the hall to the right. Can't miss it," he answers. "Want me to show you?"

"No." I wave my hand. "It's fine. You relax. I'll just be a minute." Excusing myself from the group, I make my way into the house following Jacoby's directions.

When I'm finished, I open the door to walk back down the hall, but stop when I hear voices coming from the room across the hall.

"God I've wanted you all day. You've got those tits on display for me. It's taken everything to not just rip your clothes off in front of everyone out there," a male voice says.

My eyes widen as I stand in the bathroom doorway, frozen in place at the sound of what is obvious kissing coupled with zippers moving up or down. The female in the room moans, giving me the most uncomfortable feeling. I'm stuck here not knowing which choice to make. Do I run down the hall to get away from whatever is going on? Or do I step back and shut the door and just stay here until they're finished?

Ew, ew, ew!

"Andy." The female painstakingly moans. "What if someone walks in?" Her words make me wince. How did I get so lucky? The one time I choose to use the restroom and I step out to hear Andy and Sarah clearly going at it in the next room. The only thing that makes me feel better is reassuring myself that now that the stupid drunk is getting his fix for the day, maybe he'll leave me the hell alone. I roll my eyes and start back down the hall to find Jacoby.

"Crystal, I'm going to come, baby," he says. "I'm going to come. Open up. I want to watch you swallow every last drop of me."

Crystal?

Crystal and Andy?

I know I was sort of thrown in to the family introductions pretty quickly, but I remember enough to know that Andy is married to Sarah, not Crystal.

What the ever-loving fuck?

Here?

At his son's birthday party?

I try my hardest to tip toe back down the hall, praying that the floors don't squeak as I walk. I don't want to hear any more. I didn't want to hear what I heard in the first place. I don't want to be the only one who knows what's going on. I don't want to know someone else's secrets. I don't want to be involved at all. I want to go back outside and drink myself into oblivion in hopes that I'll just forget the nastiness that was just going on across from where I was standing, except I can't get drunk and stupid in front of Jacoby and his family. Sighing to myself as I finally make it to the kitchen, I think that I'm in the clear.

"Have you seen Andy?" Sarah asks, in the kitchen pouring drinks into child sippy cups.

Oh good Lord, please tell me she doesn't know.

"Uh…" I feel my eyes blink several times and my mouth go dry. "Uh, no. I'm sorry I haven't. I was just in the restroom."

"Oh. Well, would you mind giving me a hand? I have no idea where he went off to and the kids are asking for cake." She gestures to the cups on the counter as she picks up several to carry outside.

"Um, sure. Yeah," I tell her. I think for just a minute I actually feel bad for Sarah. And even worse for Charlie. He's being raised by shithead of a father. I make a mental note to encourage Jacoby to spend a little more time with Charlie so that he's benefiting from the influence of a good guy. I sure as hell am not going to be the one who tells him his brother is a cheating douche.

"Hey babe. You need some help?" I hear Andy say from behind me. I turn around slightly, to see him tucking in his shirt. When I turn back around immediately I know that Sarah saw the exact same thing I saw.

"Where were you?" She says.

Andy shrugs. "Bathroom."

Knowing exactly how this conversation is about to play out, I'm frozen in place and have no idea how I'm going to get myself out of this hot mess. Sarah quickly looks back and forth from Andy to me and I know she's wondering how Andy could've been in the bathroom when I just said I was in there. I would love nothing else than to just play dumb right now, but the redness I can feel creeping up my cheeks is a dead giveaway that I know something. She just doesn't know what I know.

"Are you…" She starts to ask, staring at me. "Did you…" Automatically I feel my head shaking back and forth trying to stop her from even asking what I know she's thinking. The hallway isn't that long. There's no way there are two bathrooms down there. Andy moves forward casually, like he has no idea what's about to happen, probably because he isn't focused on the look on his wife's face. Like a perfectly choreographed daytime soap opera, Crystal enters the kitchen smoothing the back of her sundress and adjusting her strapless bra.

Oh my God.

I can't believe this is happening.

As much as I want to crack up with laughter at the absurdity of what I can feel is about to unfold, I remain calm and try my best to appear emotionless. I refuse to incriminate myself when I know I did nothing wrong.

"Crystal?" Sarah asks.

"Yeah? Do you need some help?" Crystal offers.

Sarah's head tilts in confusion. "Where were you?"

Don't say it Crystal. Please God, don't say it.

"In the bathroom," she explains. "Sorry. Did you need something?"

"Yeah, I do," Sarah says slowly. "I need someone to explain to me why it is that three of you were supposedly in the one bathroom that I know is down that hallway at the same time, because I don't remember seeing a line a moment ago, yet here you all are. And you're all telling me that you were in the bathroom."

"Babe, come on," Andy starts but she immediately puts her hands up in defense, thus dropping the sippy cups she was holding on the floor.

Thank goodness they're spill-proof.

"Don't touch me." She backs up against the counter. Her face contorts with horror, shock, anger, and grief all at the same time. Her breathing picks up as her face whitens. I can't believe I'm not only watching this go down, but because I had to freaking pee, I was in the wrong place at the wrong time and I'm now involved.

Jacoby, come save me!

"How dare you," Sarah says. I'm watching Crystal's expression change from one of shock to one of temporary relief as her head turns and she looks at me. My head snaps back to Sarah who, if looks could kill, wants to be standing over my dead body right now.

"Me?" I ask pointing to myself.

"Yes, you! You walk in here on Jacoby's arm and within a few hours you're coming on to my husband?" she accuses.

"Wait, what?" I ask. "Me? You think I'm…hahahaha no, no, no." I can't help but chuckle this time. This is all too absurd.

"You think this is funny?" Sarah shouts. From the corner of my eye I can see a few heads turn outside. "You think you can waltz in here and just fuck around with anything here with a dick? What's the matter with you?"

"No, no, no, no, no." I repeat. "Sarah, I didn't…I'm not…" I can't even say the words. I look over at Crystal like I expect her to save me, but she only gives me a pitied look like she feels bad that I got caught. Only it wasn't me! The French doors to the patio open and Jacoby steps in. My body relaxes at the mere sight of him. "What's going on?" he asks. "Sarah, everyone out there can hear you shouting. What the hell is your problem?" He looks to Andy for some kind of explanation but of course the cum-bubble doesn't have one so he looks at me.

"I'll tell you what's going on!" Sarah announces. She moves to pick up the sippy cups she dropped on the floor and begins to carry them outside. To my dismay, we all seem to follow her even though I just want to grab Jacoby and leave. "Your whore of a girlfriend…" she starts.

"Hey. Watch it," Jacoby warns in my favor.

"…or whatever you want to call her," Sarah says angrily. "Just came on to my husband in the bathroom!"

"I did no such thing, Sarah! Are you kidding me with this?" Her words make me irate as I watch the expression on Jacoby's face turn from one of confusion to one of hurt.

"Oh my God," I gasp. "You believe her!"

"I…no." he quietly shaking his head.

Refusing to allow these people to make me look like the selfish bitch, the only thing I can do is tell the truth, even if that means hurting people I don't even know.

"Ok here it is. I went to the bathroom about five minutes ago, and when I came out there were noises going on across the hall." I nod to Andy and Crystal. "Clearly *they* were going at it. He was talking to her about her tits being on display and she was asking him to hurry up. I'm sorry that I don't know any of you and you have no reason to believe me over them, but that's the honest to God truth. I didn't touch Andy. I just needed to freaking pee."

"Ridiculous," Andy guffaws. "You came on to me back there and you know it."

"Shut the fuck up, Andy," Jacoby says.

"Yeah? Well why should I believe you huh?" Sarah says to me. "Give me one good reason."

I don't know what makes the words come out of my mouth so unabashedly, but holding up my hands I shout, "Because my hands smell like the orange ginger hand soap from the bathroom and my breath smells like beer!" I gesture to Crystal. "Unless she had time to pop a mint in her mouth, you'll find that Crystal's breath probably smells a whole lot like jizz, and if I had to guess, Andy's fingers will smell like taco sauce!"

"You BITCH!" I hear just before something wet hits my face. My eyes close on instinct and I gasp for breath, more so at the surprise of someone throwing something at me. Jacoby's body is covering mine in an instant.

"Sarah, that's ENOUGH!" he shouts. His hands are on my face wiping away the sweet-smelling wetness from my cheeks. "It's icing, Jenna. You're okay. It's just icing."

"What the fuck?" I ask in disbelief.

"Sarah! That's Charlie's cake! What the hell are you doing?" Andy yells.

"I can't believe you're defending her, you jackass!" Sarah screams as another piece of scooped up iced cake comes hurtling in our direction, hitting Jacoby in his shoulder.

Minutes pass by as the entire group of somewhat mature adults shout at each other over who is right and who is lying. Finally, Jack steps in, whistling loudly until we all stop arguing. "Whoa! Okay. Please! Out of respect for your mother, this conversation needs to stop! Now the only way I can see this argument being put to rest is looking at the evidence presented," he says with his most lawyer-like flare. "You may not believe her, but the defendant is innocent until proven guilty, so, perhaps I should just take one for the team and plant a nice big kiss on Crystal over there to see if Jenna's argument has any truth to it."

"What? No!" Crystal says.

"Not a chance." Nate chimes in, puffing his chest in front of Jack. "If anyone is going to kiss my wife, it will be me!"

"Nate, please," Crystal pleads. The fact that she obviously doesn't want to be kissed right now should tell everyone what they need to know but it looks, for now, like everyone is playing along.

"Relax babe, it's just a kiss," he says, walking over to her. He stops though when Crystal starts crying as she backs up against the door with her hand over her mouth.

"Crystal?" Nate whispers.

"Oh, for Christ's sake," Andy murmurs from the other side of the room.

I feel Jacoby squeeze my hand in support as we all watch in horror as the soap opera that is his family unfolds in front of us. Jack gives me a wink followed by a cat-ate-the-canary grin.

"I'm sorry Nate. I'm so sorry. He made me do it. He's been making me do it for a long time. He told me he would fire me if I ever told you and I knew we needed the money and…"

"Oh fuck," Jacoby whispers to himself.

Her words continue but nobody hears them when Nate turns around and runs full force into Andy, pushing him across the patio and right into what was left of Charlie's birthday cake-the cake we never even got to cut. Jacoby immediately pulls my hand and leads me off the patio and onto the grass to a safe space.

"I'm sorry Jenna. My family is a hot mess and I'm sorry I brought you here to meet them," he says.

"Kiss me," I beg him. He grins curiously at me, probably inwardly questioning whether this is the best time to be kissing me, but he doesn't have to be asked twice. His lips are on mine gentle and loving. He tenderly holds my face, even slipping in the icing all over my cheek. While we stand off to the side kissing, I can't help but imagine what this scene must look like from above. Two men are fighting, one woman is screaming at her husband as she watches him get his ass kicked, one woman is crying her eyes out and Jacoby and I are just over here taking this moment to share in an emotional kiss. A giggle escapes my mouth mid-kiss.

"What's so funny?" Jacoby asks.

"This is." I gesture to the circus going on around us. "I suppose Andy and Sarah picked the appropriate theme for this birthday party, huh?"

"KitKat, I do believe you've got a point." We both stand together laughing as we watch the show develop.

What I wouldn't give for a lawn chair and an ice-cold beer.

Jack finally joins us a moment later with three beers in his hands. The man can read my mind. "I knew that would come up eventually," he says shaking his head.

"What's that?" Jacoby asks.

"Their little…fling, or whatever you call it. It's been going on way too long, though if what she's saying is true, I had no idea."

"What? You knew about it?" Jacoby questions him. "Why didn't you ever say anything?"

"Dude, if there's anyone in our office who doesn't know about it, I would be shocked," he answers nonchalantly. "But he's big wig in his firm and none of us want to risk our jobs to call out an affair that has nothing to do with us. He's got judge influence, man. And your dad…"

"Say no more. Fuck!" Jacoby fumes. "I always knew he was a loser. I actually wish Dad were here to see what a loser he is." He scoffs. "Except it wouldn't surprise me in the least if he already knew. Hell, he probably gave Andy the idea in the first place."

His words create a softness in my heart for Mrs. Malloy. Her husband is a politician after all. I suppose I can't be surprised at the fact that he may have had an affair or two in his time. "Poor Sarah," I whisper to myself.

"Yeah," Jacoby answers to my surprise. "She may have turned into a bit of a diva but she doesn't come from money. She doesn't deserve this. I should go talk to her."

That softness in my heart turns to jealousy in an instant. Does he still love her? Will he want to be there for her? Will he want her back if she leaves Andy? Will he forget about me? I let go of Jacoby's hand and gulp over half of my beer, spitting some of it out when a child starts screaming.

"NOOOOOO!!!! WHERE'S MY CAKE MOMMY?" Charlie and his buddies have come around the corner to see the disaster that is a completely smashed cake laying all over the picnic table. Everyone stops whatever it was they were doing and freezes in place, staring at Charlie and the rest of the kids with him. There's an uncomfortable silence across the yard.

Quietly I whisper to Jacoby, "Do something."

"Huh?" he asks.

"You have to do something for Charlie. Look at the look on his face. He'll be devastated."

"Okay, okay…umm." Jacoby thinks for a second, surveying everyone in the yard before finally speaking up.

"Hey Charlie." Jacoby runs across the yard to where the kids are standing. "We just thought this circus needed something really fun," he says as he looks around.

"Like what, Uncle Jacoby?"

"Like…a FOOD FIGHT! Look! Your mom got me good right in the shoulder!" He points to the icing all over his shirt.

"Cool!" Charlie exclaims.

"Yeah! Now we need to get her back! It's war! Grab some cake and let's have some fun!" Jacoby tells them.

"YEAH!!" The kids scream and run for the patio as fast as they can to get in on the action. In minutes, they're a mess, covered in cake and icing from head to toe. Jacoby looks over toward me and all I can do is smile at the way he easily saved Charlie's birthday from turning into a catastrophic event for this young boy. I smile, that is, until Jacoby flings a handful of cake in my direction that lands right on my left boob.

Oh, no he didn't.

Laughing right along with him, I jog over to the patio to scoop up whatever kind of cake mess I can find and smear it all over Jacoby's face. Before we know it, everyone is laughing and screaming and we're all covered in smashed chocolate and vanilla cake with loads of colored icing. This is definitely the most circus-like birthday party I've ever been to. Reaching down to the ground I'm able to scoop up one more large handful of smashed cake. Like a weak discus thrower, I wind up to throw my scoop in Charlie's direction. It's so great to see him having so much fun. Score one for Uncle Jacoby. My body pivots to release my weapon and when the cake flies out of my hand, the world around me moves in a heart wrenching, anxiety driven slow motion. It seems my throw may have been a little high. Too high to hit Charlie, but I watch in horror as my handful of cake slop makes a direct hit to the chest of an older gentleman now standing on the back patio. He's dressed in a three-piece navy blue business suit with a red striped tie.

Oh God.

Don't tell me.

"Dad! What are you doing here?"

CHAPTER 17
Drop It Like It's Hot
Jenna

Andy looks as shocked as the rest of us at his father's presence. "I thought you had a meeting all day."

Governor Malloy is clearly pissed off, but tries to reign himself in, most likely because there are children present. When he speaks, it's with an eerie calm that makes me feel like I should go directly to jail. No passing GO, and no collecting two hundred dollars.

"Does someone want to explain what in the hell is going on out here?" He demands as he reaches inside his jacket pocket. He pulls out a handkerchief – do people even still use those? – and wipes the goop off of his now ruined suit coat, dress shirt and tie. My cheeks turn beet red in embarrassment. It'll take me months at The Hole Punch to make enough money to repay him for the damage I just caused.

"Uncle Jacoby let us have a food fight, Pap! It was so cool!" Charlie says, jumping up and down. I honestly can't tell if he's excited, or if he just needs to pee. Governor Malloy looks up to survey everyone standing around until his eyes land on Jacoby. The sour look he gives Jacoby surprises me even though it shouldn't. Jacoby's told me all about their relationship. I guess I just assumed he would play nice to save political face.

"I'm guessing that must be your yellow toy out front? That must've cost a pretty penny," he says. I can feel Jacoby stiffen next to me. He doesn't say anything at first; he simply stares at his father. The tension around us is immediately palpable which makes me uncomfortable. We were all having so much fun until now.

"What's your point?" Jacoby asks his father. The governor shrugs with a bored expression on his face.

"Let me guess, you're here because you spent all your money on some stupid car…" he starts.

"I don't need a damn thing from you, Governor." Jacoby spits out. "I'm here for Charlie. In case you've forgotten, it's your grandson's birthday."

"I'm your father, Jacoby. You're welcome to address me as such."

Jacoby takes one step forward with a sneer on his face. "When was the last time you acted like a father to me, *Governor*?" he stresses again.

Mr. Malloy is silent for a moment as he assesses the situation around us. My heart drops when he looks at his sweet wife, Mrs. Malloy, who with obvious tears in her eyes, excuses herself inside. Sarah and Erica motion for the kids to follow inside so that they can get cleaned up. Nate and Andy both stand up and brush themselves off, though Nate is still very clearly pissed at Andy. Nate follows the group inside, chasing after a sobbing Crystal. Andy thinks he's going to stand here while my Jacoby and Mr. Malloy speak. No way in hell will I let that happen.

"Andy, would you excuse us, please? I think Sarah might need to see you," I tell him.

Or kill you.

"Who's this?" the governor asks, nodding to me.

"She's with me," Jacoby says.

"Is that so?"

I step forward reaching out my hand to Governor Malloy. "I'm Jenna, sir. Jenna Zimmerman. It's a pleasure to meet you." For a moment, the governor seems to rein in his attitude as if I haven't been standing here watching this altercation the entire time.

"The pleasure is all mine Ms. Zimmerman, and what is it you do?"

"And there it is," Jacoby mutters. I look back at him as he shakes his head in disbelief.

"There what is?" his father goads.

"Never mind," he scoffs.

"I'm a manager at The Hole Punch, sir. I'm the sales manager there." Smiling, I step back, placing my hands in my back pockets. Mr. Malloy watches me with a keen eye before bursting out in laughter. Jacoby and I exchange glances, waiting to find out why he's laughing.

"That's a good one, Ms. Zimmerman! You had me going there for a second. Come now, what is it you really do?"

Who the hell is this guy?

Feeling the tension rise even more in Jacoby, and seeing the embarrassment on Jack's face standing next to him, I square my shoulders and decide to see how the governor likes my one hundred percent honesty.

"Really? Well really, I spend my nights designing lingerie, which I then market and sell to local boutiques. One day I hope to own my own fashion line, but until then, I soak up all the retail information I can managing sales numbers at The Hole Punch."

"Lingerie?" the governor repeats.

"Yes, sir."

He nods not disapprovingly, but not approvingly either. "That's an interesting line of work."

"It's a passion sir. And one that I work very hard for," I tell him.

"Yes well, that's all very good. Perhaps one day my son here will take a few pointers from you about passion."

"Fuck you, *Father,*" Jacoby seethes. "You know nothing about passion."

The governor points his finger at Jacoby. "You watch your mouth, son. You will not disrespect me in my home. If you were half the man your brother is…" he starts, but I can't hold back. Not one more minute.

"Excuse me sir, do you mean Andy? Andy, the brother who has been cheating on his wife for who the hell knows how long with his secretary? The brother who has been ordering his secretary to perform sexual favors for him lest she lose her job? The one who was coming in her mouth not even thirty minutes ago, right here in your own home? That brother? Because if that's the case, then Jacoby is right. You don't know jack shit about passion, or about working hard for something you believe in, or about being a decent human being for that matter."

"Jenna…" I hear Jacoby say behind me.

"NO, Jacoby! Your father is treating you like shit and I think it's preposterous and it needs to stop!"

"Jenna it's…"

I look Governor Malloy right in the eye when I speak again, the anger building inside. "Do you even know what your son does? Do you know the kind, gentle, passionate man that he is? Do you know anything about the world that he has created for himself? The world he chooses to keep a secret and not tell anyone about, because of how it might affect *you*?"

"Jenna, don't…" Jacoby pleads.

"Oh, this ought to be good," Governor Malloy bellows. "He has a secret life? Please, tell me, does he dress like one of those drag queen freaks in New York City, or does he spend his days and nights playing Dungeons and Dragons in his basement?"

All I see is red.

"HE'S A NEW YORK TIMES BEST SELLING AUTHOR, Governor Douchebag! With more money to his name than you could ever hope of seeing and I love him with all my heart, and I would still love him even if he didn't have a damn dime!" I shout. "Which is so much more than I can say for you."

The tug on my arm is instant. "We're leaving." Jacoby growls. "Right now."

I don't even have time to say anything more, and there was so much more I wanted to say. "Jacoby, wait!" I try to say but my words fall on deaf ears. Holding tightly to my upper arm, Jacoby walks me around to the front of the house where he opens the passenger door of the car for me.

"Get in, now," he snaps. His voice is gruff and dare I say, intimidating. If I had a tail, it would be between my legs right now. Clearly, I've pissed him off.

"Jacoby, I'm sorry, I…"

"Don't say another word." He hisses as he peels out of the driveway.

Oh, God, I've messed up. I close my eyes, and inhale a deep breath, letting it out slowly so that Jacoby doesn't know that I'm about to lose it. My eyes become a watery mess, and as I keep my face turned away from him, all the words I just vomited to Governor Malloy come rushing back to my brain.

Governor Douchebag!

New York Times Best Selling Author.

Secret life.

I betrayed him. The one secret Jacoby entrusted me with and I blew it. I ruined everything without even giving the repercussions of my actions any thought whatsoever. I knew that one day, my inability to filter my words would come back to bite me. I just didn't think the bite would be a deadly blow to anyone else but me, certainly not someone that I love.

We spend the next few minutes driving along the coast, silently brooding to ourselves. I look out at the sound that I know leads to the ocean. The waters are so calm and peaceful. Ironic since it feels like there's a hurricane brewing in the front seat of this car. Reaching up to my cheek and hoping Jacoby doesn't notice, I wipe the tear that had escaped and was sliding down my face. Without warning, Jacoby pulls over to the left-hand side of the road. We're in a semi-deserted area. There's no traffic, and no houses. Just a hill between us and the water down below. Jacoby opens his door and once out of the car, slams it shut. I watch, in anxious wonderment as he walks a few yards away pacing in front of the car, his hands both on his head. Clearly, he's working out some anger. I only wish it hadn't been caused by me.

"Shit. I'm so sorry," I whisper to Jacoby from inside the car as I continue to watch him for any clues as to what's happening. I hate that he's not talking to me. I hate that he won't just argue with me. If anyone deserves to be screamed at, it's me. Jacoby picks up a stone and throws it, as hard as he can, into the water. I count three full seconds before I watch the stone hit the water. Distracted by the small waves hitting the shoreline, I miss that Jacoby turns around and stalks back to the car.

To my side of the car.

He opens my door and, offering his hand, snaps at me to get out. All sorts of thoughts run though my head. Is he going to leave me here? Are we here so he can scream at me and nobody will hear us? Is he going to push me down that hill so nobody will ever see any evidence? Is he going to hurt me? Surely, he wouldn't hurt me. I've trusted him so many times before, but then again, he trusted me too, and look what happened.

Once out of the car, we stand an arm's length apart from one another. I cross my arms in front of me instinctively to protect myself, but Jacoby's hands are in his pockets. "Did you mean what you said?" he asks.

My eyes filled with unease, I try to respond. "I…Jacoby…"

"Answer me," he demands.

"I don't know what you want me to…"

"For Christ's sake, Jenna," he storms. "I NEED you to tell me if you meant what you said."

"YES! YES, I meant what I said!" I shout back, arms flailing. "I meant every goddamn word! From the fact that I think your father is a douchebag who treats you like shit, to the fact that I love you and don't care what anyone else fucking thinks! YES! I meant it! Alright?"

"God, dammit, you just said it again!"

"Said what?" My body starts to tremble. Why does this feel like history repeating itself? "Jacoby, you're scaring me." I cry.

"You said that you love me," he reveals.

"I do! I do love you! What's wrong with that?" I shout exasperatingly. "I'm sorry it came out of my mouth at a time when maybe you least expected to hear it, but you deserve to be told that someone loves you and for God's sake, that someone is ME!"

"I love you, too."

"I'm sorry that I hurt you today okay?" I continue shouting, the emotions finally pouring out of me, complete with the waterfall of tears. "I'm sorry that I potentially ruined your writing career." Sniffle. "I'm sorry that I had to freaking pee and got mixed up in whatever the hell kind of hot mess your brother has started." Sniffle. "I'm sorry your father showed up and rained on Charlie's parade." Sniffle. "And I'm sorry that I caused you to leave without saying goodbye to your family, and I'll completely understand if you just want to…"

"KitKat!" Jacoby interrupts, shifting forward and placing both his hands on my face, his thumbs wiping away my tears. Somewhere I missed that he calmed himself down, and now I'm all riled up.

"What?"

The shameless force of his mouth on mine takes me by surprise. I thought we were arguing here, and now, suddenly our tongues are twisting together, licking, tasting each other, in an emotionally fueled kiss that I never saw coming.

"I said, I love you, too," he confesses between breathes.

"What? Why? Stop it." I object, trying to push him away from me, but he just leans harder into me. "You can't love me right now."

"Oh, yes I can," he says.

"No, you can't. Please don't. I'm not good enough for you," I plead.

Jacoby chuckles endearingly as he rubs his hands up and down my arms. "Give me one reason why not."

"Because I vomit words out of my mouth like Linda Blair vomits pea soup in *The Exorcist*."

Trying to hold in his laugh at my outburst, Jacoby shakes his head, smiling. "KitKat, you could be a possessed, pea soup vomiting, trash-bag-diaper-wearing, taco-muncher and I would still love you."

"But I ruined your career." I cry.

"You didn't ruin anything, KitKat." His forehead falls to mine. "You set me free."

"What do you mean?" I sniffle.

"Jenna, you were right. You've been right all along, and I was just too scared of the unknown to do anything about it. There's no reason I can't tell people who I am. There's no reason a man can't write a great love story. There are many out there who do it every day. So, when you said what you did to my dad, you immediately made me realize that I don't need to hide anymore. I should never have put you in the position of having to keep such a stupid secret. It's not your responsibility. Who gives a shit what anyone in my family thinks? I'm a good person. I've always strived to be a good person and I let my father allow me to feel like I was never good enough; that what I did was never good enough."

I let Chad do the same thing to me.

"But you are good enough," I tell him.

"I know that now." Jacoby softly trails his fingers down my face. "I know it because you made me see it for myself. You did that, and let me tell you something. I don't mean to sound like a pussy but I've never had a girl…I don't know…stick up for me before. I mean – not that I've ever really needed it, or wanted it, but – I guess what I mean is, I've never had a girl show that much emotion for me before. It might have been the hottest thing I've ever seen."

"Jacoby." I sigh.

"Jenna," he whispers as his arms fold around my waist in a tight hug. The tightness of our embrace almost takes my breath away. "I love you Jenna Zimmerman." I try to respond but my words are choppy as his lips attach to the side of my neck, sucking, and kissing that favorite spot we girls all have right behind our ears.

"I…love…you…mmmm." Jacoby's lips are warm on my skin, causing tiny goose bumps to raise up on my arms. I feel his hands slip underneath me before he jacks me up like one of the cars in his garage, into his arms, wrapping my legs around his waist. His kisses are fierce but not frantic. His rough tongue is sinfully suggestive with its every move.

"I need you," he says to me as the hand he has near my neck reaches up into my hair. It's the best feeling in the world when he plays with my hair, but this time he pulls it just a tiny bit so I that I feel just enough pain to gasp as he simultaneously bites my bottom lip. "I'm going to take us somewhere where we can be alone okay?" He's not really asking, though I suppose I could object.

If I was an idiot.

With a rapid swiftness, Jacoby has opened my car door and lowered me down to my seat, all the while, continuing to lock his lips with mine. "I'm going to take us somewhere that nobody can interrupt us. No cell phones. No computers. Just us and our naked bodies and the ebb and flow of the ocean water."

The Jovi!

"I think that sounds perfect," I reply.

CHAPTER 18

Take Her Down Below

Jacoby

In less than five minutes we're pulling into a parking space and walking hand-in-hand on the dock toward The Jovi, my pride and joy that I share with my best friend, Jack. I lead Jenna onto the boat, motioning for her to have a seat up front on the benches. It only takes me a few seconds before I'm back with her, holding two glasses of wine.

"Hold mine for me for a second, okay?" I ask her.

"Sure." She smiles.

She watches me as I untie the boat from the dock, take my place at the Captain's chair, and turn the ignition. The Jovi roars to life and I'm all smiles as I navigate us through the other docked boats until we are free out on the water.

"You want to drive?" I offer once we're out farther into the sound.

"I don't really know how," she tells me, shaking her head.

"It's easy." I motion for her to join me. "Come on."

When she reaches me, she hands me my drink, which I effectively chug so that I can lose the glass. I wrap my arm around her, pulling her onto my lap and placing her hands on the wheel.

"It's not exactly like driving a car, but for the most part, it is. We're not close enough to land for you to crash anytime soon so I think we're okay." I joke. Thank God she laughs.

"This is so cool, Jacoby!" The warm evening wind hits our faces as the smell of salt water permeates my senses. I love the ocean, and I love being out here with someone who means the world to me. Finally, I can take a deep breath and relax knowing that I have her here with me, all to myself, for as long as she'll stay with me.

"Thank you for bringing me out here."

I hear her words, the sincerity in her voice, but I can't bring myself to answer her. Instead, I close my eyes and let my hands do all the talking. I slip them under her shirt, my warm fingers caressing her skin, immediately waking up the horn-ball in my body that's been dormant all day. Being with her at Charlie's party and not having my hands on her all day was much harder than expected, but now? Now it's just us. I dart my eyes around us as much as I can without being obvious to be sure that nobody is around. Thank God, we're alone in this part of the sound. I take my foot off the gas pedal to slow down the Jovi as my hands continue to explore the upper half of her exquisite body.

"Your skin is so soft, KitKat." I whisper in her ear as I trail kisses across the back of her neck. "I'll never get over how attractive you are, how you make me feel, how my body awakens every time you're near me." The heat of my hands on her cool skin causes her nipples to come out of hibernation. It only takes a light flick of my forefingers on two of the most sensitive parts of her body to send her into a scorching storm of desire. Her breathing quickens, her skin heats up and I can feel her melt against my chest. The guttural groan that escapes her tells me that I'm not the only one with primal urges.

Without hesitation or warning, I swiftly lift her shirt off, right here on the open water, where thankfully, we are very much alone.

Good Lord she is beautiful.

"Mmmm." She groans as my hands tighten around her breasts. I've never been one to try adult toys of any kind but damn if I'm not questioning what nipple clamps might look like on her. "Yessss..." She arches her back, pushing her chest away from me. It's a move that I'm certain heightens the sensation for her, but I have other plans. Rocking us forward on my lap, I clutch her even tighter against me.

"I want to feel you, Kit Kat. Turn around. Straddle me." When she turns around, she kicks off her sandals before straddling my lap, tightly warming herself against my chest.

Dammit, my balls.

She must see my wince as she moves against me, because she starts to back up off me, but I grab her again.

"No. It's okay," I say. "I just…need to make an adjustment." I wink and shift myself around until my dick is comfortable enough in these jeans. "Sorry." I chuckle. "It's just what you do to me."

"I'd like to do a lot of things to you, Jacoby." She purrs against my ear.

"Yeah?"

"Mmm hmmm," she replies as she wriggles her bottom half against mine. Her suggestiveness is irresistible. Hearing this woman tell my father, the one man in this world that I can't seem to please no matter what I do, that she loves me, and would love me regardless of what I have or don't have made my heart grow about six sizes larger today. It took all the control I could muster to not bend her over right there in the back yard and pump her full of everything I could possibly give her in return for the words she said.

I love him.

It's quiet out here with nobody around us. All I can hear besides the breathing of the beautiful girl sitting on my lap, is the lapping of the water as it hits the side of the boat. I kiss Jenna's lips softly once, twice, three times before nipping her bottom lip with my teeth. When she gasps, I don't hesitate to graze the inside of her mouth with my tongue. I want this moment of intimacy with her to be a promise to her. My promise of love, and commitment. The gentle tenderness of my tongue against hers promising her that I'll never hurt her. My breathing, in tandem with hers, a promise to her that she'll never have to feel alone. My hands gliding up her back and unsnapping her bra so that I can feel her body, my promise that I will cherish her and protect her. Like I've wanted to do for so long now. Like I've wanted to do since the first day I saw her standing behind the counter.

"I love you, KitKat." The words tumble easily from my mouth as she smiles against me.

"I love you too, Jacoby. Take me down below," she replies.

This time it's my turn to smile.

"What?" she asks, clearly not hearing her double entendre.

"Are you asking me to take you down *below*, or are you asking me to *take* you down below?" I shrug. "Honestly, regardless of how you answer, it's not going to stop me from feeling like I just won the lottery."

When she laughs at my question, her tits move up and down against my chest, and now there's no holding back. The untamed horn-ball inside me awakens with a heated groan. I have to have her. Clothes need to come off. Skin needs to be touched, and sucked, and licked, and kissed, for hours if we can stand it. Jenna's hands move down my chest until they reach the pulsing monster screaming to be freed from the confines of my jeans. Now I'm the one gasping.

Holy hell, she can keep her hand there all night.

"I'm asking you take me down *below,* so that you *can* take me down below." She smirks.

I clear my throat and shake my head at her, in awe of her lack of inhibition. "Yes ma'am." I steady her body in my hands and rise from my chair, carrying her down the steps to the cabin below. Without needing to turn on a light, because I know this cabin like the back of my hand, I lay her down gently on the bed along the back wall. She grabs at the bottom hem of my t-shirt, but I'm one step ahead of her as I reach behind me and pull my shirt up and over my head. I kick off my shoes and then bend over her as she arches her back so that I can easily slide off her jeans. It's too dark to see what kind of panties she's wearing since I didn't bother to turn off the light, but my fingers run across the soft satin material with what feels like lace on the sides.

Good Lord she's wearing lace.

I need to see this.

"KitKat, I need to turn on the light," I tell her.

"Are you okay?" Her high-pitched question full of concern.

"Hell yeah I'm okay, baby. I just need to see what you're wearing."

"Umm…no, it's…it's okay…you don't have to…" She stammers, but it's too late. I've switched the light on only to find her sitting up with her arms around her knees.

"Jenna?"

"I'm sorry...I…I knew…I shouldn't have worn them…" She shakes her head, her eyes filled with remorse and I think, embarrassment. I'm on my knees in front of her in the blink of an eye, my hands on her hands.

"Jenna, look at me." When her eyes find mine, I can tell they're filling with tears. My brain spins a mile a minute while I think of anything and everything I could've done just then to have upset her.

And then it dawns on me. "You made them."

She nods.

I take a deep breath, realizing that this is the first time she's ever worn one of her own creations for me, and I just called mega attention to it, like I didn't like what I was touching. Little does she know I was thinking the exact opposite.

"KitKat, I need you to understand something," I plead to her. "I need you to understand that I love you. I love everything about you, including the fact that you have an unbelievable talent for creating magnificent pieces of what I would call 'sexual art.' My fingers went from satin to lace, and call me old fashioned, but damn if I don't have an affinity for lacey things, so I just…wanted to see it."

She remains silent except for a light sniffle. It breaks my heart that she thinks I would think negatively of her at all. "I'm going to hold your hands, KitKat, and I'm going to help you lay back, okay?" I don't wait long for a response; instead, I squeeze her hands softly in mine so she knows I'm with her and lean her back against the mattress, keeping my eyes on her the entire time. I wait for her to give me a nod before swallowing the knot in my throat and allowing my eyes to divert to the beautiful piece of peach satin with cream colored lace hanging along her hips.

With a deep steadying breath, I'm able to mumble, "Dear God, I think I just found my kryptonite."

"You like it?" Her voice is timid.

"Like it?" I shake my head in complete fascination of her beauty. "KitKat, you wore a plastic garbage bag around your waist and I thought you were gorgeous, so this?" I trail my finger along the lace that goes from the side of her pelvis back around her hip. "This makes me feel like a teenage boy watching the Phoebe Cates scene from *Fast Times At Ridgemont High* for the first time."

"What's *Fast Times At Ridgemont High*? Is that a show?" Jenna shakes her head, perplexed. I can't help but chuckle.

"I'll tell you all about it later, but first, I need to get you out of these panties."

"So, you like doilies?" What had to have been some of the best sex of my life just ended not five minutes ago. With her head resting on my warm and now sweaty chest, her question takes me by surprise.

"Doilies?"

"Yeah, doilies," she responds.

"You mean like, those knitted circles that old ladies usually have all over their houses? Those doilies?" I confirm.

"Yeah, except I'm pretty sure they're not knitted. They're crocheted, but I'll give you a pass on that." Her fingers swirl around the top of my chest. How is she lying here so calmly after the sex we just had and asking me about doilies?

"Umm, well, I guess I never gave much thought to doilies before. Can I ask what spurred that question?"

She shrugs in my arms, smiling. "You said you had an affinity for lace, so, you know."

Ah. She's witty, this one.

"Touché, KitKat." I laugh, running my hands up and down her naked back. Her skin is smooth and warm to the touch. I could lull myself to sleep doing this. "I guess I should've clarified. I have an affinity for lacey undergarments, especially when the woman I love is wearing them. In fact, I think I'll keep the ones you were wearing."

She gasps as her head lifts off my chest. "If you take my panties, I won't have anything to wear home."

"Oh…" I smirk. "Damn. Whatever will you do?"

She laughs lightly and places a small kiss on my cheek. "I guess I'll be going commando then. That will feel great as the juices you just pumped me with trickle down my leg."

"Yes, well, welcome to the life of a teenage boy who blows his junk for the very first time and never sees it coming…pun unintended." I laugh with her.

"Oh my God! Does that really happen? I mean, seriously?"

"Sure does. Like a Mentos in a coke." I confirm. She breaks out into laughter and I can't help but smile at the sound of her giggle. If someone would've told me six months ago that I would soon be lying naked in bed with the girl I've had my eye on for at least that long, I would never have believed it. Life is good, but she showed me today that I can make it even better.

"Jenna, I want to go to New York," I spit out.

"Okay. What's in New York?" she asks.

"A book signing."

Resting her forearm on my chest, she props her head up to look at me while we talk. "A book signing for you?"

"Yeah. Remember the phone call I took that very first night I brought you back to the garage with me?"

"Mm-hmm. Double-O-Seven."

"Yeah. It was my agent trying to talk me into doing it but I firmly told him it was a no-go. There was no way I was ready to let the world know who I was," I explain.

"And you're ready now?" Her question should scare the shit out of me, but it doesn't. I don't know why. Maybe it's her. Maybe it's knowing I don't have to feel alone. Maybe it's knowing that she loves me regardless of my decision here. I smooth her hair back away from her face, taking in her beauty for a few seconds before I respond.

"Yeah. I think I am…if you promise to go with me."

She smiles and leans down to place a kiss on my chest, right above my heart. "It would be an honor and my pleasure Ashton Jacobs."

I kiss her on the top of her head. "It's a date then. I'll call my agent in the morning."

"Okay." She yawns, snuggling into the corner of my chest.

"KitKat?"

"Hmm?"

"Thank you…for today." She's silent and for a minute I'm not sure if she just doesn't know what to say or if she's already fallen asleep.

"I love you," she murmurs. I can already tell she's drifting to sleep. Her breathing evens out and her body feels heavier against my chest.

"I love you too, KitKat," I whisper before drifting off to sleep.

CHAPTER 19
Ashton Jacobs Has A Penis!

Jenna

It only took a little over twenty-four hours for Jacoby's agent to set up the signing in New York City with his publisher. The last few weeks have been a little more anxiety-driven for each of us as both of our important events approach, but so far, we've handled every twist and turn with ease and are now excitedly anticipating the epic event that is Ashton Jacobs' very first book signing. She has millions of fans and not one of them has ever gotten to meet the famous author. I can tell that Jacoby is nervous about how his fans are going to respond when they find out that *she* is actually a *he*. Call me naïve, but I tend to think they're going to go crazy – in a good way – when they see him. I mean, what's not to love? Dark hair? Beautiful eyes? A kick-ass body, and he writes about steamy sex? Umm, yes, please!

"Penny for your thoughts?" he inquires. I smile to myself because I don't want to tell him that I was just thinking about his sexy body that keeps me warm most nights, and his dreamy eyes that pierce my heart with every stare.

"The coastline is gorgeous this morning," I tell him instead. I may have been daydreaming about the likes of the sexy guy driving us to New York City, but telling him that may distract his driving and I'm excited to be able to spend the whole evening in the city with him before his big day tomorrow.

"Perfect, isn't it? I wish it weren't getting colder now. I love spending time on the Jovi," he responds. "Especially with you." His hand squeezes my knee ever so slightly.

"Sooo, I have a question," I tell him.

"Ok. Shoot."

"How do you get your ideas for all the steamy scenes in your books?" I ask.

Jacoby's head turns quickly toward me, I'm guessing, so he can judge my facial expression. "Uh, are you wanting to know if the sexual encounters I write about are ones I've actually had?"

"No. Not really."

Yes. Totally yes.

"Because they're not. So, if that's why you're asking you can calm down the voices in that beautiful head of yours." He laughs.

"Okay so they're not. Then how do you come up with them? Do you watch a lot of porn?"

Jacoby shrugs. "I don't know. I just, write what feels right I guess. I can't even tell you that I write all the words that I would say to a woman, because the characters I write about aren't me."

"What do you mean?" I prompt.

"I mean each character is their own person. They have their own personality, their own physical features, their own thoughts and fears, likes and dislikes. So when I'm writing, I have to think like that character would think. I have to respond the way they would respond, even if that means saying something I would never say personally out of my own mouth," he explains.

"So you've never actually had sex on the New York subway?"

Jacoby laughs, shaking his head back and forth. "No ma'am, I have not…but you have to admit, that was a pretty good scene."

"Uh, yeah. You could say that again." I smile.

"You know, we'll be there in a couple hours if you want to give it a go."

"Hahaha! I think I'll pass, thanks."

Shrugging again, Jacoby answers, "Suit yourself KitKat."

"So what if you were writing a book about me?" I ask him.

"You?"

"Well, us, I guess. A story about us," I respond. "What would you call it?"

Jacoby is silent for a couple minutes. I can tell he's pondering my question. I give him a few minutes while I, myself, try to come up with a good title.

"For the Love of Jizz." I suggest. "Ew, no. scratch that. How about *Jacked Up?"*

"Nope. Not right," Jacoby responds.

"Oooh" I giggle. "I have another one! How about *Jacoby's Jizz?"* I can't help but laugh at my own suggestions. This could be fun. I need a job where I come up with book titles all day long.

Jacoby squeezes my knee a little tighter. "Now there's something to think about. We can talk about my jizz anytime you want."

Suddenly, a sly looking smirk crosses his face. "I got it."

"Okay." I smile. "Let's hear it."

"I would call it *Hole-Punched*. It's the perfect double entendre for a romance book, particularly about you, if you know what I'm saying." He winks.

"Oh, my God! Hahaha! You are a huge goofball…and a genius because that's perfect! And I don't think I've ever told you this before, but I totally referred to your penis once as a grade-A hole punch."

Jacoby's eyebrows shoot up. "You did, eh? Is that written on a bathroom stall somewhere? Is my phone going to start ringing off the hook?"

"In your dreams, Mr. Malloy. The only people I know who know how good our sex is are Linda and Bethy. Girl talk, you know."

"Ah. Right, of course. Well, I'm happy to hear that you think my penis is grade-A. I'm going to assume that that's a good thing since you're still with me," he says.

"Yes, Jacoby. That's a very good thing." I lean over and kiss his cheek, yet unable to wipe the smitten smile off my face.

Last night was like another dream come true. I've been to the Big Apple many times, but only ever with my mom and sister, or some girlfriends. Never with the love of my life. We spent the entire day, doing touristy cliché things that I've never gotten to do. We held hands as we walked through Central Park. We ate bagels and hot dogs from corner vendors. I stood under a Broadway street sign and sang "Twinkle, Twinkle Little Star" so I could say I that I've sung on Broadway. I was even brave enough to let Jacoby feel me up on the subway since we had been joking about it earlier. Talk about foreplay. That little make-out session turned into some book-worthy shower sex a couple hours later, which then turned into second round hotel-bedroom sex after that. Seriously, this trip has been phenomenally fun and the signing is only about to happen. I'm pumped for Jacoby. I've had his hand all morning and hopefully have been a sense of calm for his anxious self. I can only imagine what's going through his mind, so I try not to intrude on his thoughts, but make sure that I'm here when he needs me.

"Are you ready for this?" I ask him when we reach the elevator of our building.

"Mmm-hmm," he answers. He's been chewing his fingernails all morning, a nervous habit that I hadn't noticed before. It's almost cute to see him so nervous, except things are usually the other way around. He's my rock when I'm an emotionally hot mess, but this time…it's my turn to be strong for him.

"You know being nervous is totally natural, right? It means you're passionate and you care very much about what you do. Great things never come from comfort zones," I remind him.

He ponders my words for a minute and repeats, "Great things never come from comfort zones. That's good. Where did you hear that? Did you just come up with that yourself?" he asks.

I shrug. "Saw it on Pinterest…doesn't mean it's not true." I wink as I squeeze his hand in mine, but he doesn't squeeze back.

He's more nervous than I thought.

"Jacoby?"

"Hmm?"

I step in front of him so that I can hold both of his hands and look him in the eye when I speak. "Every single person at your signing could boo you and walk away and it wouldn't change a damn thing about my feelings for you. I just want you to hear that come out of m…." I don't even get to finish my sentence before Jacoby backs me up against the wall of the elevator and fiercely kisses me, grabbing tightly to my sides and pulling me against his body. He stops just as abruptly as he started, resting his forehead against mine.

"I love you, KitKat. I love you more right now, in this moment, than I think I've ever loved anybody, and I need *you* to understand that I may meet a shit ton of people today, but there is nobody I would rather have lying next to me at the end of tonight, than you." He reaches up slightly to lay a soft kiss on my forehead and when he does, my left hand reaches up to his cheek so that I can hold his face.

"I love you too Ashton Jacobs. Now let's go kick ass and take names." The elevator doors open and we step out into the lobby of our hotel, just a couple of nobodies drawing no attention from passersby whatsoever. We step out on to the street to catch a cab that drives us to Fifth Avenue, coming to a halt right in front of New York Books, the city's largest commercial book store. We walk inside the gargantuan store, again, unnoticed by anyone, except for two men who look excited by our presence, or at least, Jacoby's presence.

"Jacoby." He greets us very professionally, shaking Jacoby's hand as we reach him.

"James. Good to see you again. I'd like to introduce you to my girlfriend, Jenna. Jenna, this is James Forlow, my agent."

"The man behind the ringtone." I smile as I offer my handshake.

A low chuckle comes from Jacoby before he explains to James. "007. Long story."

"Ah, yes. Perfect, obviously," James responds. "It's a pleasure to meet you Jenna." He gestures to the other man standing with him. "This is Matthew, the Events Manager here at the book store. He'll be taking care of you today."

"Hi," Matthew says, shaking our hands. "Pleasure to meet you, sir, ma'am. Why don't you guys come with me? I'll get you all set up and ready. I should probably warn you that there are no less than four hundred people downstairs anxiously awaiting your arrival."

"Four…hundred…" I murmur.

"Four hundred people want to meet me?" Jacoby asks, astounded. "Good Lord, I hope they're ready for what's coming."

James laughs. "No Jacoby, I think you have that backwards. Let's hope *you* are ready for what's coming."

We're led into a huge amphitheater type room inside the bookstore. I can hear the dull murmuring of voices on the other side of the wall. "We use this room for many of our forum talks when we host them, or for signings when we get someone like you to join us. I promise you, when I open the main doors, this room will be hopping," Matthew informs us. "There's plenty of water for you in the mini fridge located under the counter where you'll be seated, and if there's anything you desire while you're here, don't hesitate to ask."

"Thank you," Jacoby says. He inhales a deep breath and turns to me, squeezing my hand in his. "Are you ready for this, KitKat?"

"Ready for you to be ogled by hundreds of horny women who read your sex scenes over and over again?" I tease. "Bring it." With one last heart-stopping kiss, we both situate ourselves behind the counter where there are piles upon piles of Ashton Jacobs books.

Matthew nods to the sheets of paper lying on the counter. "I was going to have someone from the store be available to be your right-hand man, but…"

"She's got this." Jacoby winks at me.

Matthew laughs. "I'm sure she does. This is a pre-order list, Jenna. Just cross off the names as they pick up their books. Easy as that."

"Got it," I tell him. "Thank you."

"Alright, if you two are ready, let's get this show on the road, shall we?"

Matthew makes his way to the back of the room where the main doors are located. As soon as they open, a line of women make a beeline for the stage area where Jacoby and I are sitting. A woman, I'm guessing to be in her early thirties, is the first one to the table. She smiles broadly and hands me one of the four books she has in her hands.

"Would you please make it out to Heather?" she asks me. I look at her dumbfounded for a second before I shake my head, realizing that she thinks I am Ashton Jacobs. Without saying a word, I slide her book over to my right so that it's in front of Jacoby. He clears his throat, smiles, and greets the poor confused lady.

"Hi Heather. I'm Ashton Jacobs," he says proudly. "And you, are the very first person I have ever signed a book for in public." Her mouth hangs open as she looks from Jacoby to me, and then back to Jacoby, and then back to me.

"You're not Ashton Jacobs?" Her voice raises in pitch when she speaks to me.

"Nope. Sorry." I apologize, grinning. "I'm just the help. The one you want is this guy right here." I nod to Jacoby.

The next lady in line pokes her head over the first lady's shoulder. "Did you just say that he is Ashton Jacobs? Ashton Jacobs is a guy?"

"Yes ma'am. Ashton Jacobs does indeed have a penis." I announce to the laughter of many standing in front of us. Wincing, I cover my mouth with my hand, a little embarrassed to have just said that.

"Well holy crap on a cracker, you learn something new every day!" The lady exclaims. "I'm so glad to finally meet you Mr. Jacobs, and, I just need to tell you that your books light a fire in me that I didn't know needed stoked. Thank you so very much for your writing and for your message of love and passion and commitment. I've been reading your books for years. Never miss a single one."

"Well that deserves a hug!" Jacoby announces. "Thank you so much for coming here today to meet me, and for uh, being ok with the fact that I have a penis, I guess." He turns back to me and winks, making me blush all over again.

The news of who Ashton Jacobs really is travels like wild fire through the line of waiting women. I can watch it happen like a game of telephone, one woman turning to the one standing behind her to tell the now outed secret. The look of surprise on their faces humors me, as does the group of women who immediately whip out their compact mirrors to apply lipstick, fix their hair, check their complexion, and yes, even unbutton a few top buttons here and there. It takes a great deal of self-control to not roll my eyes at all of them.

I watch in awe as Jacoby sits for hours upon hours signing books, talking about his books, meeting fans, listening to them go on and on about their favorite characters, or scenes, or quotes. I can see how this world, this life, can become very overwhelming, especially for a man like Jacoby who has always remained hidden away in his private life. I have to imagine that traveling to New York City for this signing, thereby outing himself as an author, wasn't an easy decision to make, but I'm so proud of him for finally taking the leap so that he can be true to himself in all aspects of his life.

It's late in the day when the line to see Jacoby has finally dwindled down to a few remaining guests. The last woman in line, a timid looking girl with a slim frame, dark hair, and green eyes stands before Jacoby holding one book in her hands. I notice that she has a bandage wrapped around her left hand, and what look like a few small scars on her neck and face, but what stands out the most to me, is the look in her eye. It's one I know I've seen before. It's an expression that looked back at me one day when I looked in the mirror.

"Hello there," Jacoby greets her. "Thank you so much for waiting all this time. You must've been here for hours."

The woman smiles meekly as she nods. She looks between Jacoby and me before looking back down at the book in her hands. It's a copy of *Falling To Pieces*, one of my favorite books of his. "I don't mind the wait, Mr. Jacobs." She says almost too quietly to hear her. "You saved my life."

Jacoby turns his head toward me momentarily before turning back to the woman. "I'm sorry? I don't understand." He shakes his head slowly back and forth.

The woman clears her throat. "My name is Summer, and I live at the Safe Horizon House not too far from here with my two children." Her eyes begin to well up with tears. "Three weeks ago, my kids and I left our home for what we could only pray would be a safer environment than what we were in. My husband drinks, you see. And sometimes, he drinks too much and when that happens..." She doesn't need to finish her sentence before Jacoby is up out of his chair, taking Summer by the hand and leading her to his seat. We don't have to say the words to know that when she says Safe Horizon, she's talking about a battered women's shelter. Not knowing what else to do to for her in this very moment, I grab a bottle of water from the cooler beside us and hand it to her.

"Thank you." She smiles and takes a small sip before continuing her explanation. "It was your book, Mr. Jacobs. I had just finished reading a book that had been gifted to me, a copy of *Falling to Pieces*, the night my husband came home drunker and angrier than anything I had ever seen before. He never used to be like that." She whimpers. "We had such a happy marriage, but when he lost his job, depression took over, and he never recovered. But that night...that night it wasn't me he went after." She sniffles. "It was my children."

A small gasp escapes me as my heart fills with empathy for this beautifully brave woman. "That was it for me, Mr. Jacobs," she says, wiping tears off her face. "I had just read Tina's story of strength and hope during a time in her life that eerily mirrored my own and all I could think about was that if she could take the leap, I could too. I could finally tell myself that I deserved better than a life of pain and fear. My kids deserved better than a life of pain and fear. I was strong enough to take the slaps and the punches and the shoves and the hurtful words from my husband, but I couldn't let him touch my kids, so we left the minute he fell asleep, just like Tina did in your book. They all grabbed a few items, their favorite stuffed animals and a change of clothes and we were out the door."

I watch Jacoby's expression as she talks, but I can't read him. He seems stunned. "Summer," he says, crouching down in front of her, holding her hand. "Does your husband know where you are? Are you safe now?"

"Yes, sir." She nods. "My kids and I are safe. I don't know if he's looking for me or not. We try to keep a pretty low profile and Safe Horizons moved us to a different location so we're farther away from him."

Jacoby assesses her before asking, "He did this to you?" I can tell he wants to beat the shit out of the man who hurt her, but he keeps himself calm for her sake.

"Yes, sir, but I'm okay now. I'll be fine. When I heard at the library that you were going to be in town for this event, I knew I had to try to get here to thank you in person. Your words gave me strength, and they continue to give me hope that a better, happier life is out there for me and my kids."

"I – I don't even know what to say, Summer," Jacoby stammers.

"Honestly," she sniffles. "I thought I was coming here to thank a woman and to talk to her about my story, but to know now that it was a man who wrote Tina's story…" She shakes her head back and forth flabbergasted. "Well, it means even more to me now. It's nice to know that there are men out there who have the ability to show compassion, and love."

Jacoby gives her a comforting smile. "Summer, I'm so…I…I'm so sorry for all you've gone through. For what your kids have gone through, what they continue to go through. I want to do something to help. Do you have a plan? What happens next now that you're out?"

"No, no, Mr. Jacobs." She argues. "I didn't come here for anything other than your signature on this book and to say thank you from the bottom of my heart for saving my life, and for saving my kids' lives. We're going to be just fine once we figure out what comes next."

"Do you have a job?" Jacoby asks her.

She nods. "Yes. I'm on staff at the Children's Museum. I've been there twelve years now. They're very good to me there. My job used to be relatively high profile in terms of community involvement but since I've had to tell my boss what's been going on, she gave me some paid time off and then helped move my job away from being involved with the community so my husband couldn't find me."

Jacoby pulls his wallet out of his back pocket, opens it, and fishes out a white business card with blue wording on it. "I want you to take this." He says offering her the card. "It's a close friend of mine. He's a lawyer and can help you with anything you might need, questions you may have. Anything. Anything at all. It's all pro-bono."

"Umm…thank you," she says softly, taking the card into her hand.

"How old are your kids?" I ask her.

"My son, Alex, is seven and my daughter, April, is ten." She smiles. "They're my life. My everything."

I watch as Jacoby pulls money out of his wallet, a small amount of crisp one hundred dollar bills. "Please, take this too," he says, handing her the money.

"Oh no." She shakes her head adamantly. "Please, Mr. Jacobs, I really didn't come here for this."

"I know you didn't, Summer. You came here to thank me, but what you don't realize is that I should be thanking you," he explains.

"Thanking me? For what?"

"I wasn't going to do this event. I was content to never come out to the public about who I really am…a man writing under a female penname. I was perfectly fine living a life of solitude, until this girl…" he says, pointing to me, "She convinced me to be proud of who I am regardless of what some may think. So, I took the leap and here I am…and now here *you* are…standing here in front of me, coming all this way just to thank me for my words." He shakes his head, overwhelmed with emotion. "You have no idea how much your presence here today means to me. You, Summer, you made my decision to come here today totally worth all the anxiety, so please, let me help you just a little bit. If not for yourself, then for your children. Christmas will be here before you know it. Take this and get whatever you need; clothes, food, a night out to the movies. Whatever you want. Please."

All three of us look at one another, tears rolling down our cheeks. Summer lifts her hand slowly to accept Jacoby's gift. He places the bills in her hand and folds his hand over top. "Thank you." She cries. "Just – thank you."

"Thank *you,* Summer. I'm so proud of you. Tina would be so proud of you for being strong enough to escape your hell. You're not alone. You'll never be alone in this new life. Remember that."

After what ended up being an emotionally charged afternoon, Jacoby and I finally make our way back to our hotel, too physically and emotionally exhausted to do much of anything.

"I'm starving. How about a shit ton of room service, a bottle of wine, and a hot bath?" he suggests.

"I think that sounds like heaven." I watch him unload his pockets onto the dresser in our room. "You okay? You've been kind of quiet since we left the bookstore."

"Yeah, I just…" He plops himself on the edge of the bed. "I had no idea."

"No idea about what?"

"I had no idea that readers really took words so seriously, you know? I mean they're just stories. Love stories. I thought women just wanted steamy sex scenes and short plots, or maybe the occasional dramatic storyline that still included hot sex. I never in a million years thought that someone would thank me for saving their life, that my words might inspire someone or touch them in an emotional way."

Sitting next to him on the edge of the bed, I reach up and run my hand down the left side of his head. "A lot of people probably think that romances are nothing but smutty stories for soccer moms, but they're wrong. At least, mostly wrong. I imagine there are some poorly written smutty books out there for those who are looking for them, but for the most part, romances are filled with just the right amount of angst, and passion, and raw emotion, and maybe even a little bit of laughter for the stories to feel completely real to many readers. It has to be the greatest feeling in the world, for someone like Summer to talk to you like she did today."

"Humbling," he mutters.

"Yeah. I'm sure it is, but you've never been anything but humble in this endeavor, Jacoby. I'm so proud of you for going through with the signing. Oh! And I almost forgot to show you." I pull my cell phone out of my back pocket and open up my Twitter app. "Look! You're trending on Twitter! You get to officially be you, now!" I close the app after letting him read a few of the posts, and open the camera on my phone. Holding the phone up in front of us, I lean toward him so I can snap a selfie of the two of us.

Jacoby chuckles. "You want to see trending?" He grabs my phone and tosses it on my bag laying on the floor. He places a hand in the middle of my chest and pushes me down onto the bed and rises over me. "I'll show you something worth being a trending topic," he says as his lips connect with mine.

CHAPTER 20
Tainted
Jenna

Time flies when you're having fun, or in my case, when you're so insanely busy you don't have time to eat, or sleep, or breathe, because the biggest event of your life is coming up way faster than you ever imagined. October has been a whirlwind of activity as Bethy and I work every waking minute on the designs being used for the upcoming bridal fashion show. Tomorrow is the big day. I've had nervous flutters in my stomach all week anticipating the doors that could open for us with this event. It's the biggest bridal show in the state, so it's bound to attract a lot of people. Daydreaming about it is fun and all, but only makes me more nervous. To top off my anxiety, something is going on down below this morning that has me questioning if I might have cancer of the inner-thigh – if that's even a thing. What started out as a small pimply bump - in a place where girls don't like pimply bumps - is quickly growing into an invasive tumor-like thing. I tried to take a quick break to check and see what's going on but was called to the copy center for help with a project so my possible inner-thigh cancerous tumor will have to wait.

"OOOOh! That one is a keeper!" I'm distracted from my daydream when the old woman standing at the counter speaks up again. She found me working at the copy center about fifteen minutes ago and asked me to print some emails for her that contained documents about plantar fasciitis for the nursing home where she worked. I handed her the order, but she just huddled over her phone at the customer self-service desk telling me she would have a few more emails to send me for printing.

"Okay young lady," she says to me in what sounds like an old lady southern accent. "I'm gonna send you just a few more now. Some pictures." I open one email and soon hear the alert to three, four, and then finally ten more emails. "I just want a single print of each, please, darlin'."

"Yes Ma'am," I reply. I finish her printing order and hand her the small package of pictures, watching as she flips through them again and again, giddy and laughing. "It looks like it was a fun party." I smile.

"Yeah, it does," she replies.

"Was it a family reunion?" I follow up as I ring out her transaction at the register.

"Oh, you know, I'm not sure. I don't know these people. I just found these pictures on that Faceweb thingy and thought they looked like such nice people. I'm going to hang them up in my house!" she says, taking her receipt from my hand. "Thank you Darlin'. You have yourself a nice day." All I can do is stand here, slack jawed, as I watch her take her prints and head for the door.

What in the hell just happened?

"Jenna, you're needed at the tech-desk please," Linda says in my ear. She's obviously standing in front of a customer since she used my real name.

"On my way." I tell her before walking across the store to where Linda is standing with a bemused looking gentleman in a business suit.

Fantastic. He probably can't remember a password.

"Jenna here should be able to help you, sir. Have a good day," Linda says before winking at me and walking away.

BEEP, BEEP, BEEP! RED FLAG! RED FLAG! Linda never walks away from a good -looking guy no matter what he's wearing, and she certainly wouldn't throw him at me knowing that I'm very much taken. Something is up. Am I being punked?

"Hi there. I'm Jenna. What can I do for you?" I offer.

"Well I brought in my laptop and my wife's laptop. I was hoping you could help me out," he starts.

"Sure. What seems to be the problem?"

"Well I started watching uhh…well…some porn this morning on my laptop," he whispers. "Only it locked up on me and quit."

"Okay," I say.

"But, I wasn't done watching, so I opened my wife's laptop so I could, you know, finish, except then her laptop locked up on me too, and now I can't use either of them."

You have got to be kidding.

I am being punked.

"Hahahaha! That's a good one," I say. Hitting the button for my ear piece I say, "Good one Linda." I'm still laughing when I look over to the copy center where Linda took my place to see her shaking her head back and forth with a serious look on her face. She nods past me, causing me to look back at my customer who isn't laughing.

Not even a little bit.

"Please, I need your help," he begs. "My wife hates when I watch porn and she'll kill me if she finds out that I locked up her laptop. She needs it for her second job."

Oh God. I'm not being punked. This is real. Is it a full moon or something?

"Oh, my God, I'm so sorry, I thought…" I turn my head toward Linda once more. "Never mind what I thought. Yes, sir, I can help you. I can run a virus scan on both computers, I'll just need you to pay the service fee for both before I do anything."

"Sure. Yeah. No problem." He reaches into his wallet.

Once I ring out his transaction, and because we're a little dead tonight and I have time, I hook up both of his laptops to begin scanning and removing any viruses. From looking at his credit card, I've learned that this good looking perv's name is Tim Johnson.

Oh, the irony.

"Hey, while you're working on that, can I ask you another question?" Tim asks.

"Absolutely."

"When I'm watching porn on my phone, like when I'm in the can or something like that, and that little box pops up that says I won a new iPhone, should I click it?"

I love my job. I love my job. I love my job.

There's a flurry of activity happening in my house right now. Garments are being tagged, covered, hung, and categorized for tomorrow's fashion show. Bethy is crunching numbers over in the corner of the room, Jacoby and I have been packing inventory and labeling everything I'll need for my models, and Linda has been stuffing food into my mouth every time I walk to her side of the room, which, I might add, has become increasingly more painful throughout the day because of this inner-thigh-now-raging-tumor thing growing ever closer to my lady bits. I'm trying not to freak out because I know, after some quick research, that it's just an ingrown hair but holy shit, an ingrown hair…THERE…is not something I wanted to be dealing with right now, the night before the biggest day of my life. It's now easily the size of a silver dollar with a bubble forming that I can only imagine will end in a disgusting eruption of God only knows what.

"Take another bite," Linda demands, forcing a fork into my mouth. "Can't have you getting hangry on us. The night is young."

"Thanks Linda," I say through my stuffed mouth. "It's great by the way." Homemade macaroni and cheese has always been a comfort food for me. It's just what I need to keep me going for a while.

"Ok KitKat, this box is sealed, labeled, and ready to go," Jacoby announces.

"Great. That makes four down, one more to go." I tell him as I awkwardly head to the last box, picking it up and placing it on the coffee table in front of me. Grabbing my clip board to check my notes on what needs packed next, I go to sit next to the box, but end up yelping in pain as I spring up from the coffee table, alarming everyone in the room.

"What's wrong Jizza? Did you sit on a pair of scissors or something?" Linda asks amused.

"No. I'm fine. It's fine." I wince at the sharp pain I had just felt.

"What's fine?" Jacoby asks.

"I'm fine." I repeat, feeling a little frustrated and a whole lot embarrassed. "Everything's fine. It's fine. Fine. Okay?"

"Then why are you wincing, Jizz?" asks Linda.

"I'm not wincing?"

"You totally winced," she argues.

"What did you do to her Jacoby?" Linda winks. "A little too hot and heavy last night?" She gasps. "Oh my gosh, did you two just get it on before we even got here? That so…"

"OH MY GOSH, STOP! It's a TAINT TUMOR okay? I have a fucking TAINT TUMOR and it hurts like a damn bitch and there's nothing I can do about it right now so can we please get back to work?" I shout.

The room is silent as my eyes move from Linda, to Jacoby, to Bethy at the back table. Each of them is staring at me like I just spoke a different language. Bethy is the first one to crack and starts cackling, she's laughing so hard.

"What the hell, Jenna? A taint tumor? Is that what you said?" She laughs more. "'Cause I'm pretty sure there's no such thing." I watch as she grabs her phone off the table to undoubtedly Google the term taint-tumor.

Linda scrunches her face, but continues to chuckle. "Whatever the hell a taint-tumor is, it doesn't sound good. What is that? Like, a hemorrhoid or something? You have 'roids?"

"No. I don't have 'roids." I huff, tossing my clipboard onto the couch. I catch sight of Jacoby who is trying damn hard to not laugh at me, but also seems a bit confused.

Ugh!

"It's just an ingrown hair," I explain.

A collective and understanding "Oooh" is given by Bethy and Linda. Every female who shaves must have experienced an ingrown hair at least once in her life. It's not fun. Finally, they get it, even though neither one of them has stopped laughing.

"You have an ingrown hair on your taint?" Linda asks looking horrified. "You're a taint-shaver? How have I never known?"

Jacoby chokes on the water he just sipped from the bottle in his hand. "Wait, what? Are we really talking about KitKat's taint?"

"No," I say, while Linda says, "Yes. Yes, we are."

"Would someone please tell me what's going on?" Jacoby pleads. "What do you mean you have an ingrown hair on your taint?"

"Ugh! It's not really on my…" I start with a huff and then take a deep breath to continue. "I shaved okay? I shaved all over because I thought that after tomorrow we might want to celebrate only…only now I have this ingrown hair that is on my inner thigh, like, deep back in my very inner thigh, and it's done nothing but grow all day like the hugest pimple I've ever seen, and I really want to just squeeze the shit out of it, but I'm going to have to be in the shower when I do, because OH MY GOD, I really don't know what might happen, but I'm pretty sure it might be like having a mini vagicano on my thigh!"

I watch Jacoby's facial expression contort from serious concern to outright hilarity, by the time I'm done explaining myself to him. "I'm sorry." He laughs "I'm sorry. I don't mean to laugh. You're obviously in some pain, but damn if you're not the cutest thing right now."

"Girl, you should go put a band-aid on that sucker," Linda suggests.

"Linda!" I shout. "It would be like putting a band-aid right along my ass-crack! Do you know how much that is going to hurt?" I ask her, but I may as well not be talking. All three of them are laughing again.

I get it. I can see the humor in my situation enough to allow myself to chuckle with them, but seriously, I have to do something before tomorrow or I will be miserable all day.

"Come on, Jizza. I'll help you figure out a solution." Linda grabs me by the hand and leads me towards my bedroom.

"Hold up!" Jacoby asserts. "I believe KitKat's taint or anything in that general area belongs to me." He winks. "I'll be more than happy to help her take care of it."

"No." I shake my head. "Jacoby, you don't have to do…"

"Stop right there, babe. Whatever it is you were going to say, you're wrong."

"How do you know what I was going to say?" I huff.

"You were going to say that it's gross and you don't want me to have to see it because it's nasty and it's a turn off blah, blah, blah, am I right?" He shrugs. "But no matter what, that's where you're wrong, because love isn't always hearts, and flowers, and sex, and rainbows, and all that shit you read about in Hallmark cards. Sometimes love is holding your hair back while you puke, or listening to you have the Hershey squirts in the middle of the night because you ate the mushrooms anyway, and sometimes, sometimes love means helping out with taint tumors, so come on. Let's go see what we're dealing with before Mount St. Jenna erupts all over the place."

I'm smiling so hard that I don't notice Linda picking her jaw up off the floor. "I don't know about you, but I'm pretty sure sexier words have never been spoken," she whispers to me.

"I have to agree," I whisper back before Jacoby takes my hand, squeezes it, and leads me down the hall.

CHAPTER 21
Top Drawer
Jacoby

The fashion show has been an astounding success so far. When Jenna asked me to accompany her here, my mind pictured something to the effect of one of those community craft shows my mom used to take us to when we were little, only with women wearing dresses with big bows and puffy sleeves. I guess, being an unmarried man, I never pay much attention to the wedding scene, nor to how many ladies flock to this city just to watch models walk down the runway. I guess I shouldn't be surprised. I hear it's all out chaos in New York City during fashion week, why shouldn't this be the same way, just on a slightly smaller scale? Since before the show started, I've been backstage with Jenna as she fits each model with the appropriate piece of beautifully made lingerie. I watched as each girl floated up and down the runway showing off Jenna's art to an impressive and excited crowd. And since the show has ended, I've gotten to be the proud partner, holding her hand, kissing her temple, handing her another glass of champagne and standing with her as prospective mentors and industry professionals chat with her about her lingerie line. I don't think I could be prouder.

Seeing semi-naked women waltzing down a runway in exquisite lingerie should've given me a woody to end all woodies. What guy doesn't want to study the merchandise when he sees a Victoria's Secret model on TV? To my surprise though, I'm more turned on by the fact that each of those beautiful pieces of fabric art were thought up and designed by my girl. The detailed designs that spring from her head and end up on the female body are a wonder to behold. I don't know how she does it, but I'm so proud of her for being unique, and chasing her dream.

"In case I don't get to tell you a couple hundred times tonight, you did a fabulous job," I whisper into her ear.

"Thank you, Jacoby." She blushes. Feeling the warmth of her hand in mine makes me want to hold on to her all night long, or better yet, push her up against a wall and give her a hole punch that she won't soon forget, but I know this is a professional event for her. People are interested in her tonight. They want to talk to her, listen to her, and learn about her. It's Jenna's night to shine and she is indeed sparkling. I'm simply the rock she can lean on if or when she needs me.

"Jenna!" We're just about to meet up with Bethy and Linda when a woman calls to Jenna from a few feet away, her hand in the air waving. I recognize her, but can't recall her name. She's the owner of the boutique where Jenna sells her pieces.

"Leslie!" Jenna calls to her.

That's right. Her name is Leslie.

"Is everything okay?" Jenna asks her as Bethy and Linda approach us to give their congratulations to Jenna. "Do you need help with something at the booth?"

Leslie smiles broadly. "No! Well, that is, not unless you have an extra fifty pieces hanging around to sell, because we sold out of everything!" she exclaims.

"WHAT?" All three girls shout simultaneously. "That's incredible!" They all jump up and down excitedly. I must admit, their excitement is contagious, and in Jenna's case, it's ridiculously cute.

"I know, right? As soon as your portion of the show was over, ladies were flocking there to get their hands on anything they could. And FYI, the black corset piece…genius! Everyone wants one. They love the pink ruffles! Nicely done!"

"Oh, my gosh, Leslie, thank you so much for all of your help," Jenna gushes.

Beth shakes her head stunned. "I can't believe we sold out! There was a ton of inventory."

"Well I can believe it." Linda winks. "That shit would make a possessed Linda Blair look like a fucking sex goddess."

She doesn't know why, and maybe she never will, as it was a moment just between us, but Jenna and I look at each other at Linda's mention of Linda Blair and bust out in laughter.

"What's so funny?" Linda asks.

"Nothing," I tell her. "Inside vomit joke."

"Excuse me, Ms. Zimmerman?" We turn to find a man and a woman standing before us, dressed immaculately in what can only be described, by me, as very expensive suits.

"Uh, yes. Yes, that's me. I'm umm. I'm Jenna Zimmerman," she responds, looking a little star-struck. Okay, a lot star-struck.

The woman extends her hand to Jenna. "My name is Melinda Wexing, I'm a buyer and the Director of Design for…"

"Top Drawer." Jenna interrupts her, shaking her hand. I can see the blush of embarrassment creeping up her cheeks. "I'm sorry. I didn't mean to interrupt you. It's just that, well, I'm sure you know that your reputation precedes you. The Top Drawer Lingerie Boutique is the most well respected lingerie company in the country. We used to study the company when I was in school."

Melinda smiles warmly. "Ah, I'm glad to see that you are as excited to meet us as we are to meet you."

"Absolutely," Jenna replies.

"Your part of the fashion show today was tremendous, Ms. Zimmerman. You really have an eye for detail and your designs are like nothing we've ever seen before in the lingerie world, and trust me when I say, we've seen some pretty out-there ideas." She winks.

"Thank you very much." Jenna looks shocked to even be speaking to these people.

"If you're not already in contract negotiations with another company, we would like to set up a meeting with you about purchasing your line. Honestly, even if you are already in contract talks with someone else, I would still like to meet with you."

"No, I – uh - I mean, no, I haven't talked to anyone yet about the line," Jenna stammers.

"Great. We would also like to extend you the invitation of interning with our company. You're just the kind of person we are looking for to join our team of designers. In many cases our internships turn into full time positions in the company." Melinda tells her. I watch as Jenna's jaw practically hits the floor and tears well up in her eyes. This is an opportunity of a lifetime for her.

"Oh, my God, that's wonderful!" She cries. "I'm honored. Truly, I'm … I'm more than appreciative that you would even consider me for an opportunity like this, but…"

But?

She said but?

"The Top Drawer is in New York City. Obviously, I would be expected to relocate to the city for a job like that, correct?"

"Naturally, yes." Melinda says. "We would like to have you with us in New York City. For someone with your career aspirations, that's where you would want to be anyway to find your success. We could show you around some of the safer neighborhoods, help you find a place, get you settled, of course."

I can see the sparkle and excitement leave Jenna's eyes as I catch on to what she must be thinking. She doesn't think she can leave Mystic. Her family and friends are here.

She would be leaving me.

Like hell she's leaving me.

"She'll take it." The words expel themselves from my mouth before I even realize I opened it. I think I just word-vomited for the very first time. Is this what it feels like? Everyone's eyes fly to me, standing there like we're having an everyday conversation about who is going to get milk on the way home.

"What?" Jenna says, tears in her eyes. "Jacoby, I can't take the job. I can't just up and leave Mystic."

Linda and Beth both gasp simultaneously. "Why not?" they ask her.

"Jizza don't be stupid" Linda whispers. "This is your big shot! It's what you've always wanted."

"I…I don't think I…"

"We'll do it together," I interrupt.

"What?" she asks, her eyes growing huge.

"Marry me, KitKat." Fuck! I just did it again with the word vomit, but damn if I'm not crazy in love with this girl. I would be stupid to let her leave for New York City without me by her side.

"Wait, what? Are you even serious right now?" She's looking at me like I'm goddamn crazy.

"I don't have a damn ring. I'm sorry. We'll go pick one out together or something. Obviously, I didn't plan to do it this way, but yeah, I'm serious. Marry me, and we'll do this together. We'll take the leap. We'll move to the city. I'll keep my place here so we can always come back for the weekend. It's only a couple hours. I can write from anywhere and there's no way I'm letting you go to New York City without being my wife, so just say yes and let's get this show on the road. You made me see how important it was to be true to myself and show the world who I was. This is your dream, KitKat. Show the world who Jenna Irene Zimmerman is. Don't throw it away so easily." Whoa…now that was some word vomit. I think she's beginning to rub off on me.

"Sooo…is that a yes?" Melinda says with a smirk on her face and a tilt to her head.

Jenna's eyes haven't left mine since I started talking. There are beads of tears sliding down her beautiful cheeks but she hasn't stopped staring at me, nor I at her. It's as if our souls are connecting, binding themselves to each other, amongst the chaos that is this day.

"Yes," I hear her whisper. "Yes, I'll marry you."

"And?" I prompt her.

She smiles, wiping the tears off her face with her hands. "And I'll take the job." She turns to Melinda who is smiling as well. "I'll do it. Thank you so much for the offer."

"Fantastic," she says. "We'll get started at the beginning of the new year so that you have time to tie up loose ends around here, and get situated in the city. I'll have paperwork emailed to you in the meantime so you can read through a few things."

"Sounds great. Thank you, again. I'm honored, really," Jenna tells her.

"It was a pleasure to meet you Jenna." Melinda extends her hand to shake Jenna's. "I'll be in touch with you soon. Congratulations to you both, and once you're in the city, I know a great place to look for that ring." She winks, making us both laugh.

"It's a deal," I tell her. We watch Melinda and her silent assistant walk away, at which point Jenna turns, throwing herself at me, nearly knocking me off balance.

"I love you Jacoby Malloy. I love you so much," she says in my ear. I wrap my arms around her, squeezing her as tightly as I can without hurting her. This feeling right here, the feeling of her warm body against mine, the feeling of comfort we both get from our embrace, the feeling that all our life's excitement could end tomorrow and she would still love me, it's worth everything to me.

"I love you too, KitKat. There is nobody I would rather take the leap with than you. I'm so damn proud of you."

"Well isn't this just the best day any of us could have asked for?" Linda announces. "Jacoby came out of the author's closet and is still just as successful and loved as ever, Beth and Jizza are going to make a shit-ton of money from the sale of their lingerie line, Jenna is chasing after her dream, and I have a hot date tonight!"

When I let go of Jenna she turns to Linda, astounded to be hearing Linda's latest news. "You what? You have a date? You didn't tell me you had a date!"

"Yeah well, I do!" Linda responds.

"With who?" she asks.

"A super mega hot guy named Jack. He's kind of quiet, a little quirky, but different from most of the guys I've dated before. I'm kind of excited."

"Quiet, quirky, hot guy named Jack…" I repeat. "I bet his last name is Schmidt." I elbow Jenna and she laughs.

Linda's jaw flies open. "As a matter of fact, it is Schmidt. You know him?"

I can't help but laugh. "Know him? I grew up with him! He's my best friend."

"Shut up. You're joking," Linda says.

I pull out my phone, hit the home button and pull up a picture of Jack and I together. "Is this the guy you're seeing tonight?"

Linda's hand flies to her forehead. "Yeah. It is. Holy shit! How did this happen? Oh, my God. Did you plan this? Did you plan for us to meet? You totally did, Malloy, didn't you?"

Continuing to laugh I answer her. "No ma'am, I did not. I swear. Where did you two meet?"

"Uh…" Linda blushes. "On an online dating site."

"What?" Jenna laughs. "Since when?"

"I know, I know. It's not my usual M.O. but I was bored one night and thought I would give it a try just for shits and giggles. It was actually something I was going to have us both do before this guy hole-punched his way into your life," she says. "Anyway, then I was matched with him and we've been talking, and one thing led to another, and once we learned we were in the same town we knew we wanted to see what happens. I mean, it'll be fine, right? He's hot. He seems nice, and if I'm lucky, I may even get laid!" She winks at Jenna.

"Mmm…I don't know about that," I tell her.

"What do you mean?"

"Nothing. You just don't know Jack Schmidt," I tell her.

She listens to my words but stops short of responding and cracks up laughing instead.

"What's so funny?" I ask her.

"You don't know Jack Schmidt! That's what's funny!" She snorts. "Sounds like you're saying…hahaha you know what? That would make a great title for your next best seller."

You don't know Jack Schmidt.

Yes. Yes, it would.

The End

Acknowledgements

Writing a romantic comedy is fucking hard. It's hard to be funny, or even want to be funny when your day just isn't going the way you want it to. I felt like this book took me a long time to write because life just kept happening, but in the end, I'm happy with the final product! Writing this taught me many things that I'm happy to have learned. Most importantly, writing teaches me each and every time that it takes a village. It's never just a one-woman show. At least not for me. I couldn't even begin to do what I love without the help and support of those in my inner book circle. I owe you ALL a great deal of thanks.

Kandy, I still don't know the right things to have a PA do, but regardless, you are badass at doing all of the things that never even cross my mind. Thank you for throwing yourself into Facebook jail just for me! Haha! I owe you a drink…or six! Seriously, you're the perfect addition to our little team.

Nikki Rose, you make my words pretty and for that I am SUUUPER thankful! I don't write with any type of format. I simply type words on paper and somehow, from that hot mess, you put things together for me in a way that still keeps my voice real and sincere. (Fyi to my readers, my editor doesn't edit my acknowledgements…can you tell?) Thank you for the countless hours of conversation shooting ideas and thoughts back and forth. Also, you're a much prettier book bitch than my husband!

Samantha, as if you needed another thing on your plate this year, you took time to compile all of the whacky cover ideas I had and came up with something that I love! I know it sounds crazy being a romance writer, but I'm a firm believer (because I have a young impressionable daughter) that romance books don't have to have nearly naked people on the covers for them to be good. That's my goal every time when I think about a cover, and you, once again, helped pull off the perfect idea! Thank you so much for being willing to stretch the limits and for encouraging me to do the same!

Brandi, I also believe that people walk into your life for a reason, but I have no fucking clue why you walked into mine. Oh wait…yes, I do. You needed a pen and so I graciously gave up mine for you, and thus started a blooming love/hate-ship ☺ Just kidding. I adore you and I'm so glad you're now in my life. I'm hereby announcing to the world that you are the newest member of the Susan Renee Book Bitches. Welcome to our group. Sit down and stay a while, but don't you dare touch my fucking pen.

Doug, I know I'm a pissy bitch sometimes. I blame Brandi, (see above), but I can't tell you how much I appreciate you for encouraging me to keep doing what I'm doing. You tell me to trust my gut, put my faith in my circle of book friends and to never look back. You hug me when I'm frustrated and you talk out plot lines with me like it's every day conversation. I'm always grateful for you and love you more than words can ever say.

To my readers, I continue to do this because you write to me and tell me how excited you are to read "whatever is next." I do this because you all keep me laughing and you all keep me real. I do this because I want to give a voice to all those out there who don't feel like they have one. Thank you for reading my words. Thank you for leaving your reviews, for sharing my social media posts, for stopping by my tables and getting to know me, for EVERYTHING that you do. It absolutely does NOT go unnoticed and I'm honored to be a part of a world of people such as yourselves who just want to snuggle under a blanket with a good book once in a while. I love you all more than my words could ever say. Thank you.

About the Author

Susan Renee wants to live in a world where paint doesn't smell, Hogwarts is open twenty-four/seven, and everything is covered in glitter. An indie romance author, Susan has written about everything from lawn mowers to thick colossal bottles of wine, and has won a Snuggle Buddy award for her nonfiction book, *The Hula Hoop Tester's Guide to Jumping*. She lives in Ohio with her family and seven tiny donkeys. She's a Pet Whispering major from OMGU with a Masters in medical care for inanimate objects (a la Doc McStuffins). Susan enjoys crab-walking through the Swiss Alps, drinking Muscle Milk, and doing the Care Bear stare with her closest friends.

Website: www.authorsusanrenee.com
Facebook: www.facebook.com/authorsusanrenee
Goodreads: www.goodreads.com/SusanRenee
Instagram: authorsusanrenee
Twitter: @indiesusanrenee
Spotify: susan_renee

Stay tuned!!

The Schmidt Load series

Begins in 2017!

Made in the USA
Middletown, DE
27 August 2019